Heroes
of the 21st
century

Heroes of
the 21st Century

by

Peter Mason

HOLON

Heroes of the 21st Century

Copyright © 2013 by Peter Mason

Cover by: Kari Hicks
Art direction: Jeremy Gotwals

ISBN: 978-0-9853027-7-1

Published by:
Holon Publishing & Collective Press
www.Holonpublishing.com

103 N. College Ave. Bloomington, IN 47404

Printed in U.S.A

Heroes of the 21st Century is dedicated in memory of my great friend David M. Weir, who unfortunately did not live long enough to witness its actual publication, yet whose brave fight against increasing odds helped give me the courage to see the project through to completion. His encouragement, advice and honesty were always on the mark and delivered with just the right amount of sarcasm and exasperation and love as to allow me to do just one more rewrite.

Special thanks for the loving support of my wife Louise, who had the good sense to remain serenely detached through it all, as well as my sons, Will and Forrest, who over the years observed the fitful progress of the novel with detached amusement and gentle giddying. I would also like to thank Barb Noble for having the courage (nay, the foolishness) to read the book in too embryonic a form. Barb, how you must have suffered!

Also special thanks to all the dedicated folks at Holon Publishing, Jeremy Gotwals and Kari Hicks who put up with me and were instrumental in getting this book into your hands

Chapter 1

BEL AIR

The Nethermann estate basked in the warmth of a brilliant, mid-afternoon sun. The only indication that it was late November was the ominous shadow consuming more and more of the mansion's grounds in an inexorable advance down toward a palatial swimming pool situated on one side of the main house. In a short time, as temperatures dropped to something more seasonal, the throngs of mostly twenty and thirty-somethings cavorting poolside at Cecil Lumley's regular Sunday "open house" would have to seek shelter under sweat shirts and cotton sweaters.

Simon Gordon was slowly making his way toward the pool area along on a serpentine, gravel path that ran down from the front side of the house and on through the manicured lawns and gardens. His gait was robotic, the result of a poor night's sleep from an overnight flight from Buenos Aires. Despite his disjointedness that afternoon, Simon had decided on his habitual Sunday visit to his friends, Cecil Lumley and Samantha Hewitt, two fellow Brits who were trying to insinuate themselves into the Hollywood scene. As he was emerging from the shadows, and coming in sight of the pool, an unmistakable voice called out.

"Simon, over here, do come join us, haven't seen you in ages." The rotund caller with a languidly waving arm beckoned from the direction of a small rise at a corner of the vast lawn.

After several seconds of attempting to get a fix on the familiar voice, Simon caught sight of Lionel Vesey in the center of a small belvedere. More precisely, his eyes took in the expansive contours of the screenwriter's unmistakable silhouette, which seemed from afar to fully occupy the space between the folly's two front pillars. Simon jerkily made his way up the rise where the self-appointed doyen of Hollywood's British colony held court. Despite the fine weather, it was a diminished court, consisting of only Vesey's Filipino valet, Juco, and Mimi Neville, a once famous designer from the fifties and sixties whose creations adorned the likes of Vivien Leigh, Jennifer Jones, Carol Baker and Elizabeth Taylor and a host of other prominent actresses of the era. Closing in her late eighties, Miss Neville had succumbed to the amber warmth of the afternoon sun and a shaker of liquid refreshment that stood empty on the little table by her wicker chair.

"Lionel, how have you been, a pleasure to see you again," Simon said, shaking the pudgy hand limply extended to him. Simon, like virtually everyone in Hollywood, enjoyed chatting with the acerbic two-time Oscar winning screenwriter. Looking down toward the pool from his new vantage point, Simon exclaimed with some distaste in his voice, "Who are these people, Lionel? They seem like a totally new crowd. And where is our host and liege lord, Cecil Lumley? No one answered the door when I arrived; haven't seen Sam either, for that matter."

Lionel leaned over the side of the lounge chair, his ponderous bulk draping itself over the arm of the chair; in low conspiratorial tones, he launched into an analysis of the rise and fall of their titular host. "Well, like you, dear boy, I've been away on location. Young Albert insisted, don't cha know, that I accompany him to the wilds of East Borneo, just in case I had to change a comma or rewrite a speaking part for one of the coolies. It was absolutely dreadful, the food, the heat, and of course those neurotic actors. Well, be that as it may," Lionel said hurriedly, hoping that Simon hadn't taken the slight too personally, "When I returned to Sodom about three weeks ago, the word about town was that old Cecil was on the skids, and desperate for the big score, was getting himself mixed up with some unsavory characters. Naturally, everyone who was anyone started to decamp the sinking yacht, pardon my mixed metaphors. So, ma'dear, the great slide was on, the course set, and a terrible dénouement fated.

"Now, as you can see, we are surrounded by cast members and habitués of the next to the lowest dregs of our exalted industry, just one step up from the soft porn guilds. I mean, really now, denizens of cable TV, I can't bring myself to use the word stars, and even personalities is too affirming an appellation. I shall settle on the word 'creatures' for the time being – creatures of shows like 'Housewives of Lubbock, Texas' and Bravo's 'America's Next Top Yodeler'. It is all too much for a fellow of my refined nature to bear. I can tell you one thing, my dear Simon: this is the last time you'll see me attending one of these sordid jamborees. My boy, one mustn't allow oneself to be ruined by association with people of the third declension."

Breathless, and in need of rejuvenation, Lionel fumbled for his watermelon-colored drink and took several long drafts from the orchid bowl-size snifter.

"And what about you, did everything go swimmingly in Argentina? Did you see that old Virginian, Bobby Duval, sweeping up Nevis's dance partner in one of those dockside tango joints? And what is the dirt on your beautiful co-star, the divine Miss. Arabella? My readers are dying to know," concluded Lionel with a mock leer.

Simon's normally serious expression was transformed upon taking a seat next to one of Hollywood's most enduring fixtures; in place of his usual slight frown, he now wore a broad and relaxed smile. What did it matter that Lionel's Sidney Greenstreet shtick had long ago missed the mark. Since the late eighties the Aussies had become the top dogs in the foreign stable. The days of Basil Rathbone, Herbert Marshall and Claude Rains had come and gone, replaced by the likes of Russell Crowe, Cate Blanchett, Nicole Kidman and Guy Pearce. Yet the town would be a much duller place if Lionel Vesey ever departed and repaired to an Orthodox monastery on Mount Athos, something he threatened to do from time to time. "It went quite well actually, everyone was reasonably well behaved. We were in the foothills of the Andes; in Patagonia. A lot like Switzerland but a bit but wilder, more remote. I just came back on Wednesday; Sam asked me to stop over. And, yes, I have to agree with you that the current crop of hangers-on is a trifle louche, even by my flexible standards." And as if to add her own stamp of opprobrium on the crowd down by the pools, a still sleeping Mimi Neville punctuated the rarified banter of the belvedere with a series of loud, brisk snorts.

Lionel, ignoring for the moment his companion's nasal murmurings, was about to support Simon's observations when he was abruptly cut short by a loud thwacking sound. The strange noise, reminiscent of wood being stressed to the utmost just prior to cracking, came from behind the high, well-tended cypress tree hedge that surrounded the property on the west side. Lionel and Simon looked up as an object appeared over the pool. Seen against the haze of a weak afternoon sun, details were initially hard to discern, except to say it was large and coming down fast. Just as it reached its apogee, a few feet above the high hedge of well-tended cypress trees, Lionel made visual contact with the unidentified intruder. "I believe that's Viscount Cecil Lumley of Radnor now."

The erstwhile host, now formally making his entrance, proceeded to slam into the middle of the pool with a tremendous splash, narrowly missing two thong-clad lovelies who were engaged in a swimming contest across its considerable width. Screams of astonishment and horror erupted from the crowd as the fully clothed body of Cecil surfaced from the pool's depths to float serenely on its back for a few seconds before turning turtle and rolling over.

"Simon, please run down there and see what is going on, I'm afraid my rotundity prevents me from a timely personal inspection. Please remember to secure for my delectation a couple of lovelies to console me over our great loss, preferably ones who are made up of something less than fifty percent plastic," but by then Simon was too far away for him to hear Lionel's last entreaty.

Just as Cecil Montagu Egmont Lumley, the seventh Viscount of Radnor and son and heir of the eleventh Marquis of Simsbury, was about to begin his swift decent, his girlfriend of the past year, Samantha Howard Hewitt, was in a heated conversation with the leasing agent for the Nethermann estate. "Mr. Abrams, I fully appreciate what you are telling me and have told me repeatedly for the last five minutes, but I know virtually nothing about Lord Radnor's finances, let alone having any fiduciary authority over them. You will simply have to wait until he returns from Seattle; it should be later this evening. I will be happy to pass on to him the fact that you urgently wish to speak with him; other than that there is little I can do." Sam spoke in calm and measured tones, the kind of voice one would use in talking to a cornered psychopath who is holding a pistol to a child's head.

"You must appreciate that I have the opportunity to lease the Nethermann property for an entire year but the interested party is very impatient and needs some type of decision. Lord Radnor's lease runs out in two months, but he has the option to renew. That option expires on Monday; I must have his decision no later than Sunday evening to enable me to tell the other party where they stand. This is all I'm asking, and it's all I've been asking for the past several weeks," answered Mr. Abrams in a harsh, frustrated voice.

Samantha was just about to beg off, when from her vantage point in the morning room on the main floor, something momentarily blocked out the sun, casting the room into a temporary twilight. As she casually glanced out the French door she caught the unmistakable sight of the air borne Cecil. Samantha was immediately able to identify the aerial traveler by the blue double-breasted silk blazer and the muted yellow trousers the figure was wearing. The real giveaway, however, were the reddish-brown alligator leather loafers by Maxwell that the Viscount loved to clump around in. The tasteful ensemble was indeed the very same getup that he had worn when he left to catch his plane on Thursday afternoon.

Samantha automatically rose from the love seat and stared out the door in utter disbelief. Numbed, she politely told Mr. Abrams that he would indeed have an answer for him by next morning and to call around 11:00. She then ran out through the French doors and onto the circular stairs that connected the upper balcony to a large terrace and garden at the end of the pool. Samantha did not know what to think or how she would react when she came upon him. The truth of the matter was that their relationship had become increasingly frayed over the last couple of months, his annoyingly childish refusal to accept the reality of his situation merely added to the tension between them. It was obvious to her, and to all their friends, that no one was interested in turning Simon Raven's Alms for Oblivion saga into a twelve part package deal for TV, and that it would be best to move on to a more commercially viable project.

Cecil, however, refused to give up on his vision. Increasingly, he began to see himself in the tradition of one of the great misunderstood personalities of the film industry: An unacknowledged genius initially ignored and ridiculed by the oafish rabble who ran things, only to be belatedly appreciated by his peers as one of the seminal visionaries of the modern "cinema". His descent down the financial pecking order – from the large banks and respected investor pools down to the grubby money laundering operations and slush funds controlled by loan sharks and other sorts – was in Cecil's eyes not to be interpreted as a fall from respectability, but merely the Via Delarosa he was destined to tread for the sake of his art. "As heir to great and ancient name and sizeable fortune, I was never told that failure was a consideration in any of my ventures," he primly retorted after Samantha dared to question his association with Macho Antonio "The Gay Blade" Camacho, one of LA's most notorious hoods. By the time the ashen-faced Samantha appeared at poolside, Simon and a couple of others had managed to push

Cecil's remains to the edge of the pool and were in the process of making one final tug to fish him out altogether. Seeing the substantial and sodden corpse of Cecil deposited directly at her feet with a squishy thud, Sam decided the best thing she could do was to faint dead away.

~

A deep sigh came out of Simon Gordon as he watched the last LA County Sheriff's forensics van slip away down the long, winding drive to the unseen street below. Allowing the curtains to fall back into place, he decided to make his way to the living room where the others were holed-up. He and Lionel had remained behind after the police had questioned them to give what aid and comfort they could to their grieving fellow Brit. He was still amazed by the length of time it took for the police to go over the crime scene, examine and cart off the body, and interview all forty-five guests. All those hours frittered away in a near meaningless police procedure, when it was clear to everyone that Cecil had been disposed of somewhere other than at the house.

It was now 11:45, almost Sunday. As Simon entered the study he was struck by the exhausted expressions engraved on everyone's faces. Lionel was sitting at the end of the large, bluish Jacquard covered couch, the ever-loyal Juco standing against the wall directly behind him. The jowly-faced writer had lapsed into a Buddha-like silence, a sure indication that his system was now overly lubricated by the day's alcohol intake. Anne Blumenthal, Samantha's close friend, had shown up within twenty minutes of getting a sob-filled call, and was doing her best to console her still shell-shocked friend. She occupied an uncomfortable looking high-backed chair across from the end of the couch where Samantha sat. Feeling as if he were intruding on a scene of sacerdotal silence, Simon entered the room as unobtrusively as possible, made his way to an armchair across from Lionel, and waited for something to happen.

A minute or two later, the house telephone rang, startling Samantha out of her trance-like state. She leaned over and picked up the phone on the end table; her movements were automatic, almost robotic. "Yes, hello, whom may I ask is calling? Oh, mother, thank God," the recognition of her mother's voice jarring Samantha into animation. "Then I suppose you've heard? Just a moment please." She excitedly asked Simon if he would hold the receiver until she reached her bedroom. When he insisted that they could all go off into another room, she signaled her wish not to inconvenience her guests by continuing to head straight for the sweeping marble staircase in the entrance hall.

"Thank you, Simon, I have it now," she heard the extension click off and was about to begin the conversation when the Mrs. Hewitt started in.

"Is it true what we're hearing over here? How absolutely dreadful! How are you holding up, Samantha? I see yes, quite right. One or two of those things are quite all right during times like these, but you mustn't become too reliant on them. Yes, we first heard what happened on the BBC morning program. Every station is carrying something about it; all a lot of terrible gossip mongering, I'm sure. Cecil's father, Bernard, gave a statement, says he's going to be flying over for the inquest and to bring Cecil back and all that. Didn't seem particularly grieved by the whole affair but those families are so completely around the bend one

9

never knows what's going on up in their brains, assuming, of course, that they have any." Mrs. Hewitt spoke in clipped and nervous fashion, squelching as best she could her concern for her only daughter, and the fact that she was feeling helpless in being unable to extend anything beyond simple verbal support.

Samantha lay upright on the king-sized bed in the master bedroom suite. Her mid-length auburn hair was becoming more and more disheveled as she continually ran her hand through it, twisting some of the strands backwards and forwards. "I'm so happy you called, I didn't want to wake you. Yes, I suppose it is nonsense at a time like this to worry about something so stupid. The press finally left, you could see those parasitical slugs over the wall at the front of the place, or at least their camera lights and what have you. Oh, I just want to get out of here and come home for Christmas. It is just going to get more awful with the police and courts and the baying hounds of the paparazzi."

"My dear, as much as I can appreciate your distress and loss, I don't really think it would be wise to come home over this, not right now at least. Remember, Cecil's family is far better known here than over there, if word gets out about your relationship, it will be just as hot in Britain, if not more so. My suggestion is that you leave Los Angeles as soon as practicable and move to some inconspicuous place like Chicago or Seattle and finish off your tour abroad there. Here's your father, he has been dying to talk to you, I'll get on the other line in a bit." Sam could detect the relief in her mother's voice as she signed off in favor of the Cornelius Xavier Howard Hewitt, Professor Emeritus of Eastern European Medieval Political and Economic History at the University of London.

"My poor daughter, terrible, terrible to hear about old

Cecil, terrible blow indeed; do they know who did it? I must say I warned you about the rampant lawlessness in America and the country's preoccupation with violence. It is, I'm afraid, a malignancy that affects all aspects of their social, economic and political behavior. I am also afraid that Hollywood, the city where you and Cecil chose to set up shop, is the epicenter for the glamorization of violence and sex, and as such is at the very crucible of evil which everyone calls America," said the good professor in the same tone he used to lecture undergraduates about the follies of Poland's Jagiellon Dynasty.

"Is it true that they used a portable trebuchet to fling him over the wall? Really quite clever, when you think about it. We're hearing that the police suspect that it was attached to a tow lorry of some sort, a wrecker I believe they're called in the states." Cornelius Hewitt then caught himself, deciding quickly to head on to subjects that would spare Sam from recounting the messier aspects of her bereavement.

"Unlike your mother, whom I gather has urged you to stick it out in that land of vipers and gangsters, I, as your father, must insist that you return home immediately, proceed then to Geneva and put your Cambridge degree to work in the aid and succor of the world's disenfranchised masses. If you had followed your father's humble advice from the start, you wouldn't have become so self-absorbed with your own pleasures."

Samantha didn't know whether to laugh or cry at all of this. The fact that her father, generally a good, if not always very sensible man, could be so entirely clueless regarding the emotional needs of his daughter under the current circumstances struck Samantha as both horrifying and comical. But in a strange way, his loony rantings and the familiar fussy tone of his voice made Sam feel a connection with a more solid and permanent world.

"Oh, Cornelius, please do shut up. Can't you understand your daughter is still in shock and grieving? Get off the line this minute until it's time to say goodbye. Really now!" demanded his wife from an upstairs phone.

"Listen, my dear, on the way upstairs, I suddenly remembered that Uncle Robbie has a very good friend in New York, a Mr. Leuven. He's a pretty big fish from the way Robbie was going on, owns companies all over the country. Let me call your uncle later today and see if he thinks Mr. Leuven might be able to help in some way."

The initial relief Samantha enjoyed from talking with her parents gradually faded, replaced by a thin layer of depression and increasing frustration and disappointment. She wished that they had not offered advice or editorialized about her tragedy, and had just tried to be supportive and soothing. That her mother suggested a place like Chicago or Seattle didn't make any sense. It was one thing to avoid England, but quite another to run off to a rainy or northern clime; it was, after all, getting on to December, and by the time she could leave town it would be January, the dead of winter.

After she had rung off, Samantha asked herself what living in LA would be like without Cecil. There would be a great comedown in living standards; the income from her grandfather's trust would not allow her to live the life she had enjoyed for the last year. Instead of Bel Air and Beverly Hills it would be West Hollywood or Westwood, maybe one of the Canyons. Certainly, any new residence would be nothing like the Nethermann place. Should she go into pictures? Everyone told her she had the looks and style currently in demand, but she had no great interest in acting just for the sake of being able to stay with her few remaining A-list friends. Most of the people she met in the business didn't really appeal to her: vain, insecure, ruthless and uncouth was her take on most of them. Only a few were really to her liking. And then she asked herself: Why put up with all the hassles of living here if you weren't in the business? LA in most respects, aside from the weather and the fun of Hollywood, was a difficult city in which to live.

Before she nodded off, Sam remembered Cecil. Samantha had known him since she was a teenager. His father, the Marquis, had a hunting establishment in Lincolnshire near her Uncle's, and Cecil was pretty good friends with her brother Alistair, but the meetings were only once or twice a year, and then brief. So it came as a big surprise to her that during the first leg of her post graduation American odyssey she should run into him at a weekend house party in Middleburg, Virginia. He started talking about his determination to become a producer in LA and all the hopes he had of making quality movies for the masses. Since it was late October, Samantha felt that LA might be more fun than self-important Washington, and agreed to come out there in a few weeks to give California a try.

Cecil had been so much the type; not overly bright, unaware of other people's agendas unless they were spelled out for him on large billboards, and then surprised that anyone would want to do something that ran counter to his own interests. His hopeless naiveté about the workings of the movie business were touching at first but after a while, as it became plain that he wasn't catching on, some of his associates began to take open advantage of him, and the more honest people simply slipped away. Samantha could see it all happening, but he never listened to her because she was a woman and he a man, and a lord besides.

"It was fun while it lasted, but I'm glad it's over," Samantha mumbled to herself as her mind gently ground to a halt and drifted off into a deep sleep; exhaustion, pills and a couple of drinks finally showering her with the miracle of oblivion.

Chapter 2

NEW YORK

Bryce Lysander Leuven was a lean and tall man. What made him truly imposing, however, was not his height but his thin face with its chiseled features, set off by cobalt blue eyes and a striking aquiline nose. His face seemed to have been taken out of a David painting, celebrating the austere rectitude of a Roman senator during the early Republic. Framing his remarkable countenance was a head of thick, wavy, white hair, combed straight back to just above his collar and feathered to cover the top of his long, pendulous ears.

He had come to New York right after his tour of duty in Korea. His only apparent assets were a degree from Tulane, a few names in a tattered address book, and some poker winnings. This meager endowment, plus a razor sharp mind for sniffing out the right deal at the right price, had allowed him to accumulate a considerable fortune over the years. In time, he became known as a man of good reputation and appreciated instincts, a fair-minded confidant and advisor to all whom respectfully sought his growing reputation for wise and not too self-serving counsel.

One of those who sought his counsel was Stephan Gartner, a man of uncertain background, though the rumor with the most staying power had his family migrating from Turkey via Greece in the twenties. He was one of many whom Bunny had befriended over the years. Starting together in the early 60's, the

15

two bought up a number of radio and smaller city TV stations. In the seventies and early eighties they picked up a string of equally small cable TV networks. Over the last several years, they had sold off most of the cable systems to the likes of Times-Warner, Cox and Comcast. At the end of the cycle of acquiring and divesting they still managed to hold onto or control an odd assortment of independent radio and TV properties as well as two small cable networks which no one seemed to want or know what to do with, one of which was WEBCO – the Weather and Environmental Broadcasting Corporation.

Bunny, as he was called by his intimates, was beginning his second organized sweep through the main floor of the townhouse. He was trying to locate the prospectus he had misplaced a day or two ago. A thorough inspection of the dining and morning rooms had yielded nothing. The table and chairs in the main hallway were also bare. In a fit of exasperation, he finally decided that the missing paper must be in the living room, probably in one of the numerous chairs or sofas. Methodically moving from the hallway into the far end of the living room, Bunny spied what he thought was the lost folder sticking out between the seat cushion and arm of a sofa, one of a pair perpendicular to the imposing stone fireplace. While striding over to retrieve the document, Bunny caught sight of his son, Charlie, at the opposite end of the room. He was in the process of snapping back the silk drapes covering one of the French windows overlooking the side street that ran into Fifth Avenue. He guessed that Charlie was put off by the weather. He had boasted to his father before leaving Milwaukee that his staff had forecasted sunny skies and highs in the low fifties – great weather for New York in late November – weather that would be lingering around for the entire Thanksgiving weekend.

16

Instead, what he got was the same sullen mixture of sleet and heavy, cold showers that had hounded him all the way from the Midwest. Compounding Charlie's rather sour mood was an early flu outbreak that had laid the only old girlfriend he hungrily wanted to see again, and who he believed was equally as famished to see him as well. With everything that was going wrong, Charlie was wondering why he had bothered to come back at all.

After enduring four days of hanging around his father's house and putting up with the occasional visits of his brothers and sister, Charlie was feeling the need to ask his father's advice on how to reorder his unsatisfying life before returning to Milwaukee. Just as he was turning his back on the curtained window, Charlie caught sight of his father moving across the far end of the spacious room. Deciding not to hesitate, he loudly blurted out, "Dad, I wonder if we can have a talk? Do you have a minute?"

"Yes, of course, Charlie. Let me gather up my toys and we'll meet in the library," Bryce Leuven affably replied, as he deftly slid the file under his arm without unduly disturbing the contents of the heavy highball glass that contained his habitual after-dinner Bourbon.

Charlie had always loved the library. The light colored wood paneling was formal but not forbidding like those of some of his friends' fathers. The gloss on the paneling gave off a subtle airiness, even on days like this when the weather was uninviting. Here there was a welcoming lightness about the room, accented now by the soft luminescence of two antique lamps, positioned near the two club chairs. Amid the volumes on the bookshelves beckoned a wealth of things that boys found irresistible – exotic display cases containing daggers and pistols, model ships, small tableaus of miniature soldiers, and stuffed varmints and birds. Charlie slumped easily into the creased leather of one of the chairs and faced his father across the small coffee table piled high with magazines.

Charlie decided that the best strategy would be to come right out with it and make a direct plea. "Dad, I'm at the end of my tether; I simply can't see myself living in Milwaukee for much longer. It's driving me nuts! I think I've served my time in hell. I have to get back to New York and start over." Charlie stopped and waited for a response that he hoped would contain the tidy solution to all of his problems.

Bunny looked at his son with a mixture of exasperation and affection. He was not surprised in the least about the topic weighing on his youngest; over the last couple of years they had seemed to have discussed little else. Each time the issue was raised, Leuven Sr. urged his son to stick it out, and make the best of it. A contract was a contract, after all, and Charlie had signed it. No, he wouldn't directly intercede on Charlie's behalf with Stephan Gartner, even though he was aware his refusal would mean another long, drab winter in Wisconsin for the boy. He would, however, attempt to augment firmness with hope; or the expectation of hope that in the not too distant future Charlie might well enjoy full manumission.

"Now son, I know losing a wife is hard, and Cynthia Gartner was a wonderful girl", he began in what was left of his central Mississippi drawl, "and we all know that it's been about two years since you were sent out there to allow things to settle down after her death. However, I truthfully can't say the Gartners are any better disposed toward you today than when they first hatched the idea of shipping you out to Wisconsin for five years."

18

Bryce Leuven honed in on his son's face, especially Charlie's hazel eyes. "Now you've been out there running WEBCO for all that time, and I've finally seen some real progress. You've begun turning that loser around. I might say that you've done as well as anyone could, given a less than supportive ownership." Bryce paused, took a sip of his bourbon and continued, keeping his eyes on Charlie.

"But you aren't going to get a reprieve from Stephan Gartner just by boosting WEBCO's ratings by a point or two; you're simply going to have to do something spectacular with that old horse. Further, you're going to have to accept that the odds are stacked against you, and so you may as well go for broke. In a word son, you gotta' put the network into play by pulling off something big, really big. You've simply got to get the damn thing noticed; do something to put the spotlight on it. Otherwise, I am afraid you're going to have to buckle-down and learn German, because I know that Stephan is not over the death of his poor little Cynthia, and probably never will be. However, there is something he warms to, and that is money, and plenty of it. If you can make him boatloads of it, he might just turn his forgiving side on you for a change."

Charlie listened with flagging hope and interest as his father spun out the reasons for not granting him a parole from his sentence. He had heard them all before. The only real difference this time was that his father offered a suggestion beyond the routine "grin and bear it" advice of the past. The suggestion that he somehow put WEBCO in play was great, but how? How to make a third place twenty-four hour-a-day weather network a hot property? "Dad, any suggestions about how to put this train back on the track?" Charlie asked in a sheepish voice.

The father quizzically eyed his youngest son. Charlie's face was broader and more refined than his father's, but it lacked the drama of the older man's. In contrast to his father's almost nonexistent lips, Charlie's were full, almost sensual. He had an easy, approachable manner that tempted some to mistakenly write him off as just another amiable rich boy. Even his father was not sure whether Charlie had what it took to make his way in the world, or if he was simply a rambunctious mediocrity. God knows he had tried to instill in him the right values, tried to give the boy the encouragement and the benefit of his wisdom and long experience, especially after the death of his mother. Bunny, nevertheless, lived uneasily with the feeling that his time and energies had been insufficient in turning out a serious man.

"Listen here, Charlie, one thing certain about the weather is that it changes, and it's in that change where you can make your opportunity. Something will present itself one day, it may need a nudge from you, maybe a big one, but it will appear, I swear to you on that," Bunny said, hunching his body towards his son in the opposite chair. "Here's another thing going in your favor. The Gartners don't have that much time left; they're a spent force. All their rantin' and ravin' is just them trying to cover up the sounds of their chains rattlin' against the cell walls. I've seen this thing happen before: a man works hard, gets rich, thinks he has everything, then one day he looks around and sees his wife for what she is, his kids for what they are and he realizes that it's all for shit and there ain't nothing he can do about it. All the money in the world won't make a hateful wife love you; all the money in the world won't give you sons who respect you, either. It's not gonna happen and everyone knows it. What occurs in more cases than not is that the man begins to get sloppy, he starts giving up

20

and dying little by little. He knows the game is pretty well over and there's nothin' he can do about it but sit and watch it all slip away. He's already started with all that drinking he's been up to; it's only the first rung of what will turn out to be a thoroughly squalid slide. But then, I could be utterly wrong," chuckled Bryce, his eyes twinkling for the first time that evening.

"You sound positively pleased by it all," observed Charlie, moving forward to in the direction of his father.

"Well, I'm not pleased, just realistic. We've made a lot of money together over the years, he and I, but I've made a lot of money with a lot of other people, too. The only difference is I never had my kids marry any of my other partners' children. And the fact that I did has complicated matters; but it has also heightened my personal interest in the outcome of this little drama."

"Dad, why don't I just quit and be done with it. I can always do something else."

"I don't know? Why don't you?" Bryce Senior shot back, his eyes renewing their inquisition. "Nothing wrong with starting over, if you do it right, but we both know that they will come after you and sue you for breach of contract, and with that hanging over your head you might find it harder than you think to start your second act. But if you play your cards right, we can get you out of Milwaukee and make a pile of money from this mess called WEBCO. All you've got to do is remain vigilant and patient; the rest will take care of itself. Just remember, where Gartner goes there isn't much in the way of talent in that family to keep things moving on," Bryce's eyes flashed hungrily.

"What about James? He's a decent sort, and he might return one of these days" Charles queried his dad, excited by the conversation's conspiratorial tone, but still not quite believing a successful outcome was very likely.

"No doubt, no doubt, a bright and good man. Only one thing though, James isn't coming back. He's happy livin' the life he's livin'. He doesn't want to be bothered by meetings, financials and all the rest. All he wants is a monthly check sent to the bank nearest his latest playground. Who's to blame him? It ain't bad work if you can get it."

"You might be right, Dad."

"Shoot, you're damn straight I'm right." Bryce said almost laughing. "And that Roger, well he's a poor no-account. He'll be blown away in the first stiff breeze. Now this is what I want you to do. Go back to Milwaukee, continue to make that outfit appear respectable, and carefully cook up some big play that you can run with when the right time comes along. Then you can come back here as a real hero," Bryce said with a barely detectable smile, "Now is that a deal my boy?"

"Deal, I guess, but it still seems like it will take a lot of luck to have everything fall into place just-so," Charles said with a voice that betrayed the low estimation of his abilities in pulling something off successfully, given the nebulous game plan that his father had just outlined.

"Son, the big things are always the easiest. They'll take care of themselves because they're big and you can see all the moving parts. If something starts going wrong, all you need to do is stick your hand in to make some type of coarse adjustment. No, there's no luck when it comes to the big picture. It's the damn little things that are the devil. At first they seem too small to matter until they rail up on their hind legs as if out of nowhere. Then it's too late, and you're prone to overreact and lose your balance."

A few minutes after his father took a phone call from London, Charlie was up in his old bedroom, a room unrecognizable since his mother's radical redecoration efforts had changed it from a young man's room to one more befitting its new designation as the third guest room. He still liked it though and didn't feel displaced by the changes. He was, after all, thirty-one and had a place of his own just a few blocks away, rented out for the past two years to an old friend from Cornell. Besides, his mother had had excellent taste and had managed to put together a pleasing arrangement of Italian provincial pieces with an odd eclectic touch here and there to give the room its simple and inviting character.

Charlie flopped into one of the room's two chairs and turned on the small TV, flicking through the channels until coming to the Military History Channel. Its feature that evening was a tale of a young naval officer sent out on a secret mission during World War II. As the narrator provided a brief biographical sketch of the young man, Charlie became more attentive. He easily related, at least on a superficial level, with the hero of the tale, a one Lieutenant Lex Crowell. Crowell was a young man from an old Philadelphia family whose father commanded him to volunteer for military service after a sexual escapade with the daughter of one of his law partners. In an effort to redeem his family's honor, Lt. Crowell had at the first opportunity volunteered for a secret and highly dangerous assignment. The mission would take him behind enemy lines just prior to the invasion of Sicily in order to organize and coordinate partisan band activities before the landing. It was a mission that all but guaranteed the young Philadelphian some sort of posthumous medal.

As the show continued, Charlie increasingly identified with the program's hero, readily comparing his exile to the Midwest with Crowell's virtual banishment from Philadelphia; Crowell's secret mission with the vague counsel his father had just given him about something "big". Granted there were obvious differences, the two lives didn't exactly run on parallel tracks. The similarities, however, were real enough in Charlie's mind for him to embrace the Lieutenant as a fellow comrade in arms, who, like Charlie, had been seeking redemption via a high-stakes gamble. For a second, he pictured the two of them sharing the back of an open limousine, their chests bedecked by special ribbons and medals, cruising slowly up Broadway, ticker tape cascading furiously down from the office towers, delirious crowds cheering wildly, their progress occasionally punctuated by a delirious worshipper breaking through the police lines in a desperate effort to touch the heroic young men.

Later in the show, the documentary featured an interview with Lt. Crowell, now a man in his late seventies, done shortly before his death in 1999. As in the war time photographs, the old warrior retained the same square-jawed good looks, the same flinty, penetrating stare, and the same mocking smile of someone who had cheated death on a whim, and in turn for his daring had received a long reprieve from a bemused Grim Reaper. As the elderly Crowell began to talk about the operation and what was going on in his head at the time, Charlie was suddenly struck by the absurdity in comparing their respective "exploits". Crowell had volunteered for a virtual suicide mission that in all likelihood would leave him dead on some lonely beach, if he was lucky, or, if not, facing the agony of prolonged torture followed by a summary hanging at the hands of a jaded SS executioner – all for the sake of honor and duty. Charlie, on the other hand, had only agreed to take up the presidential reins of a faltering weather network in Milwaukee. Lt. Lex Crowell had faced violent storms, real gunfire, hand-to-hand combat and two hazardous escapes in the course of his adventure. In contrast, Charlie had neatly inherited a corner office in a skyscraper and lucked into a stylish condo at a cut-rate price within days of arriving in town, and survived two bleak but average Midwest winters.

The questions raised by the show became sharper and more urgent in Charlie's mind. The somber wartime realities endured by Crowell, where one's decisions held real consequences of life and death, were something he had never encountered. "Shit, could I do that, what that guy did?" Charlie muttered out loud, allowing the rhetorical silence to answer his own question. He shriveled back into the chair, his fantasy completely deflated by relentless reality. Whereas just a few minutes ago he had pictured himself in a ticker tape parade, figuratively sharing the crowd's enthusiasm with his daring predecessor, he was now just a guy sitting in his dad's home spinning kid dreams.

Charlie had visited this mental terrain before. He was a great one for dreaming up elaborate, adolescent scenarios in which he would invariably play center stage. Sometimes he was a character who brought about important historic changes; others were more personal, in which he would rescue the love of his life or save a family stricken by horrendous tragedy. Regardless of their scope, in the end these fantasies always collapsed in on themselves, leaving him closer to the despair he was trying to escape and feeling more diminished than when he had started. And so the cycle repeats itself, a Ferris wheel of momentary elations, inevitably followed, as if on cue, by downward, depressive downdraft. Charlie could feel his time running out to make a big splash in life, and that he would either have to do something truly notable or be cast back yet again into an endless, negative feedback loop of his own making.

"Am I a gutless fucking coward," he asked himself, "unfit for anything real?" Charlie continued his self-flagellation regarding his personal inadequacies. "God I wish we weren't so rich and lived in one of those new 'luxury' high rises in the 90's where the walls were made of sheetrock instead of plaster. Then I could punch the shit out of them all night, punch them until I exhausted myself and fell asleep. Christ, I don't even have the guts to tell everyone to go fuck themselves," he whined. Charlie, exhausted by the outburst, listlessly reached for the remote control in hopes that a PBS repeat of an inane British comedy or a detective mystery might sooth his torment.

In the midst of trying to get the old remote to work, between still more curses and whines, Charlie's mind seemed suddenly to be hijacked by a voice coming from the middle of his brain. It was a quiet and kind voice but also firm and authoritative, one that was meant to be listened to. Its message was clear and spoken only once – "Though you are man only in form, go forth without fear."

Alarmed and speechless, Charlie allowed the remote to fall to the floor. Was someone in the room or in the hall? No, the words came from deep inside his head but they weren't his words, and certainly not his voice. Though sexless, the voice in quality and timbre had many of the characteristics of Cynthia's. "What's going on?" Charlie blurted out. After a few moments he began to question whether he really had heard a voice at all, and whether even the words were really words or some noise made by the

26

old house. Finally, overtaken by fatigue, he threw a blanket over himself, curled up into a fetal position on the bed, and allowed himself to be led off into a profound sleep.

Chapter 3

MILWAUKEE

"You *bastard!*" screamed Samantha as she hurled an arabesque-styled candelabra at Charlie's head, "You are absolutely the worst human being who ever walked upright!" He ducked in time to hear the prized piece whiz by his head and straight into the new, wall-mounted, 48-inch plasma TV. Dark black bits of glass shot out from the screen, littering a wide swath of the floor. The noise and the loss of his new toy made Charlie stop for a second before going after her. Samantha, in contrast, did not pause for a second; the next addition to her fusillade was a heavy, oddly-shaped wine bottle that rested on a small bookcase; it too became immediately airborne. Unlike the candelabra, this objét connected, glancing off the left side of Charlie's head before falling to the hardwood floor, unbroken. The bottle managed to draw the minimum amount of blood required for scoring purposes while forcing a grimace to spread across the face of the intended victim.

Charlie had anticipated a small row after breaking the news to Samantha, but he completely underestimated the depth of her reaction to his idea of making their relationship mutually nonexclusive. The first indication that the fight was serious was when Sam, winding up and letting go with a lamp, caused her chemise to ride up on her hip to reveal for a second her auburn muff. Under the normal rules of engagement, this would be stimulus enough for Charlie to beat a strategic retreat toward the bedroom and end the squabble in a round of mock-violent lovemaking. But not today; things were too far out of hand for that type of happy resolution. Now, seemingly fighting for his life, he didn't know exactly what to do except keep moving in hopes that Sam would, in time, run out of things to throw at him.

"I will kill you now; I have the range, you bastard!" Samantha shrieked, as she picked up a side chair and swung it at Charlie's groin. Then Sam, as if suddenly recalling her English birth, became embarrassed by her surrender to primitive passions. Stopping for a second, she then began to sob uncontrollably, stumbling around for a few brief moments before collapsing into a suitable chair in order to finish her breakdown in comfort.

Charlie, puzzled by the sudden change coming over Samantha, stood in the rubble of the room gawking at this beautiful woman. He knew he had made a terrible mistake. Besides being beautiful, Samantha was charming, intelligent, good-humored, and normally well mannered and simply comfortable to be around. She had all the makings of a real pal for life, maybe even a wife. He realized he had been a fool and as he stood there in his black silk boxers, he felt utterly stupid and completely unable to make any sense of why a few brief minutes ago he had thought that his proposal of mutual unlimited unfaithfulness had seemed like such a brilliant idea.

"Sam, listen. I'm really sorry. Honest, I am. I really want to take back what I said; I didn't really mean it. I want to be with you and no one else. Please forgive me; I just got scared about being so in love with you. That's all." Charlie knew it sounded weak, but for once his plea fairly well matched his feelings.

She stopped sobbing and in a voice of bitter, mocking acerbity mimicked Charlie's lame crie de coeur. "I just got scared about being in love with you. You fucking worm. My father was right about you Yanks, you're all a bunch of spoiled brats. Charles Duquesne Leuven, you are nothing but a turd. Now go and fetch my robe."

Charlie meekly went off to do her bidding. Eventually they both got dressed and started to clean things up. They didn't speak, what little communication occurred was done via curt nods and terse grunts. It was awkward for Charlie, but more so, he suspected for Sam, who was, after all, on his turf. All his attempts to be the caring gentleman were ignored or resolutely rebuffed.

Still seething, Samantha grimly made her way to the kitchen to make some tea. While waiting for the water to boil, she looked out over downtown from the small window over the sink. Samantha wondered why she had ever come to this provincial burg in the first place when there were so many more interesting places to live. Milwaukee! She must have lost her mind completely. She could not help but feel disheartened by the seemingly inexorably downward course her life had taken since her decision to flee LA. Why had she left the comfortable LA life of unusual and fascinating people, the warm climate, the mixing bowl of cultures, and, of course, her good friends, to move out here of all places. Milwaukee with its stolid German/Slavic population, horrible weather, and completely boring social scene was like moving from London to Sheffield. Despite her job, which she did love, the year spent here had been one of the most boring of her life.

Life seemed so unfair; Samantha felt she was beginning to lose her grip entirely. Why should she have to bear the trauma

30

of Cecil's death and then within a few short weeks meet good old Charlie only to be abandoned yet again? Why did the men she was attracted to always turn out to be no better than rich prats? She had finally spotted the pattern; was it a fatal flaw in her personality to be unerringly attracted to the superficial or merely part and parcel of being twenty-four? All her decisions seemed to her to be right in the beginning but they invariably sent her down the wrong path in the end. What to do now? What to do with Charlie, Milwaukee, and the whole bucket of shit?

Unable to decide, Samantha's thoughts returned to her past life in LA. Even though it had been just over a year since she pulled up stakes and moved, her memories of the last few weeks there were beginning to blur. She could recall a few people and incidents but most of it just ran together. One person she recalled was McGuire, the short, wiry LA detective, who came snooping around the house on the flimsiest of excuses, either asking a question he had asked the day before or making a query about something that had no logical link to anything associated with Cecil's death. Inane questions like "does the maid do the laundry or do you send it out?" rolled out of his little mouth with crashing seriousness, forcing Sam to cover her mouth in hopes of suppressing a smile.

Then there were the paparazzi who hung around the estate both day and night. Anne Blumenthal told her they were probably third stringers, trying to hype up the "mystery woman" angle in hopes the evidence would eventually get around to pointing to her as the mastermind behind the "Radnor Fly Over". Since she didn't leave the house very often and there were multiple ways to get on and off the estate, it was a simple matter to elude them. In a few days the annoyance caused by their constant presence

31

only grated as a sad reminder of how her entire life had become unhinged.

The only truly vivid episode was the arrival of Cecil's father, Bernard Marquarte Lumley, the eleventh Marquis of Simsbury. Samantha took an instant dislike to the chinless man she came to label as "Lord Quart". This aversion quickly blossomed into a florid and rich detestation in the few minutes she was required to suffer his presence. It was obvious to anyone who encountered the Marquis that the bloodlines that struggled to produce such a specimen had been running thin for a considerable period of time. Anything hinting at subtlety or sensibility had been immediately calculated by his DNA as qualities too burdensome to carry on to the next generation, and so were promptly jettisoned. Stripped of everything but the frailest of intellects and the most abbreviated social awareness, the forlorn end product was the inordinately common, mildly cruel, and completely snobbish Lord Quart.

It was Samantha's good fortune that her exposure to him had been limited to a single brief phone call and one in-person encounter on a cold, rainy afternoon. On that visit, the Marquis was accompanied by a factotum by the name of Hinton, who wore his vestments of service, a black blazer and grey striped trousers with just the right combination of pride and humility; and a stooped, little man in his sixties, outfitted in a cloth cap, white shirt and black tie and apron. After gaining admittance to the entrance hall, the Marquis and his lackeys, as if on some prearranged directive, automatically formed themselves into a flying wedge to best survey the portable riches of the Nethermann house.

Despite Samantha's remonstrances and repeated insistence that the place had been leased fully furnished, the three pushed on, going through the entire house from top to bottom, the avaricious Marquis rebuffing her attempts to halt the pillage by his all-purpose rejoinders of "rubbish" and "rubbish, my good woman". They selected only the best pieces from the house's considerable offerings, taking such a proprietary interest in them that a casual observer would have thought they were the long lost furnishings from one of the Marquis's own estates which in some unexplained twist of history had been vulgarly sacked by the Nethermanns while in transit from Galicia to California in the 1920's. After fruitlessly protesting for a half hour, Samantha eventually gave up and decided to watch the trio as they scoured the contents of one of the formal sitting rooms. This triad of looters would have made Hermann Goering proud. The Marquis would enter a room and with his cane start poking at a desirable chair or desk; even paintings were not immune to his proddings. Hinton, in turn, would inspect the piece with some precision and apparent knowledge, and then in hushed tones convey to Lord Quart his best appraisal of the item. The little man in the cloth cap would then take out from a little folio a colored sticker and attach it to the object of interest. In this manner, the three went apace through all twenty-five rooms and the basement of the Italianate styled villa. By the end of their labors, Sam calculated they had selected for consignment back to the motherland over half of the paintings and furniture from the formal rooms as well as most of the silver, a good chunk of the objéts d' art, wall hangings and assorted bric-a-brac.

Not once during his remarkable visit did the good Lord inquire about Sam and the state of his son in the days preceding his death. He treated her like a servant and a whore whose sole occupation at the house was to service the limited sexual imagination of his late heir. Part of the awkward disregard that he showed her was due to his bemusement of why she was still in the house in the first place.

Satisfied that they had done a reasonably good job, the three climbed into a Lincoln Town Car and spun off down the main drive, at which point Samantha called Mr. Abrams, the leasing agent, to notify him of the Marquis's visit. She felt pleased in fulfilling the role as matchmaker between these two unpleasant people, and looked forward to witnessing their first encounter. But she had underestimated Lord Quart's zeal and organizational ability. Within minutes of hanging up the phone, two small moving vans entered the grounds and their burly crews hurriedly started to cart off the designated pieces, taking only minimum precautions to wrap and protect them. She was to learn later that the van carrying off the furniture and other large items was found in a warehouse in Long Beach while the one carrying the paintings and smaller items disappeared altogether.

Sadly, Sam also learned that Lord Quart never so much as called the police while in town. In fact, it turned out that he had made no inquiries whatsoever concerning Cecil's death, leaving the details regarding the reclamation and transport of the remains to his all-purpose man, Hinton. The public, however, was informed of the Marquis's twenty-four hour visitation when a photo of the gentleman appeared on a local Hollywood gossip website the next day. In it the mourning Lord was featured with two thoroughly wasted and almost topless young starlets in tow during an evening out at one of west LA's most celebrity-saturated haunts.

Within a week of Lord Quart's visit, the police investigation had narrowed down to a couple of lowlifes who were known to the police and the FBI as middle level money launderers and "investors" in the San Fernando porn industry. These gentlemen, in turn, had links to a prominent sundry gang and organized crime figures. Once the police had all but eliminated Samantha as a possible suspect, the enthusiasm the paparazzi had for hanging out down by the main gate quickly evaporated, and things were allowed to return to something approaching normalcy.

What still amazed Samantha was the ease by which she had been transplanted from LA to the Midwest. A call to Uncle Robbie, a call from him to Mr. Leuven in New York, and then one from Charles Leuven in Milwaukee inviting her to interview for a new opening at the network, and that was that.

By the time the lease was up at the end of January, Sam was feeling better about going to Milwaukee. She had become tired of LA's unremitting sun and traffic. Milwaukee, with all its Midwestern virtues of hard work, optimism, and its down-to-earth approach to life, was to be her first experience with "real" America, and she was going to make the best of it.

Suddenly, the water came to a head and started boiling over. Released from her revelries, Samantha got back to work on the tea. Still, she could not shake the notion that the trajectory of her life since leaving LA had been a straight shot to the bottom. She would have to think of something, and fast, if she was going to turn things around.

While Sam was ruminating about her past and "what ifs", Charlie had made himself comfortable in a corner of the living room, and stared out the massive plate glass window. A strong breeze was coming out of the west, creating a sizeable chop further out on Lake Michigan where the ice had not succeeded in petrifying the steel grey waters. The white caps were heading in the direction of the far sandy shore over the horizon. The lake was big but it was also boring, at least the bottom two-thirds of it. To Charlie it lacked character, excitement and above all romance, it was just a big patch of water that ended down around Chicago. He never understood why people valued it so much, but like many he too had decided on living in a place that featured it as a prime attraction.

Charlie had interviewed Sam less than a year ago during one of his last hiring sprees to inject new blood in the network. Sam assumed, at the time, she was interviewing for something of a clerical nature but when it turned out to be an actual on-air position, she had become positively buoyant. Even after learning that Samantha had absolutely no TV or even radio experience, Charlie remained smitten with the self-assured, naturally elegant women who sat across from his desk. He had enough confidence to know a diamond in the rough when he saw one, so he hired her on the spot. In his mind virtually anyone with reasonable quickness and poise could be a news or weather presenter. The only real problem was the green screen, and getting used to pointing to things on it that weren't really on the screen but only appeared that way to the audience sitting at home. But once that simple con job was mastered it would be off to the races for beautiful Samantha.

As Charlie predicted, Samantha learned quickly, her on-air warmth, fresh sense of humor, as well as her Oxbridge accent were the right ingredients to make her an instant minor celebrity. In five months she had become the most popular of all the WEBCO presenters, and was soon made co-anchor for the important morning time slot. Samantha, and her well-publicized face, was for many people interchangeable with their notion of

WEBCO itself. In a year or two she would be able to move to a more prestigious weather channel or as a lead weather person at a network affiliate in a major market.

While he had supported her unstintingly during her rise to fame, if not fortune, the fact that she would probably be lured away in the near future helped put a crimp in his longing to make an emotional commitment to her. A "what's the use" fatalism gradually infused itself into his thoughts regarding any long-term chances for a life together. He assumed his fears were shared by Sam as well.

"Here's your tea, *cunt hunter*," she said sharply as she practically dropped the cup and saucer into his lap. "You, Charles Leuven, are too immature for me, and I've decided to call a stop to our relationship for a while." Charlie was about to say something in his or the relationship's defense when she curtly motioned him to leave off until she had finished. "I should have known that a rich boy like you could never be a serious person. All your life you've had it too easy, everything you ever wanted was simply handed to you. No wonder you can't take life seriously if, from birth, everyone was running around trying to cater to your every whim. It really isn't your fault. I, on the other hand...."

"Please can it, Sam; how can you in good conscience go on like this? It's not like you were raised by some illiterate cockney rag pickers out of an East End alley. You've certainly had your fair share of breaks, so let's knock off the self-made woman act." Charles's refusal to put up with her occasional self-righteous posturing always impressed her, forcing Samantha to take another tack.

"I really thought we had something going here Charlie. We were getting on so well until this morning. Something is bugging you and you're not telling me, what it is?"

"I was wrong about what I said; I really do like being with you. I think we are terrific together but let's face some facts. I'm not going to stay in this town forever. I really can't stand it much longer. If you hadn't come into my life, I would have probably left months ago. And you aren't going to be happy here for much longer either. You're on your way up in this business and that means out. So why pretend; we both know that long distance romances hardly ever work out." As Charlie spoke he became more depressed, hoping that Samantha would jump in and dispel all his fears and doubts, but she just sat there listening.

"You really are a child. Don't you think I'm worth fighting for? If you're going to give up like that, you aren't the man I thought you were. You only value me if there's no inconvenience to you, only if I fit in one-hundred percent with all your plans. If you're that spoiled, it simply isn't going to work, is it now?"

Charlie looked at her wide face with its flared cheekbones and the sleek, green eyes he adored. Best of all, Charlie liked Samantha's strong chin and firm jaw line that went straight back to a slender neck. Charlie said nothing for a while; if he made a big outward play to win her back now Samantha would, in his mind, always have the upper hand. However, if he gave no hint as to his intentions, he would lose her soon enough. What to do? "You are without a doubt the most wonderful and beautiful woman I've ever known. I hope you feel that way about me. If you do, I think we should get married now and let the chips fall where they may." Charlie braced himself for Sam's reaction.

Stunned, she looked at Charlie long and hard. A proposal of marriage was the last thing that she had banked on that morning. Superficially, Charlie had all the right attributes going for him: looks, charm, money, intelligence, but for some reason those qualities never seemed to gel so as to form a man who was steady and convincing. There was something lazy and flippant about old Charlie that reminded her in some strange way of her father. But despite this, she did love him and wanted to love him more. "Charlie, I... I don't know what to say. I've never thought of us in that way, I mean not now. I'm only twenty-four; I don't know, I guess it's me who is confused," Samantha said with genuine bewilderment.

Score one, thought Charlie. I have her on the defensive at last, now be careful. "I'm not expecting an answer this second, but I want you to know how I truly feel about you. I think it's best we give it a rest for a while; we both need to sort things out more before making any decision that may prove permanent." Knowing he was sounding too much like the executive, Charlie quickly changed tactics and tone. "I mean, I want this to work and I know what I'm asking is serious and a little out of left field..." he didn't finish the sentence, letting it trail off and die on its own accord.

"Charlie, I'm very tired and can't think anymore. I should go back to my place." She leaned across the small table that separated the two chairs and kissed him on the cheek. In the condo's spacious hallway, near the elevator, Charlie helped her into her stylish coat and gave her a kiss, also on the cheek.

His eyes downcast now, Charlie, in hushed tones finally spoke, "I guess I'll see you on Tuesday, Sam."

"I guess so," came a sad, brittle reply.

Chapter 4

AN ILL WIND

Because Charlie had been out of town for a dog and pony show at a couple of Upper Peninsula TV stations all day Monday, he felt the need to come into the office early on Tuesday. Before going up to WEBCO's offices and studios on the forty-second floor of the US Bank Building, Charlie made his way over to the lobby newsstand and picked up a variety of newspapers and magazines. Once in his office, he alerted his secretary, Bobbi Shuster, not to admit anyone or transfer calls until after 9:00, by which time he hoped to have plowed through the Times, the WSJ, and the local paper before anyone got the idea in his or her head to bother him with any semi-serious questions. Listlessly thumbing through the Milwaukee Sentinel Charlie spotted a small article on the bottom of page seven in the state and local news section:

Serial Killer and Cousin Escape
Mendota State:

Madison. Authorities confirmed this evening that the notorious serial killer of the late 1970's, Carl Troutmann and his cousin, Harlan Zinter escaped from Mendota State Mental Hospital in Madison. A spokesperson for the hospital stated that the two had probably left the premises inside a food delivery truck at approximately 1:15 pm Monday afternoon. The spokesperson said that the hospital immediately alerted authorities.

State Police Headquarters confirmed that an all-persons bulletin has been issued and that citizens were alerted to be on the outlook for the two men. Lt. James Feldman, a spokesperson for the Dane County Police Department, cautioned citizens not to approach the two escapees as they are considered dangerous and possibly armed. Anyone seeing the two escapees is urged to call state or local police immediately. Police believe that the two are headed north to the Rhinelander area where they still have friends and relatives.

Troutmann (aka Norm Knutson, Carl Knutson and Norm Karl) is described as five foot eleven, heavy set and bald. Zinter is five foot seven and is of slight build with long wavy hair and a trim beard.

The article went on to summarize Knutson's rampage through northern Wisconsin during the latter part of the 70's, a rampage resulting in the deaths of seven female school teachers, earning Knutson the moniker "Mad Axe Man of Oneida County." Harlan Zinter was convicted separately in 1979, given life sentence, and incarcerated in a state mental facility for participation in at least four of the murders. Both men were described as delusional and paranoid when not on prescribed medications.

Today's break with the normal routine of coming in around 8:30 and immediately going into meetings was dictated more by Charlie's general despondency over the events of the past Sunday than with the need to catch up on any paperwork that had accumulated in his short absence. The fight with Sam had left him thoroughly bummed out and uncomfortable with being alone. He knew he was coming to a crossroads in his life, and none of the options presenting themselves were particularly attractive. He realized that because his behavior had been so selfishly manipulative, not to mention crassly stupid, it was going to take a long time to patch things up with Sam. For the time being he envisioned a period of high tension; one in which the art of instant eye dropping and reflexive cringing would have to be expertly executed in order to minimize the embarrassment of any unanticipated encounter between them. As if mutually acknowledging their need for separation, both would probably try to avoid one another in the hallways and conference rooms, barely making eye contact, and at best exchanging an embarrassed or bland pleasantry when someone else was present. In time, perhaps, the hurt feelings and the embarrassment might give way to a need for mutual reconciliation. But for now, Charlie had to face the fact that he had come off as a complete creep, one moment asking Samantha if it was OK for him to see other women, the next proposing marriage. Today he was thoroughly confused and blue; it seemed everything was smashed up beyond repair.

The second item of concern had been festering for longer: his need to move on professionally. He had been at WEBCO for almost three years. Recalling his conversation with his father a year ago at Thanksgiving, Charlie had looked in vain toward the heavens for the right series of isobars to take shape, and the best possible storm systems to line up out on the distant horizons, but to no avail. Every day, he would secretly go over the maps to see if the highs and lows were coming together to set in motion the desired meteorological cataclysm that would turn the country upside down. He was most attentive during the summer and early fall months, looking to see if the country would be hit by three or four Katrina-sized hurricanes in a row. But the past hurricane season had been unusually quiet. Now, in the full grip of winter, all of Charlie's hopes rested on a million-to-one alignment of at least two massive weather systems simultaneously occurring thousands of miles apart and converging just so to create a sweeping vortex of utter and inconvertible mayhem from coast to coast. A blizzard of 1888, 1899, 1940 or 1978 would be nice but best yet would be a combination of all four. But each time he looked, something was wrong, one system was too far south, or a polar outbreak out of Canada was moving too fast for it to hit a moisture laden low coming up from the Gulf. The confluence of the fronts didn't necessarily have to be real; they just had to look real enough to get things into play, real enough to crank up the big scare machine and get the word out to the millions who wanted and needed some excitement to get them through yet another boring winter.

All through December and most of January he kept his vigil, but except for a couple of blizzards in the Rockies, there hadn't been much serious weather all winter.

Not until late Monday evening, that is.

Then, while staring at his laptop on the flight back from Marquette, Michigan, Charlie saw what he hoped might turn into three sizeable tropical depressions meandering far off the Pacific coast. In a couple of days they might congeal into one massive system and smash into the Pacific Northwest. He also noticed a large high was just beginning to form just south of the Arctic Circle. Might this be it? It could indeed be it. No, it would be it! Charlie, by force of will, if necessary, would squeeze those fronts so they would take shape and converge just so. Then he would get

43

on TV and scare the shit out of America, and then he'd sell the albatross called WEBCO to some fool in Atlanta or Chicago, and then....

That was Charlie Leuven's grand strategy, at any rate, and that evening something deep down inside told him that, this time, he was going to get his ticket punched and get out of Dodge. He decided then and there that if over the next twenty-four hours the fronts still looked promising he was going to hype the coming "storm" for all it was worth. If it fizzled out, he would get the boot and go home and start over. On the other hand, if he turned out to be prescient or just lucky, he would appear a hero, a Tiresias of the Isobars, a Wotan of Weather, a prophet fearlessly warning the multitudes of the imminent peril awaiting them while his more fatuous competitors smugly sat around doing nothing.

As Charlie swung his chair to the left and looked out through the high windows of his office, he suddenly felt himself slipping again into the slough of self-pity, a state of mind in which he might luxuriate for days if he wasn't careful. "God this is the third winter I've spent in this place. It's like traveling to Pluto in an old VW bus and having nothing to listen to but Glenn Beck or Neil Diamond for the entire trip. Jesus, if this doesn't work, I'm going to go completely around the bend." Charles looked down from the heights of his glass eyrir onto the underwhelming panorama of Milwaukee and its environs. Since his exile from Manhattan, he had tried to adjust to living here but it was simply no good. It wasn't that the city was a dump, it had its charms but they were Midwest enchantments, predictable and unrefined attractions one might glean from the reruns of "Happy Days" or "That Seventies Show."

During the first year he was too busy to notice. The

WEBCO he took over was a distant third in every conceivable category in an industry segment that totaled only three competitors. Leuven, however, stirred himself for the first time in quite a few years. He started out with the usual cosmetics: an updated looking logo, a new advertising and promotional campaign, and brighter and more stylish sets. Charlie scoured all the markets he could think of to find new talent – people with some bounce in their step to replace the dullards and time servers who had for years been hurting the eyes and ears of WEBCO's dwindling audience. He invested in new technologies and forecasting tools, and, of course, a string of Doppler Radars strategically located throughout the network's core viewing area.

The sassier appearance of the programming helped Charlie sign up the few remaining independent cable companies who were too cheap to pony up for The Weather Channel. He also cajoled a considerable number of local independent TV stations to allow WEBCO to provide emergency weather services beyond what their limited budgets could handle. While not directly very profitable, these strategies looked good to some advertisers. Now, if Armageddon ever looked imminent these independent, small town stations would prove the lynch pin in Charlie's grand scheme.

The result of all these incremental, and what to Charlie were rather obvious tweakings, was that WEBCO was at last being taken seriously and gradually inching its way up in the ratings. Best yet, the network managed to eke out a respectable profit during the last two quarters. Audience viewing levels were up nearly nine percent in just eighteen months and demographics improved markedly as a younger and more upscale audience was starting to tune in. The payoff was that ad rates followed and increased significantly. During the most recent sweeps, WEBCO managed to come within just a hair of easing out Weather Central for the number two position. Despite Leuven's best efforts, however, The Weather Channel continued to tighten its grip on the saturated market for twenty-four hour weather news despite its bland presentations and its batch of even blander weather personalities. Its purchase by NBC would keep it solidly in the number one spot until the end of time.

It was no secret that the owners, pére and fils Gartner, were just waiting for the economy to improve and the ratings to sparkle a little more before unloading the broadcasting orphan onto any outfit which could convince itself that it had the magic formulae for creating heretofore undetectable synergies with their other media holdings. The family now knew it should have sold WEBCO off long ago, but it had been a very small part of a much bigger deal and was easily shunted aside in the rush to close on the more important assets. Ignored, it was left to quietly languish until Charlie's nemesis, Roger Gartner, rediscovered it when he was assigned the task of finding a corporate St. Helena for Charlie after the death of his beloved sister Cynthia.

Charlie sighed, ran his hands through his thick, longish hair, and swiveled his chair to take in the north view of the city, looking up along the beach and Lincoln Park. During the second year, he attempted to socialize and tried to convince himself that it wasn't all that bad living in the storied Beer Capitol. He even joined a club or two, bought a small sailboat, and tried to decorate his new condo on the park. But to little avail; the clubs were duller than dishwater, the sailing season short, the races unchallenging, and the redecorating over and done within a few months. Leuven's heart also wasn't into the usual games and gambits of the local dating scene. He was simply bored and lonely – then he met Sam and everything changed.

Attempting a momentary escape from his various conundrums, Charlie opened the pages of his recently purchased copy of Us Magazine. The cover story featured a before and after article on people who had undergone the rigors of complete facial transplants. Most of the hideously scarred folks were women but a couple were men, one a victim of fire, the other of war. The article trumpeted the fact that these poor wretches would no longer be mistaken for extras in a Wes Craven movie, and could now go about their business and attract only the minimum of stares and whispers. The transformations were indeed remarkable, and Charlie was pleased that modern plastic surgery had made such great strides in helping make a real difference in people's lives.

As he stared at the photos, Charlie wondered if he ever experienced a catastrophic failure in the looks department who he would want to emerge looking like once his face had gone through a similarly extensive refurbishing. Then he remembered a piece in Vanity Fair some months back about the changing looks of Hollywood's leading men since the 1940's and 50's. He swiveled his chair around to face his credenza and rifled through some old reports and files until he finally found it. Quickly turning the pages, his fingers eventually found the pictures of Stewart Granger and Joseph Cotton that the article used as two of several comparative examples. Since Charlie thought that most of today's leading men were simply overgrown boys, he certainly did not want to have the bandages come off only to look like a young Leonardo DiCaprio. Charlie gazed again at the two faces, Steward Granger, the great white hunter, possessing an unmistakable animal magnetism, his strong features and flowing, wavy hair resembled his own in a vague way. Charlie thought it would be a no-brainer for a good surgeon to turn him into a clone of the great "bwana."

The only problem with that solution, however, was for all of Granger's lady killing looks, there really wasn't very much apparent depth to the fellow. He seemed like a straight-ahead meat-and-potatoes guy, a sort of refined English version of John Wayne. Cotton, on the other hand, was different. You were never quite sure of what was going on with him. There was always a subtle mysteriousness, even menace beneath his good looks and studied manners, a drawing room charmer one minute and a homicidal murderer the next.

Charlie ripped out the two pictures from Vanity Fair and took them over to the full-length mirror by the door of his office. Holding them up on each side of his face, he was about to ask himself which face Sam would like best. Deciding neither would do, Charlie was about to hit on the idea of Errol Flynn when Jimmy Dasimmi opened the door and poked his big square head inside. Turning red, Charlie tried unsuccessfully to put the two photos behind his back but the old cop was too fast for him. "What do we have here, Chief," came the grinning "gotcha" smile.

Knowing he was caught, Charlie immediately posed the question of who Jimmy would like to look like in another life. The beefy ex-cop didn't hesitate, "Stuart Granger, he got all the broads, right?"

"He had that reputation. Here, look at this magazine about all these people who have gotten face transplants," Charlie said as he made his way back to his desk. "Have you located those planes I talked to you about last night?"

"They're good to go, Chief. I can have two late model Bombardier Challengers on the tarmac of your choice within six hours of your OK," Jimmy replied, a self-satisfied ring in his voice.

"Well done as usual," Charlie stared at the big man in his mid-fifties sitting across from him. He estimated Jimmy was just over six feet tall, but he looked shorter due to his box-like upper body. Contrasting Jimmy's cubic torso was a gently sloping forehead, the angle of which was accented by his longish graying black hair combed straight back. A pronounced tubular nose jutting straight out from his face and two small round ears set close to the skull awaited only the companionship of a pair of deep set, coal back eyes to complete the ensemble. The overall effect was curious but not displeasing. Most people on meeting Jimmy for the first time could not immediately sort out the overall impression that his ursine features seemed to convey. Even Charlie, when he sat down with Dasimmi after a couple days' absence, could never quite tell at first whether the person sitting across from him wasn't really a bear dressed up in a man-suit.

From the time Charlie had first set foot in Milwaukee, Jimmy had been by his side in one capacity or another. He had met him at the airport on that bleak day in November when he first arrived. It was Jimmy who had driven him to his temporary home at the Pfister Hotel and then escorted him by foot to the WEBCO offices the next morning. And so it went; in due course, Jimmy became his driver, his Mr. Fix-It, and all around go-to man. All Charlie ever discovered about Jimmy on a personal level was that he had been a sergeant on the Chicago police force, working at different times on vice, fraud and homicide. He left the force about three years after becoming a homicide detective and moved up to Milwaukee to live closer to his daughter, Stephanie.

The story around the office had it that Jimmy just showed up at WEBCO one afternoon and sat down in the news room where Stephanie worked; a few minutes later someone asked him to help move a file cabinet across the hall and from that moment on Jimmy had become a fixture. When Stephanie left WEBCO to take care of her growing brood of kids, Jimmy just stayed on. As best as Charlie could determine, Jimmy officially came on the pay roll a little over four years ago, and his official job title was listed as operations assistant.

He lived in a tidy bungalow in Shorewood, a close-in suburb on the north side, and spent a fair amount of time babysitting his grandchildren. Outside of these tidbits, Charlie knew little about him. There was a vibe about Jimmy that strongly suggested he didn't appreciate people asking too many personal questions, preferring a polite distance.

~

It was a little before 11:00 and Samantha had just returned to her desk after her 7:00 to 10:00 morning co-anchor slot. She had briefly seen Charlie in the hallway during a commercial break. She stared vacantly at her computer screen debating whether to take the rest of the day off when her cell phone rang. Samantha grabbed it on the second ring; as she had hoped it was Anne, her only true girlfriend in the States. "Oh, thank you for calling, Anne. How is everything in LA? I assume you got my text message?" Samantha asked as casually as she could.

"Same old, same old, kid; Lionel is off to a fat farm in Palm Springs. He tipped in at three-fifty last week and said that was it. I can't imagine him thin, can you? I mean he's meant to be fat. Where would Sidney Greenstreet have gotten if he looked like Ichabod Crane? Oh, well, what to do?"

Switching gears, Anne at last zeroed in on the topic that occasioned her call. "How are you doing sweets, holding up, OK? So you think Mr. WEBCO gave you the heave ho, huh? Now, tell me exactly what happened and we'll see if I can come up with some sort of game plan for you two to get back together," said Anne in a manner that seemed a cross between a therapist and a business consultant.

Samantha had hoped to hear a more consoling and comforting tone from her friend whom she hadn't seen face-to-face for over a year. Instead she was forced to wade through her tough big sister act. But Anne after all was a survivor of the Hollywood relationship wars and, by the age of thirty-two, had become inured to the effects of young passion and its inevitable triumph over common sense. Perhaps she should have called someone in England, Amanda or Ursula; they were closer to her age and hopefully not yet as jaded and detached. Anne, however, was here now and why not take advantage of it, Samantha thought as she breathlessly launched into a fifteen minute, blow-by-blow account of Sunday's breakup. Exhausted by her almost non-stop recounting of those sorry details, Samantha concluded her litany of woe by throwing her fate into the tarnished hands of Anne Blumenthal.

"I don't understand. He asked you to marry him, didn't he? So what's the problem? Why didn't you call his bluff?" asked Anne, a little puzzled by what all the excitement was about.

"Don't you think it was just a cheap ploy on his part to make me reject him? He's nothing but a manipulative little coward," answered Samantha angrily.

"Of course; listen, this is what I think darling," confided Anne distractedly as she reached over to put the fingernail gloss applicator back into its little bottle. "It is what it is, meaning that what he told you is sort of true, at least in his mind. He's afraid of making a commitment to you with everything up in the air. First, are you still interested in him? Before you say no, remember that from what you've told me he seems like quite a catch: looks, heaps of dough and a firecracker in the sack, not a bad combo my dear, so shoot."

"I don't know. I thought I did, but I think he's acted like a twenty year old spoiled brat."

"Naturally," interrupted Anne.

"I'm beginning to think that I went for him as a fall back following Cecil's death. And that I was still really in mourning for him." This bit of self-protecting rationalization did not escape Anne.

"Please, enough. You never loved that dope, Cecil was just a ticket so you could peak under the skirts of the movie set. You knew that it wouldn't last but you had the guts to go along for the ride for a while, and that's it. So don't give me that Charlie was a means for you to grieve your grief. Much too lame; you know me too well to try to pull that shit with dear old Anne.

"So, I'm concluding that you're still in love with old Charlie, and that's good or at least it's OK. So how to get him back in your life? First do nothing, do not ignore him, do not avoid him, just treat him as you would any other guy who happens to be almost exactly everything you've been looking for in a man."

Before Anne could go on, Sam interrupted. "Should I start an affair to get him jealous?"

"What, are you kidding? This is not 1985 and Charlie Leuven is not the boy next door. A guy like Charlie who can get anyone he wants is not going to go all to jelly just because you have a fling with some Joe. He'll just begin to doubt his judgment that you're the greatest and begin writing you off as a bit of flawed meat. No, don't cheapen your brand. For now you're going to have to bide your time until something comes up that will really get his attention and make him see you in a completely different way. Here's what to do."

Chapter 5

THE BIG MEETING

The darkening grey of the early night gradually enveloped the city. On the streets below, beams from headlights shot out into the darkness for a few yards before being consumed by the winter blackness. High up in the US Bank Corp tower three men and one woman sat around the elliptical table in a small, nondescript conference room. They were unconcerned about the commute home in the dark; by the time they descended to street level, the rush hour would be long over. They waited patiently for Charlie Leuven to appear and fill them in on something that he insisted was of "paramount importance." The four became five when Jimmy Dasimmi quietly entered. Nodding jerkily to the others, he took a chair against the exterior glass wall.

The conference room, adjacent to Charlie's office, enjoyed good views of the southern half of the large shallow bay that stretched past the lakeside art complex, down to a series of small buildings and pavilions comprising the Henry Maier Festival Park, concluding with the grand Marcus Amphitheatre at the lower part of the grounds. This conglomeration of buildings was snuggly jammed in between the Lake Freeway to the west and Lake Michigan to the east. Further to the south were the Port of Milwaukee and the old A&B Clock Tower; below these were the modest middle and working class towns of St. Francis and Cudahy.

Just before the waiting five began to fidget and glance nervously at their watches, Charlie Leuven made his entrance through a panel door at the far end of the room. Wasting little time with preliminaries, he hurriedly launched into what in business parlance would be termed a candid evaluation of the current viability of WEBCO.

"I've just gotten off the phone with New York. I think before we begin with the original purpose of this meeting, I need to relay to you what the feelings are at our parent, Worldwide Media. They're generally pleased with the steady progress we've achieved in improving WEBCO's profit picture and turning the network into a real industry competitor. Nevertheless, the feeling at HQ is that it makes strategic sense to explore options related to the sale of WEBCO in the near future."

Charlie stopped to let the message sink in. He looked around at the four who sat at the table: Reggie Chevis, WEBCO's Chief Meteorologist; Byron Hale, the "dean" of the network's anchors; Cal Thornquist, VP of Operations; and Susan Brownell, VP of Administration. Of the four, Byron Hale, in his natty suit and perfectly coiffed hair, was the most visibly shaken. The color in his bland industry-standard good looks had drained away, replaced by small blotches of yellowish gray. Bearing down on fifty, Hale knew that his prospects in the weather business were not very bright if his talents were jettisoned in a corporate upheaval. The other four were more in control of themselves, but there were detectable increases in thumping fingers and bouncing knees.

"I don't have to tell any of you that once we're put into play, anything can happen, and we all might find ourselves out on the street. Now I want to add that nothing has been firmly decided.

I also know that they would be interested in reconsidering things if we can give them a good reason for doing so." Charlie stopped at this point to wait for Reggie or Susan to interject but instead it was Cal, the no nonsense engineer, who spoke up.

"How in the hell are we going to make them reconsider? I mean, it's the weather, damn it. We can't do much about it. They know changes in ratings and ad revenues can only increase incrementally in a mature market." Cal concluded his pedestrian observations by running his big hand through his short bristly hair, hair so even and closely cropped that it could substitute for the flight deck of a miniature aircraft carrier.

"He has a point, you know Chief," added Reggie, WEBCO's top weather forecaster and all around meteorological guru. "We can't just make it up to suit the ratings."

Charlie looked around and saw that Bryon and Susan were in agreement. "Do you have some idea of how to save our bacon?" asked Susan expectantly.

As if waiting for his cue, Charlie rose from his seat, straightened his tie and started off on a carefully scripted offensive. "Yes, I do, but before I share my thoughts, permit me to start things off with an observation, or thesis if you will." Not waiting for a vote from his colleagues, Charlie leaped into his screed.

"If I know anything, I know this – people love fear. They love being afraid of something or even someone. They enjoy facing a potentially deadly situation and triumphing over it. It makes them feel alive, needed, united with others in some great cause. For most, the only time they feel any significance to their lives is when they somehow become part of a great historic drama. That's what I know, and that's what WEBCO is going to give them, a collective feeling of a good and godly effort that brings everyone on deck to fill the breach. A mighty and proud people reunited to overcome some unthinking, unfeeling, and malevolently primordial force of overwhelming destructive evil. An entity which, if not squarely confronted by all the citizenry, promises to destroy everything we hold dear and enslave us forever in its awful maw." Charlie quickly searched the faces of the four executives and then gave a glance toward Jimmy. Taking their stunned expressions as worshipful consent, Charlie started to move slowly around the tight confines of the room.

"Friends, I don't think it is too bold to say that in our great work fear will be our friend, our guide and our ultimate savior. We will do everything to satisfy the collective craving of our audience to be filled with terror, with a steady, seamless flow of vital and timely information that will serve both to confirm their worst apprehensions for their welfare while simultaneously applying the soothing balm of hope triumphant to our otherwise distraught viewers. I promise all of you this: the doses of fear and hope, which necessity will force us to dispense, will be distributed in responsibly measured portions to ensure that our audience is neither overwhelmed by the black dog of despair nor overly stimulated by the elixir of incandescent expectation. This, I feel, will be our storied mission, our duty to our country and to humanity at large." Satisfied that his associates were not about to run for the exits, Charlie continued to tazer them with his mass psychology theorems.

"If you don't believe that people long to be terrified, look at all these so-called horror movies that come out year after year. But it's more than that, of course. I've come to the conclusion that people need a constant sense of fear in their daily lives to feel alive. Only when an overarching sense of anxiety pervades their consciousness and threatens them do they feel really engaged with life. Now there are two caveats to all of this: first, the produced fear must be continuous but of a low intensity, at least for most of the time. The threat of terrorism is a good example: it can't be seen as something that actually disrupts the flow of everyday life very much. Only on rare occasions can fear by allowed to spike and become all-pervasive. Now, the second related caveat is this: at its core, the foundation of this fear must be something with a fairly low objective probability of actually happening.

"Now, some of you are old enough to have lived through some of the Cold War; at times the fear of nuclear holocaust was a very real thing. During Berlin, and especially the Cuban Missile Crisis, things were pretty bleak, no question. But for most of the time the doomsday cloud hung over things like a big hangover. Anyone in their right mind would have assumed that once the Cold War ended, people would be so relieved that they simply wouldn't want to think about anything so catastrophic for a long, long time. But look what happened." Charles cleared his throat so he could shoot straight through what he considered to be one of the most telling and well-crafted of his inane observations regarding human nature. "As soon as the Berlin Wall comes tumbling down and the Russians are kissing our asses – Independence Day, X Files, and all the rest of the brew telling us to prepare for a foe so powerful, so insidious that nothing we do can avert our total annihilation. Throw on top of the fear of space invaders that of a dumb piece of rock coming at us from the depths of outer space, `a la Armageddon and Deep Impact, and we're as good as toast. The chance of these things happening is of course nil, but the military-industrial-entertainment complex sees an opportunity to gin things up and viola – it's as real as a weekend visit to Aunt Polly's.

"After we got bored with this specter of annihilation from the great beyond, we're given the opportunity to contemplate death by rampaging pandemics ravaging the planet. Again, this end game is made real to us by movies like 28 Days Later, I am Legend and those yummy books on the Ebola virus.

"After 9/11, it's all about terrorism and those terrible Nickolas Cage movies. What's the chance of someone living in Omaha being splattered all over town in a terrorist attack – nada, right? But everyone gets sucked in nevertheless, made to feel a part of this big dysfunctional family we call the world community.

"All through this period we've also had to confront the 'Dates of Doom' – 1984, 1999, 2000, 2001 and 2012, and watch as endless 'History' and 'Discovery' channel programs delve into the wisdom of the Revelation, Nostradamus and the Mayan calendar.

"And who can forget about Global Warming. How true is that? Who knows really, but again we're faced with the impending doom of the planet, I mean that stupid movie The Day After Tomorrow where an ice age blows down from the Arctic in one afternoon and blankets New York. Really, who can believe that type of rubbish? But then again, who cares? Fear sells and sells big if packaged right. It has to be mixed with heroics, where a band of intrepid fighters overcomes impossible odds to save the world, or at least a deserving remnant that will carry on after the sins of the world are cleansed by flood or flame. You also have to make people feel like they're not only a part of what's going on, but that they also can participate directly in the disaster du jour and be among the few, the brave, and the chosen who walk out when everyone else is hamburger. These survivors are buoyed by the knowledge that the rubble they see all around them would have been worse if not for their own heroic efforts."

Charlie stopped again to survey the reaction of his four listeners. Expressions of the most profound wonderment seemed to sum up the little group's thinking. They eyed one another and then turned their collective blank expressions back to their maximum leader, wordlessly expressing their unanimous belief that Charlie was certifiably insane.

"What the fuck are you talking about, here, fear and redemption and all the rest of this bullshit that you're shoveling at us? Do you think we're just a bunch of rubes and idiots?" The heated and exasperated words came again from Cal, who gave every appearance that his next move would be to jump over the table and deck Charlie with a couple of round house rights.

"Cal's right, Chief – I mean what's there to be afraid of? We can't just make something up out of the blue to frighten everyone. We're a little beyond War of the Worlds these days. We would be laughed out of town; our license could even be yanked. What gives here, Charlie?" asked Chevis in a crestfallen voice.

"Here's what's up," a nonplussed Charlie retorted. "Let me give you the updates as of fifteen hundred hours." Without moving, Charlie clicked the remote control turning on the fifty-two inch TV that took up practically the entire wall behind him. He then tapped a few keys on his laptop before walking up to a current weather map of North America featured on the screen. Pointing to the west coast of the country with a thick laser pen, Charlie began the heart of his presentation with unalloyed seriousness. "We have a very unusual confluence of fronts building off the West Coast. It's not unusual to have a low or two at this time of year forming out here. This week, however, we're going to have three of them coming ashore almost simultaneously. The largest one is coming out of the northwest, and it will hit south of Seattle. It has extremely low pressure; it would be dangerous enough if it were all by itself. Unfortunately, we have two more, slightly smaller systems that are going to make for interesting surfing. The next low should come ashore south of the Bay Area, between Monterrey and Santa Cruz. Further on, the southernmost system will be coming onto the mainland around Santa Barbara, at almost the same hour.

"These systems have three salient features in common: First, they all cover a vast area and their barometric pressures are extremely low, between 27.80 inches and 27.32 inches. Second, as of now, it seems that all three will be hitting the coast within a five-hour time span. I am predicting landfall for around three o'clock Thursday, local time. Lastly, these depressions, even though their upper level winds are only about sixty knots per hour, are traveling at about fifty knots. That's very fast, needless to say. They will bring significant rain to the West Coast and heavy snowfall to the west slopes of the Rockies. However, it won't be until they hit the big Canada cold weather mass that things get interesting."

Charlie then moved over toward the middle of the big screen to explain the pattern coming down from Canada. "I'm predicting that a deep jet stream trough will shift radically south, as far down as southern Arizona and New Mexico, extending all the way east to southern Florida. In the central Canadian Rockies, a large and deepening arctic system is forming which by late Thursday night will be dipping into the western U.S. around the Boise area. It will quickly extend as far west as Billings, Montana by late Friday morning. This will of course constitute a major polar outbreak characterized by intense, and in many cases near-record low temperatures, and very high winds exceeding seventy miles per-hour in some cases. Temperatures may reach as low as minus eighty degrees in the higher elevations. In addition to its intensity, the size of the outbreak will be significant. I'm anticipating that it will eventually reach as far south as the Dallas, Jackson and Birmingham line and eventually as far east as the Carolinas. Needless to say, when this front collides with those coming out of the west, there will be one fucking big KABOOM on the ground," concluded Charlie, clapping his hands together for emphasis.

He stopped for a moment, caught his breath and then plunged on. "That's not all mates. Turning to the waters off the Yucatan, in the Gulf, I'm seeing an unusual depression forming for this time of year. Based on upper-level wind patterns, I'm predicting that this front will move north and come ashore along the western Louisiana coast by late Friday, at about which time it should reach the tropical storm category. It will then continue north, up the Mississippi before veering eastward around St. Louis, and then go up along Ohio River Valley. This one will be moving slowly, but will bring lots of moisture along with it."

Charlie was getting more and more pumped up as he envisioned cities the size of Minneapolis and Denver buried under hundreds of feet of snow; highways clogged with tens of thousands of panic-stricken motorists fleeing south in a vain attempt to escape their preordained doom. In his fervid imagination, Charlie saw planes coated with ice falling from the sky and crashing into suburban housing tracts, and above all he saw ratings soaring and money rolling in by the barrel-full, as a terrified yet fascinated nation stayed glued to WEBCO.

"In addition to the action off the Yucatan there's also a weak low brewing in the eastern Gulf, west of Cuba. Now, if that moves north and comes ashore in the panhandle of Florida, and then moves up the eastern seaboard we're talking the blizzards of 1888, 1950 and '93 all over again.

"Now let me finish here with something that may or may not affect the larger picture." As he said this he had moved further over to the far right side of the screen and turned his body so that he was pointing from his right hand. The laser's red light hit a point in the North Atlantic between Newfoundland and Greenland. "I'm hop... betting," Charlie said catching himself, "that the East Coast may be in for a very stiff Nor'easter by Sunday. If this low becomes more defined at the same rate it has been developing over the last twenty-four hours it could be significant. If it does, and what I am telling you now is still open to a lot of 'ifs', there will be little stopping it from colliding with remnants of the strong systems coming from the West. And if that happens it's BOOM and BAM, lights out, that's all she wrote! So you see gang, we very well may have something to sell besides an emotion, something big and important that can really put us on the map if we handle it right. Do you read me?

"And that's how we're going to save WEBCO from the auction block. We're going to be the first to come out with the forecast I just outlined. We're going to scare the shit out of the country in such a way that people will be talking about nothing else but WEBCO and our forecast. Everyone will be tuning in, and believe me once they do, I have some ideas on how to keep them watching." Here Charlie stopped. He was now the picture of smugness, hands on hips, head thrown back, as if daring the world to take him on, a mad glint in his eye as if he had just seen something beyond comprehension of mere mortals.

The silence in the conference room was total. For almost a minute no one exchanged looks, much less spoke. No one could believe that Charlie could have come up with this type of long range forecast on his own. He was considered by nearly all the weather people no more than an amiable dunce when it came to the nuts and bolts of the weather. Finally, Reggie screwed up the courage to offer a comment.

"You may have something there, Chief, but I gotta say I think it might be a little too early to come out with such a sweeping forecast just now; there're a lot of factors that have to fall into place before we can be sure it's going to break the way you've outlined."

Before Charlie could pounce, Susan circuitously came to Reggie's support. "Charlie that was really great and you spelled it out so clearly and all. But I'm surprised that none of the other networks have started talking about this; you know, as something they might be watching out for. What gives?"

"I'll tell you what gives; they don't have Charlie Leuven's vision, that's what gives!" Collectively the eyeballs in the room swiveled over in the direction of Byron Hale, the "Toady from Toledo" as some called him behind his back. "That was the greatest Chief; I can see it getting really hairy out there in a few days. The information that Charles just gave us imposes on all of us an enormous responsibility. If we blow this thing it's lights out for WEBCO. We got to play it straight and we got to deliver every second we're on the air. I'm with you Chief, come what may," Hale's voice quivered as he concluded his offer of unreserved support.

64

"Thanks, Byron, I knew I could count on you," Charlie said, trying to suppress any hint of sarcasm. "I need to break here for a few minutes. Let's start up again in a half-hour and wrap things up," he said as he made for the connecting to his office.

Once Charlie left the room with Jimmy in tow, Cal Thornquist was the first to speak. "I can't believe we just sat there and listened to this crazy guy ramble on for twenty minutes or whatever it was. I've known a lot of hotshot grand-standers but Charlie takes the cake. If we scoop everyone else just for the sake of keeping WEBCO as is, and the forecast turns out to be a dud, we'll all end up teaching at some community college in Oshkosh. Reggie, you're the weather guy. What do you make of all this shit?"

This time all eyes turned towards Reggie Chevis, the Barbadian professor "discovered" by Charlie, snatched out of the meteorology department at the University of Wisconsin, Milwaukee and vaulted into local media prominence. Viewers from the small towns and cities who were the heart of WEBCO's audience felt uncomfortable at first in having a black man with a funny accent talking about their heartland weather. After a few weeks, however, they gradually warmed to his intelligence and encyclopedic knowledge until he became, like Samantha, a minor regional celebrity.

Reggie enjoyed his job and his reputation in the industry of being a rock solid forecaster and a straight shooter. People trusted him, sent their kids to school in the deep winter on his say-so; farmers planted based, in part, on his forecasts, and holiday-goers carefully planned their urban escapes with his blessings. As a result, he was keenly aware of his need to be viewed as a step above the unseemliness of corporate intrigues or personal interests when it came to forecasting.

He cleared his throat and moved his hands down his face before talking. "What Charlie is telling us is possible; I mean the forecast part of it. There is an unusual alignment of fronts, at least off the Pacific and over Canada. If they do converge just so, they could produce the type of disaster Charlie is talking about. So, I'm not prepared to dismiss his ideas outright, but these things usually don't come together as neatly as Charlie thinks they do. In this case, the Pacific systems can easily get stalled in the Rockies where they dump the bulk of their snow. Admittedly, in this case, they are moving pretty fast, so they could whip over the mountains with moisture to spare." Reggie took a deep breath, trying to make it seem like normal breathing, a technique that he mastered during his first year before the cameras.

"However, due to the big polar air mass moving south, the likelihood that the Pacific system fronts can move out of the Rockies will depend upon whether or not a powerful system comes south at the right time. These systems would have to intersect just so for the Pacific Lows to move eastward. We would also need another system moving down over the Great Lakes to bring in some lake effect snow and more cold air to meet up with the Low coming from the Gulf. Now if that happens we will have a very bad winter storm. And, if the Lows in the Gulf move north at the right time, we could have a very, very bad winter storm."

"A lot of 'ifs' for me," Susan Brownell offered. As usual, she had remained silent for most of the meeting, trying to keep out of the emotional fray and assess things calmly. "From what you're saying, I would give Charlie's thesis a D, with less than a 33% chance of happening. Am I on target here, Reggie?"

"More or less."

"Not great odds when your career could go out the window if we bet wrong."

"No matter how you slice it we're probably fucked. If we sit around and do nothing we'll get canned once WEBCO gets sold. But if we go along with Charlie we just might come out on top," Bryon Hale succinctly offered. His three colleagues looked at him startled by his ready summation of their collective quandary.

Cal huffed at his end of the table, indicating he had come up with a solution. "Why don't we try this…"

While these discussions were going on in the conference room, Charlie and Jimmy were lounging in a corner of the CEO's office over an evening drink. "I love the craziness, Jimmy, but it takes it out of you. Nevertheless, I think those turtles will climb aboard. You know, my dad was right: the big things are the easiest."

"You got' em in your pocket, Chief. Don't worry, what choice do they really have?"

"Say, what's the deal with those panelists I asked about? Have you made any progress in identifying them?"

"Yeah, here's a list of the three I think might do OK," said Jimmy matter-of-factly as he handed Charlie a neatly-printed list of the candidates along with their short bios.

"Let me take a gander and I'll get back to you after the meeting," replied Charlie, a little disappointed that the pool was so limited. "Can you get me any footage of them actually making a speech or something? I mean, we can't have a bunch of crazy people up there making God knows what type of ideas and predictions. They'll have to appear reasonably sane and seem marginally together even though they're going to be shoveling a complete line of shit."

"I got you Chief. I don't know about the footage, I'll check it out. I've talked with everyone, except for Starkweather; by reputation she's a little out there, but we might be able to clean her up before she goes on."

"If all hell is really going to break loose and a big part of the good old USA is buried under miles of snow, we can't just dress up three nuts who are predicting Doomsday and causing nationwide panic. You know what I mean, Jimmy?"

"Not exactly, but here's a suggestion, don't let that fool Hale handle the panel; he'll just fuck it up and then it will really make us all look like a bunch of amateurs. I think you're going to have to step in and do it yourself. You got the moxie to steer it right if things start going screwy."

"Jimmy, you're right, absolutely right," sighed Charlie as he glanced at his watch. "Show time, let's go."

Charlie wasn't prepared for the reception he received upon rejoining the meeting. Instead of a group of bemused and worried executives, Charlie was met by a solid phalanx of corporate rioters. Cal Thornquist jumped in first, "Charlie, we've been discussing your ideas, and I think we've come up with a way to help you and WEBCO."

"Great, let me hear them," Charlie replied in a tone that indicated he would rather not hear anyone's ideas except his own. Cal quickly came to the heart of the matter. "We're prepared to go along with your amateurish forecasting scheme and give you our full and undying support in exchange for two million apiece."

"What? fuck you! No way in hell. You're talking extortion

here. I'm not going to put up with that shit; I should fire the whole lot of you and…" Charlie's face contorted into an expression resembling that of a spoiled child whose plans were being thwarted at the last minute.   "And what are you going to do without us? We're the ones who are going to make this thing work. You won't be able to find anyone to replace us before your 'Storm of the Century' comes to town," Cal countered evenly.

Sensing a standoff developing, Susan jumped in. "Charlie, it's just that we have families to support, mortgages to pay, and kids to get through college. If your forecast doesn't work out, we'll be out on the street with no prospects of getting comparable positions, if any, for that matter."   Charlie   didn't   reply immediately; his eyes scanned the occupants of the room, searing themselves into eyes of each of his senior executives. After half a minute or so of the ocular test of wills, Charlie finally spoke, "I understand your positions and concerns; frankly I hadn't taken them fully into account before presenting my plan. A plan, I would remind you, that was formulated with your best interests in mind. And while I am disappointed with what I consider to be something of a shakedown, I'm willing to meet your demands under these conditions: one, the money I set aside will go into an escrow account; two, you won't get anything if my predictions turn out to be on the money. In another words, a payout has nothing to do with whether or not World Media unloads WEBCO, provided that the sale isn't caused by an implosion caused by my call. Got it?"

Four heads bobbed in unison. "OK, enough said about this. I'm not pleased by your conduct but I guess I understand it," concluded Charlie indicating that the topic would not and could not be raised again. "Is there anyone else with a smart idea?" he asked accusingly.

"Just one thing; it's about the timing of the forecast. I'm not quite sure how it works," Susan Brownell offered pleasantly. "You said that the three systems off the coast will come ashore midday Thursday and then come over the Rockies by the next morning. Won't our competitors be putting two and two together when the Pacific Coast gets slammed? If this thing is going to work we're going to have to be the first to announce it to get the jump on everyone." Around the table the four heads bobbed in unison again while Charlie stared down at his notes.

"Damn good point Susan," Charlie said evenly, masking as best he could his building anger and exasperation. "Here's my thinking. The other weather operations have traditionally been very conservative and incremental in their reporting approach. I don't think they'll declare a national emergency just because three fronts converge off the coast. They'll temper their remarks at first, conditioning everything with 'ifs' and 'maybes' and what have you. While they're twiddling their thumbs, we'll come out with a balls-to-the-wall announcement that the end of the world is nigh. And that will be no later than Thursday afternoon, at least in time for the 5:00 evening news, Central Time. Does that work for everyone?" This time four heads were bobbing in unison, small smiles detectable on the faces gathered round the table.

Charles Leuven smiled too, pleased that he had managed to keep his far-fetched scheme on the rails. "OK, let's get down to business. Susan, have Charlotte MacMillan in marketing initiate around-the-clock monitoring of the Weather Channel, AccuWeather and the National Weather Service. Let me know immediately when that frog they have as their severe winter weather expert, or whatever it is they call him, wakes up and starts

70

yakking about all of this. At noon tomorrow morning, I want a plan ready to go about how we dump all this mayhem onto an unsuspecting nation right before Super Bowl Weekend. Meet with Reggie and Byron. All I need is the when and the how."

Turning to WEBCO's nuts and bolts man, Charlie took steady aim, and in an icy voice started up again. "Cal, we've got to be broadcasting regardless of what's coming. Check with your engineering staff to make sure this happens. Considering the worst case scenario of how things might shake out, and the fact that we're way up in this building, you may want to check out whether we can retrofit the old studio off of Hampton as an emergency fallback. Oh, just in case, work out a contingency transportation plan for getting essential personnel over to the old studio."

"I'm on it, Chief. I'll have a report on your desk by 7:30 the day after tomorrow morning," Thornquist stated grimly as he pulled his large hand through the sandy grey stubble he called hair. "We'll be fine, don't you worry Charlie."

"Great, Cal. Let's meet first thing on Thursday at 9:00 in my office."

"Right, Chief," Thornquist said with a slight trace of disgust. "9:00 o'clock, I thought this was urgent, these New Yorkers are a bunch of slackers, the lot of them," he muttered.

Pretending not to hear Thornquist's take on his Park Avenue habits, Charlie continued his rat-a-tat-tat contingency planning recital. "Susan, beginning tomorrow afternoon, we better start notifying our affiliates and cable partners of what we anticipate may be on the way. Please be careful, we don't want any leaks that could tip off the competition. Express concern but be vague about the when, etc., emphasis on 'may', 'possible', 'situation points to', etc. Got it?

"OK, what next? Right, Susan or Cal, assign someone to make sure we have enough cots, blankets, pillows, and food and drinks for thirty of us to last for four days. This all has to be finished by Thursday; ditto for the backup studio. Go to one of those warehouse places, Sam's Club or Cost Co, to get what we don't already have. All right, I think that's it for tonight, any questions? Good. Reggie will of course continually monitor the initial 'forecast' and immediately notify us if this thing looks like it's going to roar down on us like Cleveland, or whatever. OK, that's it; no one, and I mean no one, breathes a word to anyone about this until I say so. Byron, Reggie, mention the fronts on the Pacific Coast and in Canada in passing only, no forecasts are to be based on these observations until I give you the say so. All right, everyone get out of here"

~

A little drained, Charlie sighed and gazed absently out on the blackness over the lake. Well at least they're on board. That fucker Thornquist, what a scammer he is. Ah, what can you do? The show goes forward, that's the important thing. "Christ, what time is it?" he blurted out as it suddenly dawned on him that there would be a few more details to attend to before the day was done.

After a minute or so of rummaging around in his desk's center drawer, Charlie eventually found the note that Jimmy had left him earlier in the day. "Lysander Apopudouplous, 301-321-8752," it read in Jimmy's crabbed script. He quickly pounded in the number on his iPhone, remembering to save it to his contacts list as he did.

"Yeah," a distracted voice answered, "What's up, speak to me."

"Mr. Apopuldouplous, this is Charlie Leuven, Jimmy Dasimmi's friend."

"Right kid, Jimmy texted to say you might call. How is my favorite wop? Tell him to fucking call me once in a while so we can shoot the shit. What can I do for you, Charlie? And please call me Apop." came the raspy voice at the other end.   "I need to make an investment in some wheat futures, today, if possible. Can you do anything for me?"

"Market's closed and I don't see the money. We can get you in first thing at 7:00 tomorrow. Does that work?"

"I guess it will have to do. I'll have my New York bank wire you the money. Should be there shortly after 9:00 our time."

"Tomorrow then, it won't make any difference; the markets have been asleep this winter. How much do you want to buy, anyhow?" Apop asked casually.

"How many contracts can I get for twenty-five million?" As he spoke, Charlie realized for the first time that he might well have stepped over the line and entered a realm where his inexperience in the wooly world of commodity options trading would leave him an easy mark for any unscrupulous trader.

Beginning some months before, Charlie had begun selling most of his stocks and bonds, and anything outside of the trusts he could easily get his hands on in anticipation of the day when the fronts and the isobars would perfectly align, enabling him to strike with confidence. His reasoning was simple: if his harebrained prognostications proved correct, he would become even richer as panic swept the market and the price of wheat skyrocketed. If on the other hand, he was wide by a mile and his forecast turned out to be a bad joke, he would only lose at most a hundred thousand, assuming Apop's trades were structured properly.

"Are you sure kid? That's not chump change for a beginner. Before I get going on this I need to know that this is all legit. This type of money can attract the attention of the CME and Feds, especially if it's from a single individual; so no inside info on your part, right kid?"

Charlie thought for a moment. He never stopped to think that $25 million dollars would cause much of a stir in a world where every day billions in various markets were tossed around as so many wampum beads. Did he have inside information or not? After brief reflection he decided that no, he did not. He was basing his trade solely on information that any casual investor could easily glean from a laptop.

"I see what you mean. To be on the safe side, why don't we list the buyer of at least some of the contracts as Faulkner Investments. That's my family's investment arm; that might obscure things a bit if someone gets too nosey. I'll put the rest under my own name."

"Yeah, OK, I'll get some trades up for you to minimize the downside but that will cost you. But remember, if the Feds get suspicious, funneling the sales through different entities controlled by you isn't going to throw them off," Apop replied as his calculator of a mind started whirling through at least three option strategies.

"OK, but I'm only going to hold the positions for a few days."

"Sure kid, you must know something that I don't, but not to worry. I'm in my car now; can I call you back in an hour to go over this and work out the transfer details, etc.?"

"Sure, just call me at this number," Charlie had never wanted to get off a phone faster. What the hell was he doing? In the beginning, all he wanted was to find some way to get back home; the realization that he wanted more than a one-way ticket back to the good life in Manhattan only slowly dawned on him as he made his preparations to foist the "Storm of the Century" on the nation. Now good old American greed was rearing its fat head. But there was nothing as distressing in Charlie's mind as a poor hero. A man who had the smarts and the gumption to take a flyer in the grand manner should be demonstratively remunerated in a tangible as well as psychic way. And if wealth, why not add fame to the mix as well? Not the sort of fame a politician or movie actor ends up with, but one that's solid and deeply emblematic of a significant good, the fame of a Lindbergh or Neil Armstrong, the type of fame that would respectfully adorn him for his entire life? Perhaps in years to come he would be pointed out by a father to his young son, "Do you know who that elderly man was who was sitting at the next table? Why that was Charles Leuven, he single-handedly saved the country when I was about your age."

Reflecting for a moment on his escalating list of demands, Charlie sighed deeply, shrugged, pleased that he had finally steeled himself to go for the trifecta of his earthly desires.

Chapter 6

SETTING SAIL FOR THE WORLD

Milwaukee awoke on Thursday to brilliant sunshine and crisp temperatures, compliments of an overnight Alberta Clipper that had ended the short lived January thaw. Ignoring the refrozen slush, and the light powdering of fine snow, Charles Leuven made his way to the small speaker's platform set up in the general aviation area of Milwaukee International Airport.

A group of perhaps twenty-five bundled up men and women looked at him expectantly. Charlie had come up with his latest idea for hyping the "Storm of the Century" late on Tuesday night. His new brainchild was to insert twelve reporters into remote parts of the country to report on the coming storm. Hoping that a variety of unusual locations and perspectives would enhance WEBCO's reputation for cutting edge weather journalism, Charlie carefully instructed each reporter to produce their segments in a gritty documentary style so that the audience would "feel the cold" and "taste the wind." The little ceremony this morning was to be a sendoff for the brave men and women who were to double as WEBCO's Edward R. Morrows and Sergei Eisensteins.

Last night Charlie had mulled over the idea of delivering his remarks in a straightforward, unadorned style, one that stressed the importance of the group's mission, and the possible sacrifices each member might be called upon to make. Still enthralled by the historical landscape of World War II, thanks in large part to his promiscuous viewing of the various cable channels and Time/Life DVD's, Charlie decided to frame his speech in a manner reminiscent of Eisenhower talking with the GI's on the eve of D-Day, with a Churchillian flourish here and there to add some color and style. He hoped the combination would produce a speech that the late Lt. Crowell would have related to before being setting off to Sicily.

Unfortunately for his audience, Charles Leuven's intentions to opt for a direct, manly talk clashed with his natural suspicion of anything smacking of simplicity. In Charlie's mind, plain speaking was just that – plain. It ignored the complexity of things, and lacked appreciation for the rich composites of thought and deeds which gave important events their true meaning. Understatement simply missed the mark when the fate of the world was in the balance. How could simple declarative phrases move and inspire people to great deeds? They couldn't! Only the tumbling and jumbling cascade of words and metaphors, dense and abstract to the point of indecipherability could satisfy the spiritual longing of the masses. To Charlie's way of reasoning it was better to bury the listener under layers of contradictory bombast than to speak simply and from the heart. So Charlie's strategy was to weave webs of taut, yet easily misinterpreted imagery. That way each person would be allowed to take away the idea or ideas which best suited his or her needs and desires.

Due to Charlie's unusual take on his fellow humans and his ambivalence about the times in which he lived, he found it difficult at times to cope successfully in the pure present. After all, it was hard to create any drama and romance around even the great events and important people when everyone was dressed in clothes one cut above tank tops and cargo pants. How could Rembrandt have portrayed the characters in the Night Watch, or Le Gros's portrait of Napoleon crossing the Alps, in a world where people wore baseball caps to White House presidential award ceremonies? But Charlie was not one to meekly sit in a corner and accept the downward drift of his times. A while back he had decided to dedicate himself to fighting the forces of universal mediocrity by offering up to the world a more evolved and richer tapestry from which to gain inspiration.

Leuven adjusted the two microphones while trying, as unobtrusively as possible, to put his body through some quick limbering motions. He leaned forward, extending his chest up and over the podium. Then he jerked his torso from right to left to loosen up. Finally, with a shy boyish smile spreading across his face, and a slight nod to his expectant audience, Charles Duquesne Leuven II slowly twisted his upper body up to the left, and then quickly unwound it again like a rubber band. He was off.

"It is an honor to be with you on this bracing morning. I am very gratified that so many unhesitatingly answered the recent call for volunteers. It is a tribute to your courage and dedication. Today we stand together, knowing that beyond the horizon lurks a brooding colossus that nothing can withstand, should it take the full measure of its awful potential. In accordance, and in proportion to this threat, my words can only approximate and poorly express the pride everyone at WEBCO has in your willingness to volunteer for your perilous mission.

"Your decision to go forth into the epicenter of what our experts believe will be a titanic maelstrom, one not seen in the modern age, leaves those who remain behind humbled and grateful that there are such as you willing to take up the banner of accurate and unbiased meteorological reporting." Pausing for a moment, and trying to slow down his delivery a little, Charlie gazed out at the crowd, especially the twelve who were outfitted in maroon-colored down parkas, and matching ski pants. His audience seemed appreciative of the attention they were receiving; still, he wasn't sure that he was reaching them on a gut level. That's the problem with audiences, Leuven thought; you never really know what the hell they're thinking except when you're really good or really bad. Not bothering to explore the implications of his observation, Charlie plunged on.

"Before volunteering, you were fully briefed as to the dangers you might face in the coming days. As you know, the imperious forces of Mother Nature are converging in such a way as to put into question the very continuance of civilized life." With this last remark, a slight murmur rose up from the group. "You did not flinch from the call to assist our frontline affiliates. You did not cower when asked to go alone into the unknown to broadcast from key metrological vantage points. No. No. You did not! Since the very beginning you've embraced this mission with all the professional zeal in your hearts, knowing full well that the dire prospects you face may spell your utter annihilation.

"Some will say that our fears are unfounded, our predictions too bleak, too terrible to be taken seriously. Perhaps this is so. Nevertheless it is fitting that we gather here this morning at General Billy Mitchell Field. As we all know General Mitchell's early vision of airpower, before becoming a key component in this nation's strategic arsenal, was ridiculed during his lifetime as something preposterous and unreasoned. His prediction that this country would be attacked by the naval forces of the Imperial Japanese High Command was scoffed at by his superiors, derided as shear fantasy. So, it is with a similar visionary courage that we boldly proclaim in the face of scientifically gathered and analyzed information, our well-founded concern for the fate of our country in the face of an equally formidable enemy. Let us now bravely and unashamedly ring the rallying tocsin so as to galvanize all the citizenry and resources of the Republic to meet this deadly foe!"

Not allowing the small audience to cheer their unquenchable support, Charlie waved his fully extended left arm in the direction of two nearby, chunky Challenger jets, their engines gently humming behind the podium. "These chariots of the sky will soon take you to your appointed destinies. And, while we have taken the utmost care to ensure your safety, equipping you with the most advanced technology possible, we cannot deny that danger lurks in the mountains and on the Plains for all those who purposely defy the approaching holocaust. We pray you all come home to your families and friends hale and whole. But you well know that for a time you will be walking in the shadow of death. Walking on a path on which you may well be crushed under tons of snow and ice due to a collapsing roof of a school gymnasium in some half-forgotten crossroads. Perhaps you will simply die in your vehicle from hypothermia, alone in some god forsaken roadside ditch, seemingly abandoned by your WEBCO family, as you transmit your last report to a breathless nation. Others may be swept to their deaths by rampaging ice floes bearing down the main street of a quiet river hamlet. Finally, some may meet their end at the hands of ravenous wolves. Animals sensing the end of human civilization, and driven insane by the torments of hunger and cold, descend into the lush suburbs of our doomed metropolitan areas to eviscerate all who dare cross their paths."

Leuven's upper body bobbed up and down over the flimsy railing in metronomic cadence as his right fist pounded into his left palm. He practically leered at his benumbed audience, his eyes wild with boyish delight. Finally, he thought, the thing was taking wings. He no longer knew or cared what was spouting forth from his lips.

Charlie was now too wound up to take notice of the crowd's reaction, and so was unable to detect a decided cooling of their collective ardor for his words, and their mission. There were more than a few worried and queasy looks among the two silent rows. One or two, however, struggled not to break out in laughter as Leuven's bombast took wings. "But dear comrades, remember this: whatever forms your glorious sacrifices may take, you will be making broadcasting history in the profoundest sense of the term. By your courage and actions, you will ascend to Vallahalic Pantheon of meteorology's immortals."

Practically shouting, and in a state of febrile exhilaration, Charlie tore loose with a nugget he hoped would wow his bemused audience. "Allow me to conclude this morning with the words of the great Italian statesman and man of letters, Gabriele D'Annunzio 'Fit out the Prow and Set Sail for the World.' Go forth now with the knowledge that what you do is sacred work. Make no mistake of this undeniable fact – the challenges confronted, today and in the future have been shaped not by human design, but by the unseen and unknowable hand of Providence itself."

While some of his fellow WEBCONIANS may have acquired some second thoughts about what they had gotten themselves into, Stan Kelokowski was not one of them. His round face beamed back at Charles Leuven in worshipful appreciation.

The words and images all sounded wonderful, and exciting. A true call to service and sacrifice beyond his most longed-for hopes. Stan's spirits were so lifted by the speech, that he was having a hard time figuring out which ghastly end he would prefer for his very own. They all seemed so heroic and strangely inviting that it was difficult to make up one's mind. Having grown up near Lake Michigan, Stan was finding himself increasingly drawn toward being crushed to death by an inexorable glacier, or, if that wasn't available, being devoured by Canis Lupui. That was, of course, if he were allowed to pick and choose from the possibilities Charlie had just cited.

Mr. Kelokowski had been with the Weather and Environmental Broadcasting Corporation since right after its inception, nearly twenty-five years ago. He had worked mostly behind the scenes, as a cameraman and editor, but during the occasional important weather story that brought all available hands on deck, he had acted as a fill-in reporter. Stan was not particularly clever but he was well-liked, and considered by everyone to be a cheerful and dependable WEBCO fixture.

He liked his job, and had made for himself a pretty good life. He and his wife of over twenty-five years, Marlene, had raised two sons and a daughter in their small fieldstone house in Wauwatosa. Every one of the kids had turned out to be solid, self-supporting citizens with good values and a can-do spirit. So it came as no great relief to him that just three weeks ago he was informed by his physician, Dr. Swelinck, to get his affairs in order as his life would be coming to an abrupt and premature end.

Most people given news of this sort would have instinctively sought a second opinion, especially if they, like Stan, were feeling perfectly fine at the time. But Stan did not.

His reluctance was as much out of a strange stubbornness as it was from simple fatalism. Fatalism he and his brothers and sisters had been imbued with by their working class parents. He simply accepted the prognosis in the same way that he would have accepted his mechanic's opinion that he needed a new starter motor for his Dodge. If he had gone in for a second opinion he would have found that he was in fact in tip top shape. The faulty diagnosis was the result of the aged and nearsighted Dr. Swelinck not bothering to notice that the test results were those of eighty-five year old Mr. Kelnowski, rather than Stan's.

After a few days of stunned depression, Stan came to realize that by accepting his fate he had been given a special sort of gift. It was a kind of Grace that freed him of all earthly concerns, at last giving him permission to break out of his insipid routine, and dare life to tweak its nose and go for broke – but how, and when? These questions were quickly answered when, a couple of weeks later, Stan got wind that the Chief was looking for volunteers for a special assignment. Shortly after hearing the news, he ran into Charlie in the hall; losing no time, he asked Charlie if he could volunteer in what was openly being referred to as Charlie's Angels, and not so openly as Leuven's Losers.

Stan now fell eagerly into line with the others to receive the final benediction from Charles prior to boarding their "chariots of destiny". His boss had also taken some time to think about what historical pose he should strike during this final farewell tattoo.

Continuing his WWII theme, Charlie's fertile imagination had repeatedly been brought back to the last pictures of Hitler just before the fall of Berlin, and newsreels that showed him bidding farewell to the few remaining Hitler Youth left in the charred

83

capitol. Charlie had always liked the slow motion way in which the drug addled Fuhrer patted each of the doomed lads on the cheek while whispering whatever useless words of encouragement that came into his crazy head. It was both pathetic and endearing. And so it was that Charles slowly moved down the line of the twelve volunteers exhibiting a fatalistic and fatherly concern. He stopped to chat with each one in turn, exchanging words of sober encouragement with a smile, a handshake, and a pat on the back, or a soft fist to the shoulder.

Leuven came to Stan who stood in the middle of the first row. Charlie liked him well enough and appreciated his loyalty to WEBCO, and so was happy to heartily shake his extended hand. "Stan, Stan, how are things? Ready for D-Day? Don't take the blood and guts stuff too much to heart, just fillers to get everyone charged up for the main event. You'll be fine, wouldn't be sending you out to east Jesus if we really felt that there was too much to handle. See you in a couple of days." Stan hadn't heard the last words promising a speedy reunion; if he had, and if he had taken them to heart, his mood might have decidedly changed for the worst. Above all, he didn't want anything to jeopardize his longing for heroic self-sacrifice. "Thanks again for accepting me Chief. It's a great honor..." He began to stammer; as he did, he felt his hand being crushed for a second as a farewell signal from his generalissimo. Then the grip was abruptly released and Leuven was off to the next person.

Charlie couldn't make out the last volunteer; the hood of the parka was hitched up tightly around the person's face. He automatically extended his gloveless hand and seized the one offered him. He shook it vigorously and uttered his standard words of gratitude and encouragement with as much enthusiasm as he could muster after their twelfth repetition. It was while he stood there that he caught the scent of Samantha's perfume. It was unmistakable, light but with a subtle, lingering quality. She said it came from a small perfumeriere near Graz, one he could never remember by name. Startled by her unexpected presence, Charlie spoke in tense quiet tones to the hooded figure before him. "Christ, Sam, what are you doing here? You weren't on the list; we need you at the station for this thing!"

"I'm not interested in being in the station for this thing; I don't want to see any more of you than I have to. Do I make myself clear?" Sam said in a peevish, defiant voice.

"You're the most stubborn and self-willed woman I've run across in a long time, Miss Hewitt. I think you should reconsider this. It's not going to be a lot of fun out there."

"I've made my decision, Charlie, so please drop it. I'm going into the very jaws of hell itself to make 'meteorological reporting history', so please sod off, mate."

Charlie's exasperation with Samantha's behavior was beginning to be detectable in his voice, forcing him to break off their tête a tête before things got too heated. Reluctantly, Charlie gave her his farewell. "OK, OK, take care of yourself out there; it just may get a little more real than you bargained for."

Immediately after their last words were spoken, Leuven stepped back a few paces while moving toward the middle of the group. Once satisfied with his position, Charlie gave a sharp, definitive wave of his outstretched arm, his face intentionally contorted as if in the throes of a great effort at emotional suppression, a la Richard Nixon leaving the West Lawn for the last time. "God bless you and keep you all." He then turned and strode to his waiting Lincoln Town Car.

Charlie slumped in the back seat and allowed himself to exhale. After the car left the airport grounds and was well on its way to the freeway entrance ramp, Leuven perked up and shouted out to Jimmy Dasimmi what he had thought of the morning's performance. "Chief, you were great," Jimmy said in his heavily diphthongal, Chicago accent. "It was the greatest speech I've ever seen. I got really choked up. If I were a few years younger I would want to be on one of those fucking planes. But say, Chief, don't you think it was just a little over the top? I mean going on about the end of the world like you did."

"Over the top, you're fucking right it was over the top. Was it too over the top… that I don't know yet, it just depends on how bad things really get. Let's get back to the ranch."

Chapter 7

TIES THAT BIND

The double glass doors to WEBCO's corporate offices flung open as Charlie, his double-breasted brown camelhair overcoat flapping around his calves, briskly entered. He was greeted by a handful of nods and waves that he perfunctorily acknowledged before turning the corner to his office. Outside the entrance, he was met by the quizzical look of Bobbie Shuster, his wizened and dyspeptic secretary, long suspected by Charlie as a mole for the Gartners. She silently handed him a message as he whisked past her desk. He glanced at it quickly, nodded, and by the time he entered his hanger-sized office the phone on his desk was already ringing.

There was a poorly-concealed look of distaste on Charles's face as he slowly picked up the receiver. He hated talking to Roger Gartner. If there was anyone on earth that he never wanted to hear from or see again it would be Roger. In the abstract he mildly detested and pitied him in equal measure; however, when it came to actually dealing with him on a personal basis, the scales radically tipped in the direction of acute loathing. In Charlie's mind, Roger Gartner was not on any discernible scale categorically inhuman.

Roger, Stephan Gartner's heir apparent, resembled many scions of his type; he was both a prick and a coward. He was also undoubtedly the most insecure man Charlie had ever encountered. The sources of his insecurities were not hard to fathom. Stephan repaid his son's devotion and adoration by constantly comparing him unfavorably to his older and habitually absent brother, James, who resided in a variety of overseas playgrounds. Stephan was also known to mock and disparage nearly every idea Roger was incautious enough to slip past his lips, or submit on paper. On top of his father's mental abuse were the all too obvious factors of looks and brains, both of which had been sparingly doled out to the poor boy. His lumpy and pocked marked face, together with his grey sullen eyes, spoke of a man who would have probably been all right in a small time CPA firm, but who was well over his head in the hot-house world of the Gartner's business empire.

The worshipful scion had been assigned the task of overseeing the day-to-day progress of Charlie Leuven's stewardship of WEBCO, following the untimely death of Cynthia Gartner Leuven, Roger's younger sister and Charlie's wife.

Gartner Senior, upon learning of the death of his beloved daughter "Cyn Cyn," had immediately come to the irrevocable conclusion that Charlie had willfully planned and executed her tragic death. Nothing on this earth or above would ever change the old man's mind. Initially, Stephan wanted to have Charlie murdered. He would have been happy to personally carry out the beheading himself, if it hadn't been for Martin Selchase, his legal advisor. Selchase pointed out contractual clauses, and inherent legal constraints, which worked against such a neat resolution. So instead of burying Charlie up to his chin, and pouring honey on his head as an enticement to fire ants to work their magic, Stephan banished Charlie to Milwaukee, Wisconsin. With the intention of compounding Charlie's agony, he ordered him to report to Roger on a daily basis.

Roger's sole objective in carrying out his father's

instructions for "close and remorseless oversight" was to turn his erstwhile brother-in-law's life into a living hell. In this assignment, like many others he undertook, his zeal was far greater than his effectiveness. For the better part of a year, he nitpicked and questioned everything Charles thought, proposed or did. He gave his executive insane deadlines, set absurdly ambitious objectives, and established dual reporting channels, so Charlie's top staffers also reported to Roger on a wide range of issues. Roger thought he was succeeding splendidly, until one fine day, while on a visit to personally "lower the boom" on Charlie, he was ushered into the men's room at the Milwaukee airport. There Charlie turned and cold-cocked him with a sharp right upper cut, followed swiftly by a neat left jab. When Roger came-too, he found himself sprawled out in the stall designated for the handicapped.

Alerted to the new dynamic in their relationship, Roger quickly sought to modify his outrageous treatment of his rival by issuing a de facto truce. Charlie now was left more or less to his own devices, so long as he continued his steady progress in improving WEBCO's bottom line. This new arrangement, though brittle and liable to betrayal at any time, gave each a breathing space during which they could plot their next moves.

"Roger, what is going on in Big Town?" he asked with as much enthusiasm as he could muster.

"Same old, same old, Charlie; are you coming up to Minneapolis this weekend for the Super Bowl? Dad is really looking forward to it and would like you there." It was a poor attempt at disguising a half-hearted command as a polite inquiry; Leuven decided to treat it as an invitation between pals.

"Roger, I would love to be there to see you and Stephan, not to mention the game, but we're getting information here that indicates that something big is coming up weather-wise. I don't have all the data yet, but this could be a really nasty storm. I mean dangerous. I would hate for you and your dad to be trapped there for any length of time. Not to mention the flight itself could get pretty dicey." Charles hoped that the concern in his voice sounded sincere enough.

"That's funny; we haven't gotten any reports here that there might be a problem."

"Well of course not, Roger, you guys in New York sit around watching the Weather Channel all day. You've got no time for us out here on the front lines."

"Now see here, Charlie, we all watch WEBCO on the web every day. As you well know, our only problem is that the cable networks in Connecticut and the City don't carry you …us, so what are we to do?" Roger said sheepishly.

"OK, OK, I'll let you off once again. But about this storm, I want to keep up on it. Today's Thursday; you won't be going out there before Friday afternoon, am I right?"

"Yeah, that sounds right, but we might not leave until Saturday morning. We've been invited to attend a special pre-game event that night. We'll see how Dad feels; he's been a little under the weather for the past couple of days."

"I see, well that will give me plenty of time to sort all this out before you have to take off. So let's leave it this way – if the weather is reasonable, I'll be there, but if it looks like it's going to get really nasty, I won't. Either way, I'll give you a heads up about what to expect – deal?"

"OK, deal. Now I need to talk to you about these two jet charters. What the hell are they about? Dad is trying to make ends' meet you know."

"Roger you got a fair question there, but I have three ad executives from a big firm waiting for me right now. Can we get back to this a little later?" Charlie had uttered the magic word – ad executives. Admen were related to media purchases and they to ad revenues. These in turn added to cash flow, which was transfigured through the alchemy of accounting into profits, and in turn profits translated into a fleeting kind of serenity.

"I'll let you go but let's revisit this before Minneapolis."

"You got it, Roger, talk to you later."

"Well that wasn't too bad, almost pleasant, actually. Old Roger must have gotten laid since our last chat," guessed Leuven. He further consoled himself with the thought that, one way or the other, his would-be jock sniffing nemesis might very well be out of his life for good. He turned his chair to the left to catch a view of downtown Milwaukee. The sun was still brightly shining. Off in the distance, in the far westward sky, the wisps of high cirrus clouds were becoming visible. Charlie hit the intercom, "Bobbie, could you remind everyone in the Extreme Weather Group to meet in the large conference room at 12:15, and please tell them that I'll have the thing catered. Thank you." Charlie gingerly put the phone down, rose from his seat, and snatched up his tailored Milanese sports jacket. It would be a short meeting, after soliciting everyone's views and ideas; he would make the decision to announce the imminent arrival of the "Storm of the Century" by late afternoon.

~

Samantha Hewitt was also about to enjoy a catered lunch complements of WEBCO. Her meal, however, was going to be eaten from a plastic container at thirty-two thousand feet. She tried not to let these particulars bother her. After all, the food was sure to be good. Charlie Leuven's one saving grace was that he insisted on everyone enjoying the good things in life, one of which was a properly prepared meal.

"Listen up please. We'll be making our first stop in about forty minutes. I just want to go over a few last minute things while I have everyone here." Hubertus Wagner, better known as "Hub," was the baby sitter on Sam's plane. As manager of broadcast operations, he worked mostly in the background, so their paths rarely crossed in a meaningful way. He seemed to her to be a typical corporate nerd, complete with short sleeve shirts, and cell phones and pagers hanging from his belt.

"You've all had your briefing on the equipment. Just a reminder – this is expensive stuff. Please try to bring it back in one piece. As you know, this flight is carrying people up to the northwest. Remember, most of you will be working on your own since we don't have many partner stations up in these parts. Now on to the equipment; the sound boom is contained in the camera, so all you have to do is set the thing up, check the feed with the hand-held, and then report. The automatic lens has a seventy-degree turning radius. It will move in the direction of your voice and your body's heat profile, thirty-five degrees in either direction. So remember the machine's limitations while you're reporting. Don't run off out of range and think you are going to catch a great shot. You won't, there'll just be an empty picture. As a result, you're really going to have to think about each shot you upload to us. The key thing here is don't try to get too fancy. We don't need any Quentin Tarantino's.

"I won't go over all the other goodies, which out of the

92

goodness of our hearts, we have loaded you down with. You've been briefed on this stuff before, and most of you have used it in the field already. Now, regarding logistics, please look at your individual briefing books. They have all the information you will need. Just a word here though, because of the lack of air fields near some of your prepositioning sites, some of you will have a considerable drive ahead of you before actually getting to your reporting locations. This is one reason why we've left today, so everyone will be in place and well rested for the big show. If this thing is going to be as big as we think we should know about it early on Friday. So, if you're not assigned to a mountainous area you will have some down time on your hands. Sorry, can't be helped. That's why we advised you to bring a good book. Now before I sign off, are there any questions?"

"Yes, Marty."

"Is it more likely that we will be devoured by timber wolves or grey wolves, and how will we know the difference?" asked one of WEBCO's senior reporters.

A few brief scattered sniggers became audible in the cabin. "Very funny, very funny, Marty," Hub shot back testily. "Anyone else have any smart ass remarks?" No hands went up. He waited a few seconds before reluctantly giving up his role as briefer extraordinaire. Despite the uncalled outburst, Hub returned to his seat in the front of the plane, generally satisfied with his stint as the no-nonsense mission commander.

Sam stared down onto the flat farmland of Central Minnesota. Why did they give an asshole like "Dud" this job? Wagner was just a glorified techie who could barely navigate his way out of his garage each morning. Taking a deep sigh, she turned to her briefing book. Warroad, Minnesota was to be her reporting position. Looking at the enclosed copy of the Rand McNally road map, Sam exclaimed, "Jesus, I am almost in Canada," as she located the small town in the northwest part of the state. "Just my shitty luck; this must be where the ex-lovers of Charlie Leuven go to die." She then discovered that due to temporary problems with the local airport's radar, she was going to be dropped off in Fargo, North Dakota. The drive to Warroad would consume an extra couple of hours. The notebook informed her that reservations had been made for her in a small motel called the Patch. It was then that she broke down and cried. Charlie was right. She was headstrong and spoiled. What on earth had she gotten herself into? This was beginning to look like an awful mess. She tried to cover her face and eyes with her hair and right hand but the tears kept coming, occasionally accompanied by deep seismic sobs, which she tried unsuccessfully to conceal by faking a deep cough.

"Don't be afraid, everything will be fine. Where are they prepositioning you?" The calming words came from Stan Kelokowski, who was sitting perpendicular from her on the two-person divan on the other side of the aisle. "I got Mandan, North Dakota. I can't wait, that's right on the Upper Missouri. It's where Lewis and Clark spent their first winter."

Samantha glanced across the aisle, and saw the round, beaming face and slightly almond eyes of her sometimes cameraman. "Thanks, Stan. I'm not afraid, really, just incredibly bummed, that's all. My game plan didn't include this type of thing."

"That's OK, just a minor detour in a greater plan, that's all, nothing more."

"I hope so," but Sam didn't believe a word of Stan's New Age claptrap. She was on a fool's mission, an end-of-career reporting assignment concerning some non-event from Hellsville, USA. It was a small industry, and if she became associated with Charlie's farce, her price in the marketplace would drop like a barometer before an approaching hurricane. She turned to the window and beheld below her a gray and white landscape of fields and marshes interspersed with stretches of bare, scraggily trees. It was a bleak world below, and once again Sam felt that she had managed to put herself in the middle of it.

Chapter 8

THE COUSINS GRIM

The fugitive Harlan Zinter fidgeted in front of the oval mirror atop the Victorian vanity in the tidy master bedroom. His eyes were transfixed by the image staring back at him, beardless after shaving off his fine, almost manicured bristles; his gray face advertised his physical and mental exhaustion. There was no escaping the changes brought about by over thirty-five years in the state loony bin. Thirty-five years of poor food, lack of exercise, lack of purpose and the superfluity of powerful psychotropic drugs. Not only his face, but his slack shoulders, and slumped back, and extended belly attested to his universal collapse and degradation.

Even before their escape, Carl and Harlan had agreed that Harlan would assume the role of Carl's female traveling companion, perhaps as a sister or an old friend; the exact nature of their bogus relationship to be worked out by mutual consent. In order to fool the police, and anyone else who might be out to catch them, Carl insisted on a radical makeover for his reluctant cousin. The authorities would after all be looking for two middle-aged white men, not a couple, as Carl repeatedly stressed as if Harlan's humiliation would somehow be lessened by participating in this juvenile ruse.

The next thing to go after the beard was Harlan's long, wavy hair, replaced by a not unflattering bob, stylishly parted off-center so as to better obscure his face. It was a look Harlan once saw in a magazine and thought becoming. Except for a little help from Carl on the back, he had shaped and cut most of it by himself, and justly satisfied with the results of his labors. Arguably, it didn't exactly flatter the shape of his thin, bird like features, but that was OK, where they were going style could get you noticed, prompting awkward questions.

The makeup from a technical point of view wasn't much of a problem; putting some skin cream on his face was easy enough, so was highlighting his dull gray eyes and applying lipstick to his small, thin lips. He had seen his mother and sisters do it hundreds of times. He vividly recalled when, as a young boy, his two eldest sisters, Cheryl and Beth, held him in order to better put all that stuff on his squirming, tear stained face.

Harlan felt a rising disquiet slowly well up as he applied each successive layer of makeup he applied. It seemed that the closer he came to completing this transformation the more he was permanently obliterating his true identity. The more creams, mascara and eye liner he applied, the more Harlan realized how tenuous his grip was on what had always been a skittish reality. Afraid that once again he was beginning to experience the slow, downward spiral, Harlan became momentarily paralyzed by the fear that he was about to dissolve into a pool of eternal blankness.

His sense of impending doom was suddenly cut short, as he was about to daub on the final touches of rouge. A thumping sound, accompanied by a hopeless moan interrupted his concentration, abruptly causing Harlan to change his expression. The dumb, soulless creature who stared back at him from the mirror was suddenly replaced by a face of sharp and determined menace. "Carl do something about that moaning would you?

How can you expect me to do all this when I'm distracted by all that noise? I told you I needed complete silence for a while." Harlan spat out the words in a high, strident voice, struggling hard to sound human.

"OK, OK, sorry, sorry. I'll get right to it," came the sleepy, mimicking voice from the next room. Harlan could hear something heavy and metallic being noisily dragged across the wood floor. What followed was a crunching sound, followed by a hopeless moan. Harlan smiled into the mirror and visibly relaxed. "Thank, you, Carl. Just give me a few more minutes, and I'll be done," his voice was calmer now. But it still sounded disembodied, as if controlled by an entity other than Harlan Zinter.

Carl grunted from the second bedroom, and then shoved the body of the thirty-something woman under the bed. It was time for Carl to start thinking again. He made his way casually downstairs, cleaning off some blood from his hand with a yellow washcloth. He sat down on the couch in the main room with a solemnity befitting someone who was about to ponder the deepest mysteries of the universe. Comfortable now, he began to think about their next moves. It was his thinking, after all, thinking and planning, all firmly based on years of careful, painstaking observations, that had allowed them to make their escape in broad daylight from the high security unit of the hospital. He had timed it out so it went undetected for over four hours (according to the papers). And time had been well used; the first thing Carl did was to hot-wire a car in Sun Prairie (the laundry van's next stop after it left the hospital). Then they crossed into Iowa at Macgregor. There, they managed to steal some license plates from a garaged car, and drive north to Rochester by early the next morning. On a county road, just south of town, they ran out of gas, forcing them to ditch their rusted out Chevy Impala. They waited for several hours in the cold before some unsuspecting rube stopped to see if he could lend a hand. Despite being a couple years past sixty, Carl made short work of the neatly dressed bumpkin, neatly slitting his throat with a sharpened spoon he had fashioned in the hospital. It had been a great relief to kill that fellow, and get moving again in a new car. This one was a much nicer model, a Buick LaCrosse, complete with a CD player, and heated, leather seats.

It was around 8:00 in the evening on the second day when they spotted a light shining from a house tucked back off the main county road. Carl, who always did the driving, parked the LaCrosse half way up the long drive, making sure to turn off the lights immediately upon leaving the road. He made his way up the drive on his tiptoes, walking on the grassy border so as not to alert the owner by inadvertently kicking up any gravel or broken up ice. He stopped for a few seconds where the break in the trees met the small yard surrounding the house. Standing motionless, he took in what he could in the moonless night.

The two-story bungalow was fairly new, white framed with black shutters on the ground and upper level. A little sterile at first glance, perhaps it was one of those prefabs. Then he was able to make out the swing and chairs on the porch, partially covered by a green, plastic tarp. There was also the start of a garden; various types of small bushes and plants were evenly spaced on both sides of the front stairs. Carl took in these details while still focusing most of his attention on the half drawn curtains. Between the break in the curtains, the head of woman could be seen. She was sitting in an overstuffed chair, like one he had seen advertised in some furniture store circular. She was reading something, perhaps a student's paper or test. A pen in her right hand occasionally darted down from her temple to make flourishes across whatever it was she was reading, then just as suddenly it would fly back up to perch near her ear.

Something about being so close to her, being able to watch her every movement unobserved excited Carl. The prosaic scene recalled a similar one from years gone by. Only then it was early spring, the snow just beginning its long seasonal retreat, when he had come upon an isolated trailer outside of Wausau, Wisconsin. Inside there had also been a schoolteacher correcting tests for her ninth grade science class. Her name was Susan Norquist, and she was blond, and attractive in a Norwegian sort of way. It had been all over within a matter of a few minutes. He didn't, as a rule, like to linger over his victims; it was enough that they offered themselves up to him so easily, as if resigning themselves to ritual sacrifice. It made his work so much easier that way. It didn't seem right to Carl to prolong the inevitable, just kill them, and leave. The key thing, the real excitement, was not about the stalking, the hunt, or the con. No, the real satisfaction came from the frenzy of the kill itself, the more abrupt, the greater its rapidity, and the more brutal, the more satisfying. It must all be done like a bomb going off – a flash of suffocating violence that efficiently shredded the victim. Done that way, it really wasn't a crime, it would be as if the person never really existed in the first place, and so there would be no loss, Carl reassured himself.

He waited several minutes, allowing these satisfying memories to fade, before feeling confident enough about what line he would use to introduce himself. But as he waited, he became fearful, and he started to worry about something going wrong. He had been out of circulation for well over thirty years;

he was much older and slower than during his glory days. The guy in the Buick had been just plain, dumb luck. It didn't count he was only a man. This time was it different, the target was real now, and he must be on top of his game.

After a couple of overly aggressive knocks, a petite, strawberry blond hesitantly opened the door a crack to see who could be stopping by on a weeknight. She carried a nine-millimeter automatic in her right hand, hidden behind the door. Upon seeing the unsmiling face, Carl began his little spiel, stammering at first as he started explaining how his car's engine had died and how he needed to call a service station, and whether it might be possible for him to use her phone. As he spoke his eyes roamed down to his feet then up again, before darting into the house, trying to see if anyone was lurking around the corner.

Carl felt he was slowly gaining her trust, but then she asked him why he didn't have a cell phone. She asked in that way that teachers do when they intentionally want to shame a student they don't care for, sending the question shooting at him in that condescending, sarcastic way that made his mind go blank, and his body freeze up. The question wasn't fair. He hadn't ever used a cell phone, or any of that other junk that everyone talked about these days. How could he have? Thanks to smart-aleck bitches like her, he had been forced to spend half his lifetime in a state nuthouse! Hesitantly, at first, Carl managed to shunt his momentary panic into some psychic holding tank, before exploding into an incandescent rage. Bent on scorching that snarky, smirking voice to a cinder, Carl exploded through the door like a dying sun, effortlessly breaking the flimsy chain latch. Now inside, Carl's head crashed into the girl's, while at the same time his left arm smashed down on the hand holding the automatic. Before he knew what had happened, he found himself standing in the small foyer gazing dumbly down at the girl's small crumpled body, a stunned, stricken expression stamped into her face.

Dazed for a few seconds by the head butt, Carl didn't hear the sound of the gun going off, nor did he notice the bullet shattered, green slate tile. All he could hear was the dull ringing in his ears from the blast's aftershocks. He also didn't hear Harlan bounding up the porch steps, hoping he would be in time to help out his cousin, dreading as he ran that Carl had finally come up short. Finding it hard to keep his balance, Carl stumbled into the living room, sinking into a sofa across from the big easy chair where the girl had sat correcting her papers. He couldn't get himself to focus on anything for quite some time, staring first at the body on the floor, and then at the empty chair, occasionally taking in Harlan as he scurried around trying to find a blanket or something to cover her up. In a couple of minutes Carl came around; his first command to Harlan was for him to gag and bind the girl. Together they would take her upstairs, and shove her out of the way until he could think about what to do next.

After returning to the living room from the second floor, Carl began to ponder the events of the last few minutes. Contrary to all the evidence of the last two days, Carl was still convinced he lacked the stuff of his younger years. He hadn't killed her outright, he had let her live, at least temporarily, this wasn't the old Carl! Feelings of creeping vulnerability began to take hold. His underlying terror was that he wouldn't be strong or quick enough to ward off some future attack, and someday he would share same miserable fate as the girl's.

Trying to cast these doubts aside, he went to the kitchen,

opened the fridge and found some drumsticks in a Tupperware container. Taking the food, he slowly climbed the stairs and entered the same room where he and Harlan had deposited the teacher only half an hour earlier. She was still unconscious, or at least not moving. He lifted the bedspread up from her face, and saw a half congealed trickle of blood coming out of the large yellowish-green contusion on her forehead. Carl sat down on the bed and noisily ate his chicken, and then lay back on to the pillow and quickly fell into a dreamless sleep.

He awoke to the nagging shouts of Harlan from the next room; still sleepy, it took him some time to figure out what was stirring up his cousin. He then noticed that the teacher had somehow managed to wiggle out from under the bed, and into the middle of the room. She was now working to tear off the duct tape that Harlan had only haphazardly plastered over her mouth. Frustrated over his failure to kill her outright Carl vowed she was not going to get away to tell others of his recent ineptness in the only activity he took real pride in. Carl methodically made for an old, standup Hoover in the corner of the room, one eerily similar to the steel framed machine his mother had once owned. Dragging the heavy vacuum over the floor until it was right beside her, Carl nimbly swung it up above his head as if it had been no heavier than a broom. He brought it down squarely on the skull of the squirming teacher with his full weight and loathing. One blow quickly followed by another ended her futile struggle; a small red stain seeped through the blanket as Carl began kicking the lifeless body back under the bed.

It was now 9:30 on Wednesday morning by his watch. They were somewhere west and north of the Twin Cities, off of the main interstate in a mind numbingly dull country. In January it

103

was a land as barren and lifeless as the moon, a place where only grays and browns existed. Every morning a deadly thick, low and heartless deck of grey cast its gloom from horizon to horizon for days, sometime weeks on end. Carl hated the Plains with all his heart. The featureless landscape presented a drab nullity, made even worse by the roads, and telephone poles, interrupted by an occasional house and barn. The buildings were all cheap and tumbled down, all made of the worst stuff, as if built by some discount God. Carl much preferred the deep forests of his native Wisconsin; there you could track the logging roads for hours and days, not seeing anything or anyone unless you wanted to. A place you could hide and blend in to the trees, unobserved and unobservable.

Carl sighed and calculated. It would take most of the day to get up north and into Canada, assuming that the weather held. Ten hours of hard driving through the narcoleptic haze of bleak fields and crumbling roads, and further north, where scrubby pine forests interspersed with swamps and bogs all the way up to Winnipeg. The route laid out in his mind had offered advantages over heading east to the Upper Peninsula of Michigan. It took them a long way west of their northern Wisconsin home turf where the cops were sure to be looking for them. He was familiar with the westerly route though. As a young truck driver fresh out of high school, Carl had made a regular run between Stevens Point and Thief River Falls. Even before then, still further back, he had been as far north as Lake of the Woods. It was on a two week camping and canoeing trip with his Boy Scout troop. He still retained fond memories of that trip. It had been the last good thing he'd experienced before troubles started at home.

"Harlan, come down here, let me see you gorgeous," Carl

yelled up from the bottom of the narrow staircase, trying to hide the snickering tone in his voice. "I think I've worked it out."

Harlan soon made his appearance, looking down from the top of the stairs, valiantly trying to mask the forlorn hollowness he felt. His glaring eyes dared Carl to mock him further. Slowly, haltingly, he made his way down for the requisite inspection demanded by Carl.

"Good, real nice. I know you'll pass, at least from a couple of feet away, no problem. You look too good, so good I might get some bad ideas into my crazy head," Carl chuckled as his eyes took in the vision of his transformed traveling companion. Let's call you Heddy. Heddy Knutson, that's it, a real Swede moniker for you."

Upon hearing his new name spoken by an almost giddy Carl, Harlan/Heddy was overwhelmed by a strange sense of other worldliness, a feeling that everything was going to spin off and out of control, a certainty that chaos was going to directly descend on him. "What should I call you, Carl?" whispered Harlan.

"Me? I'm going by the name of Norm Knutson, that's simple enough. Yes, Norm Knutson. That way we can play brother and sister, man or wife, even cousin or cousin; it's perfect for the next few days. Now let's stay here today, we'll light out after dark. You scope out the house for guns, money and some clothes for yourself, anything else that we might need. I'll move the car back behind the house, just in case someone passes by and decides to come a-calling."

Chapter 9

DREAM AND HOPES

The two-lane road undulated between the high limestone outcrops on the right, and the open fields below, to the left. The road began to sparkle as the last rays of the setting sun bounced off the minerals captured in the softened macadam during the heat of past summers. The DB9 growled and pawed the road, ready to spring and take on the sharp turns that made up the downward serpentine. Its patience was rewarded as Charlie shifted into third, and slammed down on the accelerator coming out of the first blind curve. Unexpectedly, he felt the front wheels shimmy, and the backend violently fishtailed; immediately he downshifted into second, and gunned the engine to make the curve as tightly as possible. Then the Aston Martin skidded and became airborne, leaping off the road and heading down towards a field of brown corn stalks. As the car gained altitude it started to roll and twist over as if on a giant skewer, the rotation unexpectedly slow and even. Ascending into the early twilight, Charlie found himself completely upside down, only his seat belt harness preventing him from smashing into the roof. He took those few suspended seconds to wonder at the strangeness of the views, which were made even more enchanting by the slow motion of the car's rotation.

His musings were cut short by Cynthia's screams. He was turning his head to see what the fuss was about, as well as to scope out the view from the passenger side window, when the real accident occurred. A triangular concrete barrier, set off on the shoulder of the road, loomed up out of nowhere. It caught the capsized car on the right side, exactly at the point where the passenger's side windshield met the hood. Cynthia's screams were overwhelmed by a sickening explosion of crunching, twisting metal, shattering glass and pulverized bone, as the superstructure on the passenger's side disintegrated.

The enormous jolt of hitting the barrier launched Charlie's chest square into the steering wheel, knocking the wind out of him, as a portion of the roof curved over, practically enclosing him in a jagged, protective cage. The car's sideway motion, as it rocketed off the road, wrenched his head foursquare in the direction of the passenger's seat, granting him an awful view of the results of his amateurish driving.

Cynthia's head was gone. In its place was a bloody stump of torn and pulpy flesh clinging to the splintered vertebras of what had once been her swan-like neck. Stunned, Charlie instinctively reached for his pocket square in an attempt to daub his new sport jacket of the splattered blood and brain matter, but the car rolled over too quickly for him to perform his little bit of sartorial housekeeping.

After the final impact, the entire car, minus the passenger's side roof, ricocheted toward the rock face, partially righting itself in the process. The momentum of the initial crash was too powerful, however, and the car, after bouncing hard on its two right wheels, succumbed and tipped over again, landing upside down, a smoky, crumbled mass of dead steel.

Charlie would always remember the scrapping and clacking sounds of Cynthia's spinal column as it scored the weathered asphalt surface for the forty feet it took for the remains of the car to skitter to a stop.

In a related dream, Charlie would find himself in a sterile corridor of what he presumed was a hospital of some kind. However, in the place of a controlled melodrama, replete with doctors and nurses pushing his gurney through hospital hallways while applying the appropriate lifesaving procedures, Charlie beheld a somewhat less humanitarian spectacle. Here, Stephan Gartner was running after Charlie's gurney, his normally short white hair now blood red, and sticking straight out of his skull by at least a foot. In his bony, vein-beribboned hands he held a gleaming machete above his head. The oaths and threats he uttered were spelled out in white lights like those on top of a diner. Escaping the confines of the fluorescent tubing, they would leap out at Charlie in the form of hot licks of blue flame. To make matters worse, Roger Gartner was squatting over his head, his naked prehensile feet curved around the chrome bar at the head of the mobile bed. His hideous face resembled a World War II caricature of a Japanese soldier, bug eyed and buck toothed. As Charlie was trying to force his eyes away from this gargoyle-like tormentor, a long, thick line of yellow drool suddenly dropped out of Roger's mouth, stopped, then sprang halfway back up to his lips, like a yo-yo, before separating and falling into Charlie's eyes, burning out his corneas.

Then it was over; the clock said 3:37 A.M. Too early to get up, and too wide-awake to go back to sleep. The nightmare, which he hadn't dreamed for almost two years, had returned more vivid and powerful than ever. For months after the accident it had been an almost continual nocturnal visitor before becoming infrequent and then stopping altogether after a year. Now Charlie wondered, because of its sudden return, whether he could expect to be haunted again on a regular basis. Time would tell. All he knew was that this nightmare seemed like an exact reprise of the actual accident; at least the part about the accident itself. It was like a cheap teen movie, cheesy and realistically horrifying at the same time. The second part, the lurid scenes in the hospital with the Gartners, was decidedly otherworldly. While the general theme of familiar revenge kept constant, a great many of the details changed with each occurrence. In one particularly horrifying version, Stephan Gartner appeared for the purpose of administering a myriad of tortures, ranging from hypodermic needles filled with lye, vices, and nasty looking pliers to torment a helplessly incapacitated Charlie.

Charlie turned over on his side and let his mind go back to the first couple of months after the accident. Friends and family would stop by his father's house where he was recuperating to cheer him up. They offered various bromides – "the whole mess was just a tragic and unpredictable accident", "just one of those things", and "there was nothing to do but soldier on." But all the support in the world wouldn't have helped to assuage his sense of guilt and loss. After the excitement of the accident began to wear off, and people stopped coming by to entertain him, Charlie went into a depressive tailspin. He became more introspective, no longer interested in going out or seeing his best friends. He was satisfied with just hanging around the house, reading and watching TV.

Adding to Charlie's emotional disquiet was the seemingly contradictory sense of agitated impatience about life in general, particularly his career. These were things he hadn't paid much attention to in the past. And while he knew he had been lucky to survive the accident with no permanent injuries, the scares, nevertheless, ran deep. To be certain, his restlessness and irritability was partially based on his feelings of guilt for Cynthia's death. But in Charlie's case shame and humiliation were the real Furies that sapped his strength and former self-confidence. Cynthia had died because he couldn't handle a real car like an Aston Martin like a man should. It was, after all, his job to seen to it that Cynthia got home in one piece, and he couldn't even manage that. On these two counts he was guilty. He had been a boy masquerading as a man, and he simply hadn't measured up; and that was all there was to it.

As the stark realization that he would never see or hold Cynthia again finally began to seep in, so too did Charlie's acknowledgment of how very much he actually missed her. In his own boyish and disorganized way, Charlie really had loved the raven-haired girl with the quick laugh and adventurous spirit. Cynthia had the knack of seeing things from unexpected angles, seldom missing the absurd and humorous in almost any situation. She had simply been his pal, someone who had made everything seem so effortless and fun; without her life was just a senseless grind.

Making matters enormously more difficult, and impeding any hopes that Charlie could simply "soldier on", was the constant bombardment from the Gartners in assigning sole guilt for Cynthia's death to Charlie. Before he had even come to, Stephan was out of the gate with a full frontal assault, starting with a barrage of endless, harassing phone calls, and escalating quickly to letters, law suits, and subpoenas. Every form of official communication squarely portrayed his former son-in-law as a first-degree murderer, on par with Ted Bundy or Son of Sam, and all concluded with demands for the death penalty.

Despite being legally and morally buttressed by the findings of the police report which categorically stated that the accident was just that, an unavoidable calamity caused by a virtually invisible oil slick, Stephan Gartner refused to let matters rest. He continued to come after Charlie even after the findings of the police report were echoed by his own private investigators.

It all came to a head one day in November when Charlie called Stephan to agree to his latest demand that he leave New York and sign a five year contract to run WEBCO. People who knew Charlie, or thought they did, were baffled by his decision to submit to the Gartners – such awful people. Was Charlie so depressed and befuddled by grief not to know what he was getting himself into? He had been a rising star in the Gartner-Leuven world of interlocking companies and investment deals, why had he given in and accepted oblivion? Certainly, everyone agreed, he could have gone elsewhere, and done other things with his life.

The reason was simple: Charlie had ceased to care. It was time to do his penance on the shores of Lake Michigan. Only by caving into the unfairness of it all could he hope in time to banish his demons, and get on with his life. Or so he thought.

The phone rang; it was almost 4:30 now. Reggie was on the line – time to get up. Charlie opened the bedroom curtains and looked east through a wall of glass toward Lake Michigan. The faintest of pinkish glows could be seen off on the horizon. "It's the start of a beautiful day," groaned Charlie.

~

111

These weren't precisely Stan Kelokowski's sentiments at 6:00 in the morning as he finished packing up his Chevy Tahoe in the parking lot of the Cody, Wyoming airport. Off to the east he could make out a reddish tinge. For visual impact, however, it paled in comparison to a slowly approaching wall of startling blackness that was looming in the far western sky, stretching from north to south in a huge semi-circle. The temperature hovered around zero, and according to the local news that would be the high for the day. Stan was hoping he could get out of town before the blizzard hit. The "dark wall" as he called it was growing more ominous, changing from black to purple as it tumbled across the sky. It was suggestive of an inexorable harbinger of an absolute reckoning.

Nevertheless, he had hopes that today things would be better than yesterday, because yesterday had not gone well for Stan. Thanks to Hub Wagner's incompetent planning, Stan had spent most of Thursday on the jet, being bounced from one place to another. The first site was Pierre/Mandan; unfortunately, WEBCO's affiliate backed out at the last minute, making excuses that it couldn't properly support Stan's assignment. Then it was on to Billings, Montana where it turned out that the local cable company's contract with WEBCO had expired three days prior. Wagner then quickly put things right by denouncing the incompetence of Charlotte MacMillan for all the screw-ups. After what seemed like an eternity of nasty back-and-forth phone calls, Cody was finally selected as Stan's final destination.

As a result of the foul-ups, Stan was the last of his group to be dropped off, and when he grumpily deplaned at 7:00 pm: the promised 4x4 was nowhere in sight. Too tired to care, he found a place for his equipment at the terminal, and headed off to his motel. After a mediocre dinner and ninety minutes to locate the agent for the rental car company to arrange a drop off at the motel for 6:00 in the morning, and Stan was off to bed. At 1:30 he was awakened by the sounds of shots being fired in the hallway. After a few minutes, he realized that whatever he was hearing, it was unlikely a Colt 44 going off. When the noise had died down, Stan poked his nose out into the corridor. A few feet down the hall, he discovered two utterly soused cowboys, lying in a pool of vomit. Stan surmised, from the bull whips wrapped around the floor's coke and ice machines, the pair must have been engaged in some sort of demonstration of their whipping prowess before passing out. By the time the night manager had carted the pair off to their rooms and partially cleaned up the mess, it was 2:30.

Originally, Stan's plan for the day was to head west past the Buffalo Bill Dam and Reservoir and up into the mouth of the Wapiti Valley, but after pouring over his maps during breakfast he decided it simply wouldn't do. He was worried about being able to send and receive signals from a deep valley during a heavy storm. Reluctantly, he decided to forego the romance of the mountains and high valleys, and strike out east to Greybull. This small town would put him right on the Bighorn River, almost equidistant between the snowcapped Absarokas and the lower Bighorn range.

As he finally made his way out of town, Stan became more and more thrilled about being a part of weather history. In fact, he was so thrilled he neglected to check his rear view mirror. If he had, Stan would have seen the "dark wall" tumbling down the east slope of the Absaroka Range, erasing the hills and filling the valleys as if it was falling over itself in a mad rush to devour helpless Cody as quickly as possible before moving on to its next victim.

~

At the same hour that Stan was striking off for Greybull, Samantha Hewitt was awaking at the Patch Motel in Warroad, Minnesota. In comparison to Stan's, her Thursday had gone without a hitch. The plane had landed in Fargo, a little before noon. The Explorer was ready and waiting for her at the airport; the lunch in Fargo was better than anticipated, and the four-hour drive east, while exceedingly boring, was uneventful. Even the early trout dinner at the nearby restaurant was passable.

Yet, Sam's heretofore good fortune did not prevent her from greeting the new day with a large dose of self-reproach and pity. She was still very much confused over Charlie and their relationship. She was still amazed that she had been foolish enough to willfully finagle her way onto this assignment, while the big story was undoubtedly in Milwaukee. The unremittingly dull grayness of the area only worsened her mood. It was as if the world had been drained of color, and even black and white were too bold to be allowed to stand by themselves. Her mood of rejection and banishment eventually began to weigh on her, to the extent that she couldn't even muster the energy to stay mad at Charlie. Samantha was becoming resigned to reporting on a non-story, from a non-place, and then returning home to, what in all likelihood would be, a non-job.

In the restaurant, near the motel, she tried to assuage her deflated ego by ordering a full "English Breakfast" of bacon, eggs, waffles, and hash browns. After she had eaten, she spread out her two maps on the table and began considering an optimum

114

broadcast location to best reach her loyal viewers.

"Can I help you miss?" a soft male voice asked. "I couldn't but help notice all the maps you have there."

Momentarily startled by the unexpected offer, Sam looked up from her table with a shy smile to catch the pallid face of a bald, middle-aged man probably in his sixties, with thick clear frame glasses. "Yes, perhaps you can. Do you live here?"

"You betcha; my name is Norm Knutson," his homily face breaking out into a nice friendly smile. "I've lived in the area for most of my life. That's my sister Heddy over there," nodding his head in the direction of a small woman with bobbed hair cut just above her collar. The woman, in a brown sweater and a long paisley dress of dark blues and wine colors, shyly acknowledged Samantha's smile with a quick nod of the head, after which she turned to stare out at the two lane road running a few yards in front of the restaurant.

"Great, my name is Samantha Hewitt, and as you can see from the logo on my jacket, I'm with WEBCO." Sensing some puzzlement in Norm's eyes, Cindy quickly added, "the Weather and Environment Channel, you know sort of like the Weather Channel," she added with a tone indicating that she was trying to nudge him to the desired conclusion. Not sure of whether she had succeeded, Sam motioned Mr. Knutson to take a seat.

"Oh, I get it; you're up here to see what a real winter looks like?" Norm said, trying to appear to Sam as one of the locals with their misplaced pride in their appallingly long and hard winters. "You've come to the right place."

"Super. Say, Mr. Knutson, I wonder if you could tell me how far out you can drive on the lake? I saw all those fishing shanties out by the park yesterday, but it appears from the map that the lake is pretty big."

"Yes it is. Lake of the Woods stretches north about eighty miles. The lower portion is pretty much open water, but just south of the Angle it gets rocky with lots of small islands. Great fishin' though," Norm's last words were accompanied by a wistful smile.

"Last night when I was studying the maps, I was puzzled by a piece of land just north of here. Can you tell me about this Northwest Angle place? It appears to be part of the US, but it isn't contiguous. It looks like it's surrounded by Canadian territory," Samantha said, hoping old Norm might be useful in helping her find a suitable spot to report from, something a little different than her colleagues, something to brag about in a future job interview.

Knutson started to robotically recount the history of the Angle as if accessing some deeply imbedded memory chip. "The Angle came about because the original boundary made after the Revolutionary War was deemed to be incorrect. It stated the border was to run, and I quote – '...through the Lake of the Woods to the northwestern most point thereof and from thence on a due west course to the river Mississippi.' It was later determined that the headwaters of the Mississippi were considerably further south than originally thought. On revisiting the problem after the War of 1812, the error was remedied ..."

Norm's spiel was cut off by a flashing smile from Sam and a note of appreciation, "I see, that's very interesting. Does anyone live there?"

"Oh, sure, there're a few folks there, mostly Indians; I don't rightly know how many in winter, I'd guess about sixty. No towns though, just homes and a small store."

"Is there any way to get to the Angle without going into

116

Canada? I mean can I drive on the lake from the town park?"

"Well, you'll shave a mile or so off by going out to the Point and then cross from there, but you'll still be on the ice for quite some time."

"I see. How do I get out to this Point?" she asked as she started putting on her parka, getting some money out to pay for breakfast.

"It's only a few minutes by road. Just take a right at the light where the factory ends and follow the road north. There'll be a boat launch at the end there, and a well-used trail across the ice. It's about twenty miles to the Angle, so allow for a good hour of driving. You'll be fine but just don't drive it at night, if you can avoid it. The ice may be a little soft in some places due to the thaw, so stick to the trail." Norm responded in an authoritative but still friendly way.

"Mr. Knutson, I want to thank you for all your help and advice, especially the little history lesson." Samantha couldn't help but notice the cast of a pinkish blush moving across Norm's face. "I think I'll go and check it out. I hope you and Heddy have a lovely day."

Chapter 10

"THERE IS NO SUCH THING AS BAD
WEATHER...."
-John Ruskin

Charlie was surprised by the number of people who were up and functioning at 7:00 in the morning; he counted well over twenty milling around the elevator banks. Conditioned by years of Midwestern living, most of them seemed alert and wide eyed, ready to good-naturedly embrace the dark morn of mid-winter. What little talk there was in the elevator centered on the weekend's Super Bowl, and whether one team's pass defense would be a match for the nimble receivers of their opponents. Charlie, a bit snobbish about such things, never quite grasped what the frenzy over pro football was all about. Instead he focused his limited enthusiasm for sports in the direction of college ball, a game he mistakenly equated with the true wholesomeness of a vanishing amateurism.

Finally, the door opened and Charlie walked into a WEBCO reception area buzzing with activity. He was again startled by the number of people scurrying around, heads down, feet flying, clipped words exchanged, a real no nonsense beehive. Then he remembered that WEBCO was a twenty-four hour weather news network. He felt momentarily embarrassed for being so out of it. Largely ignored, except for a few scattered

118

nods and smiles, he made his way as unobtrusively as possible through the labyrinth of narrow hallways to his office. Then it dawned on him that most people might not even know who he was, since he never appeared in the office before 8:30, and the third shift was out the door by around 7:15.

He was almost at his office when Reggie bumped into him as he was leaving his. "Just the man I wanted to see," Charlie smiled. "What's up this morning. Is this still a go?"

"Step inside, Chief, I have everything plotted out, we can go over it in a few seconds." Reggie smiled widely as he stepped back into his cramped office. The left wall was largely monopolized by a large flat TV screen. Reggie went to his desk, picked up the remote control and tapped in the code. The monitor furthest from the door flashed up to reveal a map of North America. Charlie swiveled his chair around and waited for the show to begin.

"We're pretty much on target. The coastal area north of San Luis Obispo last night was hit with a lot of rain, up to eight inches in some places, ditto for northern California and lower Washington State. As of right now, these three fronts have breached the Sierra Nevada and Cascades and are converging along a line from eastern Nevada to western Idaho. The tip of the spear is in the corner of Wyoming, around Yellowstone. What I'm really surprised about is how fast this thing is moving. I thought it would slow down as it hit the mountains, but in fact, it's gained speed and is now moving well over fifty miles an hour," Reggie said drily, lowering his laser pointer so it made darting, red figure eights on the floor.

"What about that jet stream trough, where is it now?"

"It's dropped down over almost eight hundred miles

since yesterday afternoon. It's really plunged, right now it's resting along the southern border of Colorado, but it's going to dip further south as the day goes by. Probably as far south as northern Mexico before this thing is done and over with. We've also got record cold readings being reported throughout Western Canada and Montana. Kalispell had a record negative 66 below at 4:00 a.m."

"Jesus, that's frost on the pumpkin," Charlie chimed as a smile broadened across his face. "When and where will all of this go bang?"

"In the north, it's about ready to go now. The systems are currently breaching the Yellowstone and Grand Teton ranges. At around 7:30 local time the systems will begin to collide in the vicinity of Cody, Wyoming. Charlie I've never seen a pattern like this move so rapidly, this is really going to get crazy, and fast," Reggie said in a worried, almost deflated way.

Charlie just rubbed his hands together and leaned forward. "And the storm in the Gulf, is that still on target?"

"Yes, that too has picked up speed. Winds are about fifty to fifty-five knots. But it's a big storm and it's carrying a lot of moisture."

"OK, I've heard enough, let's make the announcement at 7:45 a.m. Reggie, you can have the honors. Just make sure that you convey to the public the seriousness of the situation, and the potential enormity of its impact, etc., etc., read me?"

"Yes, Chief. I read you."

"Say, Reggie, do we have anyone in that area," Charlie pointing to Wyoming, "you know one of the guys we sent out yesterday?" Charlie asked casually.

"I think Stan Kelokowski eventually wound up in Cody.

I'll call him now to get him in the field as soon as possible."

"Great, I'll be in my office if you need me. Good work, Reggie. The storm gods are at least toeing the line," Charlie said as he got up to leave.

Just outside his office, Charlie ran into Cal Thornquist. "Surprised to see me?" Charlie asked the visibly startled Swede. Charlie had done his best to avoid having anything to do with him after Thornquist squeezed him in that "insurance policy" scheme during Tuesday's meeting. But now that he wasn't going to have to pony up the eight million, Charlie was more amenable to talking with his flat-topped engineer.

"Christ, you know it," said Cal looking again at his watch to make sure the 7:20 time shown by the hands was not due to mechanical failure. "I've checked out the backup facilities; you want to go over it now?"

"Why not," Charlie said, nodding in the direction of his office door. "I think this will be the nerve center for the duration. It's closer to the studios than the main conference room. Take a seat."

"OK, this is the story," Cal began glancing down at his notes. "The old place is more or less operational now, at least in a bare bones kind of way. We never really made much progress in dismantling it, since there was some disagreement about whether we might move back there when our lease ran out here. We'll need to bring over some laptops and revamp some of the sets a little. Still it will look more or less like this place, before you upgraded everything, that is." Cal was looking at Charlie now, trying to see if any of what he said had registered with him at so early an hour.

"Everyone's going to know that we're operating from

Mount Doom. That's going to be part of the drama – a death defying escape from our skyscraper eyrir to a secret undisclosed storm proof redoubt. The viewers will eat it up, big time," Charlie said, his arms spread wide above his head.

"Right, Chief," Cal responded with a slight trace of disapproval. "Anyway, I'll have some of my guys over there this morning to double check everything and to start moving what we can now without cannibalizing our capabilities here. If the time comes, we're going to have to haul some of our stuff over with the personnel. I suggest this be as staggered an operation as possible."

"Agreed. We'll have to be televising from Studio B, as it were, before we make the final evacuation. We're going to have to have the place functioning to some degree by this evening, early Saturday at the latest."

"Chief, I suggest that we leave one or two engineers behind to handle some of the feeds and support operations."

"How dangerous would that be," a slight frown appeared on Charlie's face, as he pictured two huge lawsuits coming his way if the brave duo was blown off into Lake Michigan.

"I think it'll be pretty safe. I don't see the building toppling; it could get uncomfortable with no electricity, though."

"OK, sounds like you got it under control," Charlie said as he finished reading the short bulleted report that Cal had handed him at the start of their confab. "Two things we need to address. I'll need to come up with a great name for the old studio. Let's see: Wolf Lair, no too many unhappy memories. I got it, Storm Lair Two. Something like that, I'll get back to you when I finally nail it down. And, the second thing, how are we going to get back and forth from here to the old place, I mean Storm

Lair Two," Charlie asked, a sly grin beginning to stretch from ear to ear. "4x4's will be great for the early transfers but for the last couple of trips things could get pretty hairy, and Storm Lair Two is a good five miles away."

"Storm Lair Two", give me a break, thought Cal. The trouble with Charlie-boy is that I can't ever get a fix on him. One minute he's brilliant, the next he's someone straight out of a frat house. "We could use snowmobiles, but it's going to be pretty cold, and they don't carry much," offered Cal.

"I know," Charlie blurted out. "Let's get one of those things they use at ski resorts, you know, what are they called, Cats? Yeah, let's find one that'll hold ten people in reasonable comfort. It snows all the time here in the winter, there must be one or two lying around somewhere. I got it, Redoubt Alpha, that's it! Isn't it great?" Charlie was now out of his chair rubbing his hands together in profound satisfaction. He felt Redoubt Alpha was a masterful stroke; the kind of sexy hype he adored, suggestive of a top secret military installation hidden at the bottom of some lake or mountain. In his imagination he could see it on the big screen, a panorama shot, from the air, just as helicopters from some unknown group came into to strafe the place with rockets.

"Cal, this has been great, you're on top of things," Charlie said warmly as he ushered his Operations VP out the door. He always had an undying respect for engineers. They really knew how to figure things out. It was such a pity that most of them were so socially constipated; they simply hadn't a flair for anything beyond the design and application of solutions.

As soon as Cal left, Charlie ran back to his desk to grab the remote to bring up the WEBCO broadcast. The large, misleadingly sagacious face of Bryon Hale filled the TV as a banner weather alert streamed past on the bottom of the screen. "Ladies and Gentlemen, I have just been handed this important weather bulletin," intoned Hale, with a gravity befitting Earth's first contact with an alien civilization. "The Weather and Environmental Broadcasting Corporation has issued a nationwide weather emergency for the continental United States from the eastern slope of the Rocky Mountains to the Ohio River Valley. The developing storm system, I should correct myself here, and say storm systems, will be characterized by dangerously low temperatures, high winds and blizzard conditions, and with what we believe will be record amounts of potentially deadly snowfall for areas displayed on the map.

"In the interest of public safety, we are urging our viewers living in the following states: Idaho, Montana, Wyoming, Colorado and Northern Arizona and New Mexico to take shelter immediately. For those living in the Dakota's, Nebraska, Kansas, Texas, Oklahoma, Minnesota, Iowa, Missouri and Arkansas, we are recommending that you immediately begin preparing for a multi-day storm event of unusual intensity and duration. As of now it appears that the storm has the potential to envelop, besides the sixteen states mentioned, nearly the entire continental U.S. east of the Mississippi River. Due to the national scope and magnitude of the storm, the National Weather Service has given it the name Windigo. Windigo, as you might recall from your study of comparative mythology, is the name of the Inuit ice god, a terrible being that symbolizes the desolation and starvation of winter. Cannibalistic in nature, Windigo is depicted in Inuit art as an ice skeleton." Byron read the last tidbit with the calculated smugness of a middle school teacher imparting a shocking truth to his impressionable charges. At the same time as he was reading the bulletin, the two creases on his forehead darkened as they sunk deeper and deeper into his brow until, by the time he finished, they appeared as razor thin ravines seared down to his skull.

"In order to give the most detailed analysis of what this may mean for your local area, I would like to turn to our chief meteorologist, Dr. Reginald Chevis. Dr. Chevis, please tell our viewers what they may expect from this monster."

"Good," thought Charlie, right tone, ample amount of gravitas but not overwhelmingly dour. Charlie flicked the TV off, trusting that Reggie would do his usual good job. He then made a series of quick calls. Just as he was about to make the last one, his phone rang. Charlie could see from the LCD screen that it was Roger.

"Charlie, someone said WEBCO just made a very alarming forecast concerning this weekend's weather; is this true?" Roger asked plaintively.

"Yeah it's going to get pretty hairy," Charlie said matter-of-factly.

"Well, are we going to be able to get to Minneapolis in one piece if we leave Tetterboro by two, two-thirty?" Roger said in a poorly concealed huff.

"Oh, I suspect you might, but don't leave any later than that. And, expect a bumpy flight; there's a lot of upper air disturbance. Check with the national weather service before you leave. One last thing, Roger, you might be stranded there for a few days, even if you do get in."

"That bad?"

"That bad."

"Dad will go ahead regardless of the risks. It would be unmanly not to," Roger said with a hint of fretful pride in his voice. Roger shared none of his father's hell-bent-for-leather drive. He was congenitally suspicious of any approach to life that could not be minutely calibrated, and neatly fitted onto a spreadsheet.

"Come on. Roger, you'll be OK, if you leave at the right time."

"All right then, Charlie. I suppose you won't be able to get up for the game," Roger inquired in a voice barely able to conceal his relief at the thought of not having to deal with his despised rival until the annual sales meeting in June.

"Little chance of that; I'll be here for the duration, but have a good time. I'm sure you'll manage without me. Got to go, best of luck to you now. I hope your team takes home the gold, or whatever it is."

Over the next hour, Charlie fielded a deluge of calls coming in from all over the country. They were from other news organizations, state and federal agencies and private businesses all alarmed by WEBCO's weather proclamation. He enjoyed playing the oracle of Milwaukee for the first three or four inquiries, but he quickly became bored by the predictable nature of the questions, and his equally canned replies. By the sixth call, he decided to turn this now routine chore over to Charlotte, who was only too eager to get some "phone time" with representatives of the nation's media lords.

Bobby Shuster buzzed in to say that Jimmy Dasimmi and three associates were in the executive reception area. "Show Jimmy in, and make the other three comfortable. Put them in the small conference room so they can watch the action on the TVs," Charlie ordered.

Jimmy sauntered into Charlie's office, his eyes darting

from corner to corner as if he was trying to take a quick fix on a crime scene. "Say Chief, sounds like this will be bigger than the Frisco Earthquake," he said with genuine glee.

"That's what we're hoping, Jimmy. Sounds like you brought the crew with you. Are they going to be up for this? I mean will they be able to play it straight? This thing is a dangerous storm. I don't want a bunch of clowns on the screen making light of it. Did you get that through to them?"

"Don't you worry, Chief, they're onboard. In fact they've been rehearsing. They won't make a fool out of us," Jimmy promised as he swiveled around in one of the two big chairs in front of Charlie's black walnut desk.

The phone buzzed, it was Reggie. "We got Stan Kelokowski reporting from Wyoming. Turn on your TV, this is scary," the chief meteorologist said hurriedly.

Before Chevis got to his second sentence, Charlie was staring at the gauzy image of an unidentifiable face in a maroon parka shouting into the camera. Tremendous blasts of wind continually buffeted the forlorn reporter, forcing him to kneel down or risk being blown off his feet.

Chapter 11

WINDIGO COMETH

Stan was about halfway to Greybull, on US Route 20, when he noticed the Tahoe starting to act funny; the feel of the ride suddenly became brittle, and the steering stiff and unresponsive. Even the frame of the SUV started to chatter as the air in the tires condensed from the rapidly dropping temperatures.

Stan stopped fantasizing about the romance of the Old West with its noble Indians, rangy cowboys and the valiant 7th Calvary, and started to pay attention to the world around him. It was then that he noticed that the great, dark wall of the front had already engulfed Cody and was now roaring across the hill country, and bent on crashing through the rear window of the Tahoe.

The first snow band hit his windshield as fine crystals skirting across the glass before being tossed to the wayside. In the faint light of early morning, distant snow squalls to the north took on the appearance of waves rolling across a waterless sea; the lines between each successive wave casting a bluish shadow down into the troughs below. Visibility worsened as stinging gusts whipped the snow in every direction at once. The two-lane highway quickly vanished as it merged into the surrounding whiteness. Intermittently, ever-smaller islands of black asphalt would appear through the snow, only seconds later to be subsumed into the grayish haze of the blizzard. Figuring he might lose sight of the road entirely, Stan shivered and turned up the heater, but it barely managed to keep the moisture from forming on the inside of the windshield as the temperature plunged even lower.

Except for one or two instances when the wind went completely berserk, Stan luckily avoided any prolonged periods of whiteout conditions. Off in the distance, more or less straight ahead, he started to see the lights of what he thought must be Greybull. They would momentarily flicker, and then, as suddenly as they appeared, vanish in the next blast of blinding snow. "Not far now," he thought, "just keep it together a little longer."

Suddenly, Stan felt a deep rumbling thud come up from underneath the chassis, as if he had run over a small log, or even an animal. The vehicle lurched violently off the road, coming to a halt between the shoulder and a wide, roadside gully. After several unsuccessful tries to get back on the road, Stan slammed the center part of the steering wheel with his fists, and threw his head back in exasperation. The clock on the dashboard read almost forty-five past seven but the sky was as dark as Ava Gardner's eyes.

For the first time during the trip, Stan felt the grip of fear tightening around his chest, and from nowhere a flood of heat swarmed over and through his face and head. He was in the middle of nowhere, in the midst of a killer storm, in a broken down SUV; it was clear that unless he got a break his number would soon be up. Stan's longing for "meteorological martyrdom" quickly drained away, as he faced the cold, hard reality of his situation. Despite his dilemma, Stan thought there was nothing else to do but get on with it, and report on the great storm. Fortunately, he wasn't injured; just shaken up a little. He could still make his reports. Stan took a deep breath, and then mentally went through the checklist of the steps he needed to set up his equipment and begin reporting.

"This is Stan Kelokowski, over. This is Stan reporting from outside of Greybull, Wyoming, over." Although, he had been told that no matter how bad it got he would still be able to send in his report, Stan nevertheless had his doubts whether he would be able to get through. He offered up a short prayer that the link with the satellite would take. If it didn't the whole damn trip would be in vain, and he would likely die for nothing, too. Again, and again, he spoke into his military spec'd cell-phone. Then it happened, a faint, but distinct crackling

"Stan this is Reggie Chevis, over. How are you doing? We have a link up now, but we can't see you. Are you all right, over?"

"Roger, that Reggie; I'm in the SUV. It's very bad here. I think I can make a thirty second report before I have to get back inside the car, over."

"OK, Stan, can you report now? We are going to bring you into Bryon's time slot."

"Roger, Reggie. I'll be ready to broadcast in thirty seconds, over."

Down the hall, Charlie and Jimmy watched as Kelokowski gave a stirring, albeit blurred, report from the front lines. Despite being buffeted and blown about, and having his portable camera and transmitter knocked over by one particularly strong gust, Stan kept at it until Reggie told him point blank to get back in his car and warm up.

After a half an hour in front of the vehicle's anemic heater Stan was ready to make his second report. Right before his first broadcast, Stan had checked the temperature. According to his portable thermometer, it was a minus 55° Fahrenheit. A meaningless number in the abstract, that is until he left the relative warmth of his vehicle to set up his equipment in the lee of the Tahoe. It was then Stan experienced a truly primordial cold; it was like falling into a frozen lake headfirst and staying there for an hour. His breath was the first to go, sucked out of his lungs on contact with the Antarctica temps, then any exposed skin went numb on exposure with the air. Most surprising of all, however, was that Stan noticed his very mental functions congealing, as if the cold was freezing up his neural pathways, making the simplest thought processes slow and uncertain.

He made contact again with WEBCO; this time he spoke to Mary Barber, his producer. "One last thing Stan, before you go on, your wife called this morning to tell you that Dr. Swelinck had mixed up the test results with those of another patient. Anyhow, you're fine, and not to worry." A surge of indescribable relief mixed equally with shear panic rushed through Stan, leaving him overwhelmed in an emotionally indissoluble solution of elation and rage.

"Let's get this over with. I need to get out of here, pronto," Stan suddenly barked at Mary.

Just as he jumped back out of the Tahoe, Stan caught the sight of two low shapes lopping in unison further down the road. Probably stray dogs, or more probably still the wind and snow playing tricks on him. Stan dismissed it, concentrating instead on getting his equipment ready for his last reporting gig. Stan was moving back from the camera in the other worldly gloom of a premature night, when a rickety sign, warning of rock slides, decided to give up its metallic ghost and ascend skyward. Silently it whirled up, turning first to the right, then to the left, as if reconnoitering the terrain before deciding on its final flight plan.

Then it was off, and headed directly at the man in the maroon parka. The diamond shaped sign slammed square into his chest, an edge cutting into the side of his head.

Stan lay there stunned, gasping for air; he could barely recognize the dull throbbing pain that was trying to take hold. He was not fearful; however, he knew for certain now that his time would soon be over. He would either die of exposure or suffocate under the drifting snow; in any case he didn't have long. Straining to keep his head up as high as he could, Stan fumbled around trying to determine if his microphone was still attached to his parka. After a few listless passes of his hands he found it; he was ready to sign off. "This is Stan Kelokowski reporting. I'm not sure whether you can see me or not. Something has hit me and brought me down; I'm not sure what. It's getting cold now, very cold. Tell my wife and kids that I love them, and tell everyone at WEBCO what a great time it was working with all of you folks. This is Stan Kelokowski signing off."

Before Stan lost consciousness and succumbed to the elements, he thought he saw Rollo, the big German shepherd of his boyhood, lopping up to his side with another dog. As Stan raised his arm to pet his old companion, he felt a tug on his hand, followed by a quick, stinging pain in his rib cage, then blackness.

~

A unified gasp swept through the top floor of the US Bank building, as virtually the entire staff gazed with horror at Stan's last heroic moments on TV. It had indeed been riveting TV. Stan had not wavered throughout the brief couple of minutes that he was on air. There was something majestic in how the doomed man paid no attention to either the crippling pain or the intense cold he surely must have felt during his last seconds on earth. People in the newsroom could not determine whether Stan saw the two wolves coming up to him, or if he was even alive by the time they started digging in the snow. Someone thought he had seen a hand shoot up for an instant, but said he would have to review the video in slow motion before he could be sure. There were no screams or other indications of struggle before the equipment went dead. Tears and quiet sobs could, however, be seen and heard throughout headquarters. Men and women openly displayed their fond memory of the man whom everyone called a good coworker.

The collective hush that followed the collective gasp was quickly pushed aside to make room for footage of Charlie giving his valediction speech at the airport. Those in the studio, as well as the far wider viewing audience, watched in amazement as Charles Leuven spoke his prophetic words concerning the dangers facing the band of intrepid weather reporters as they were about to set out on their fateful journey. Of special inspiration was the recitation of the three possible death scenarios that might await them. The audience was left to conclude that poor Stanislaus Kelokowski had definitely fulfilled all the prerequisites for Death # 2 – death by wolf attack. The fact that he was first brought down by something else was felt, by some, to easily qualify him for Death #1, death by collapsing school roof, assuming, of course, that reasonable substitutions could be made. But there were still many hours and days left to go. There would be all sorts of ways these "anointed messengers" might fulfill the visionary destinies that Charlie Leuven had ordained for them. Certainly after the storm a proper tally would be taken, and a final winner declared.

Charlie watched the image of himself bobbing and weaving in Thursday's bright morning light. He thought he came off pretty well; if his physical gyrations were a bit exaggerated his words were telling enough. He reached for the phone and hit the three extension numbers that brought him in touch with Charlotte MacMillan's. "Charlotte, I assume you saw Stan's last report?"

"Oh. Charlie it was so horrible, I feel so responsible. It's really all my fault. It was my idea to send him to him to Cody. I feel…" She couldn't go on and broke down, a series of heavy sobs followed. Even over the phone they were loud. Charlie felt he was listening to a whale that had misplaced her calf.

"Charlotte, Charlotte, now listen to me kid, no one is blaming you for any of this. It might have been your idea but what happened to Stan was just fate. You had nothing to do with it. You gotta remember also that Stan and the others volunteered for their assignments. No one ordered them out into those wasted places." Charles spoke softly, unhurriedly in quiet tones, allowing Charlotte to take in every word, one at a time. In a few moments, he could tell she was settling down.

"Charlotte, I think we better get the others out of the line of fire. Try, at least, to get them to the nearest town where they can ride this thing out. Are you with me? Why don't you work with Susan, and see what you can do to get a hold of everyone." Charlotte's sobs had become shallower and less frequent now. Charlie sensed she would soon be on the go again. "OK? You'll do great, kid."

As soon as Charlie rang off, Jimmy Dasimmi stuck his nose in the door, despite the protests of Bobbi Shuster. "Chief, you ready? I've gone over the situation with the panel and they're all on board…" Jimmy was about to run on but Charlie motioned him to come inside and to stop talking. He did not want Bobbie to know more than the TV audience about what was going on today.

Jimmy sauntered in and sat down. "As I was saying, Chief, we're set to go. When do you think you will want to go on air with these guys? It's getting on to lunch," Jimmy stated matter-of-factly.

"Christ, Jimmy, I don't know. Ideally, I want them to go on around 4:00 this afternoon, in time to get the word out before the six o'clock news. Maybe, you should take them out for a long lunch at a good place, whatever they like. But keep them sober," Charlie warned.

"OK, Chief, but this is turning into a boring day. I thought there would be more action. Just like the army, hurry up and wait," sighing, Jimmy slowly turned and walked out, his time in the reflected limelight put off for another few hours.

Charlotte was almost finished contacting the reporters placed on the limes of civilization; only Samantha Hewitt remained on her call list. She had called three times over the last half hour. It was past noon, and she wanted to get out for a breath of fresh air, perhaps the last opportunity in a while to take a stroll around the art museum before all hell broke loose. She didn't want to talk to the girl she was surreptitiously trying to replace in Charlie's affections. But she was a good trooper, priding herself in getting the job done regardless of the personal toll or the awkwardness of the assignment. She would give it one more try before going out.

"Sam, is that you? It's Charlotte McMillan, in Milwaukee. Are you all right? Where exactly are you?" she breathlessly asked.

"I'm fine. I'm up in Warroad, near the Nor'west Angle. Make it fast, I'm on my way out to scout some sites before the weather turns bad," replied Samantha standoffishly, obviously resenting the intrusion into her preparations for her own form of martyrdom, especially by the woman she suspected of being her rival for Charlie.

"Thank heavens. Have you heard about Stan?" Samantha did not reply so Charlotte soldiered on. "He was killed in Wyoming. It was horrible. He literally froze before our eyes. He was so brave, even when the wolves attacked him," Charlotte waited for some type of acknowledgement about Stan's passing, but Sam was content to remain silent.

"Because this storm is really far more dangerous than we originally thought, Charlie has decided to pull all our reporters from the field. Those who can get to an affiliate station can help out there, but if you can't do that by tonight, we want you to take shelter in the largest town possible. Do you understand, Samantha?"

"I'm staying put. I can't believe that you're doing Charlie's dirty work. First he gets rid of me, then to salvage my career I have to take this harebrained assignment, and finally you're trying to yank me, taking away any hopes I may have of making a name for myself. You're nothing but a bloody slag, kindly go to the top of the building and fuck yourself," Samantha concluded in a cool, calm voice.

"Now you get this straight, Sam. You volunteered to go up there, and now you're ordered to lay low for a couple of days so you don't get killed, and this is what I get. I didn't dump

136

you, Charlie did, so don't go crazy on me about all this. Got it?" Charlotte was getting slowly riled; her light red hair seemed to be taking on decidedly more crimson hue the more she talked.

"I'm not coming in, my dear. I will be making my reports from this bog and you and Charlie are going to air them; understand? And if you call me again, I will personally ram that phone up your cunt the next time I see you. Have a nice day," then the line went dead.

Although Charlotte grew up in the sheltering arms of Glencoe, Illinois she had been around news people long enough not to be overly offended by their lack of manners and subtlety. They could be a crude lot to be sure, but most of them had their saving graces. Samantha, a proper English girl in many respects could, in a flash, bare her lethal fangs, becoming as boorish as all the rest given half a chance. What could Charlie have possibly seen in her?

Chapter 12

M[4]

"One, Two, Three, you're on," the director said in a soft, practiced tone.

"I'm Charles Leuven, President and General Manager of the Weather and Environment Broadcasting Company. I am speaking to you this evening from our headquarters in Milwaukee, Wisconsin. Due to the growing severity of the gigantic storm, Windigo, that has lashed the Rockies, and is now threatening to grow even more powerful as it races east, we at WEBCO feel obligated to report not only the dynamics of the storm, but also to help our viewers come to a greater appreciation of the social, environmental, and economic impact it may have on our country." Charlie digested this mouthful and continued to stare down the camera, reading the words rolling on the teleprompter in a deliberate manner. Since the storm was more and more speaking for itself, he saw no reason to hype things up any more than necessary. No reason to exacerbate the panic; now was time to put on the hard, manly and haggard look of an Edward R. Murrow. That man got us through the Blitz and McCarthy, and now Charles Leuven would get America through "The Storm of the Century".

"We also feel obligated to bring to your attention certain perspectives which our colleagues in the mainstream media may feel confident enough to express, insights and methodologies

138

heretofore too long ignored or misunderstood. Please welcome with me three eminent experts and thinkers who have graciously agreed to be a part of this unusual, and we feel, groundbreaking panel." The tight shot, which had featured only Charlie's upper body, opened to reveal a set centered on a low, crescent shaped table. Off to the left of the table was a large meteorological map of the US, and to the right, behind Charlie, was a lighted board of two groupings of ten cities each. Following the names of each city were four column headings with the latest reported current temperatures, wind chill, wind speed, and lastly, barometric pressure.

"On my immediate left is Professor Emeritus Conrad Merkulus, Doctor of Historical Actuarial Statistics at Marquette University," the camera zoomed in on a dapper, self-assured man in his late sixties. The Professor's face was long and knowing, with a tolerant twinkle in his soft gaze. His white hair just skirted his ears and edged over his collar.

"And on my immediate right please welcome Nightingale Starkweather, founder and president of the Earth League, and the World Womb Wholeness Movement. Ms. Starkweather is very active in what has come to be known as the Spiritual Gaia movement. Adherents of this belief system not only believe that the earth itself is a living entity, but that it has a reachable intelligence or consciousness, one which affords us the opportunity to directly communicate with it. I hope I've got that right Ms. Starkweather." The plump, middle age woman beamed and nodded affirmatively; as she did strands of her long curly hair escaped the restraints of her berets. Wisps of her unruly locks caught the studio lights in such a way as to form a frizzled corona around her oval face.

139

"Last, but by no means least, is Dr. Milton J. Hough, Professor of Environmental Psychology at the University of Wisconsin, Madison. Dr. Hough specializes on the effects that changes in the environment have on the behavior characteristics of advanced species, including mankind." The audience was given only three seconds to make an inspection of Dr. Hough's unremarkable physiognomy before their assessment was cut short by an urgent news bulletin flashing on the screen.

"Let's go over to Byron Hale in Weather Central to get an update on the worsening conditions on the High Plains," said Charlie evenly.

"Thank you Charles," came the sententious acknowledgement from Hale. "We have been advised that the Emergency Preparedness Agencies in the states of Montana, Wyoming and Colorado have recently lost all official communication links with the following towns and counties in their respective states." For the next minute Byron hurriedly read off a long list of municipalities virtually unknown to a national audience outside their immediate area. Upon conclusion, Hale looked dead into the camera, lowered his eyes and almost imperceptivity shook his head, as if to indicate that no one felt the loss more than he, but rest assured, he would remain at his post come what may.

"Thank you Byron," said Charlie with a hint of sincerity. "From what we are learning, I think it is obvious that this storm is taking on dimensions far greater, and potentially far more devastating than originally feared. Plainly we are becoming increasingly blind regarding the fate facing many of our fellow Americans in the areas directly in the storm's path. Now, Professor Merkulus, you have recently posited a theory or, perhaps better put, an approach, to looking at natural and manmade disasters of this magnitude. Please explain to our audience the exact nature of your theory, and how you came to formulate it."

"Yes, certainly, thank you, Charles. First off, I've grouped my research under the heading, the Merkulus Meteorological Mortality Metric, or M^4 for short. Central to my approach is the observation that the traditional method of enumerating the number of fatalities from a large disaster is woefully inadequate. The current method merely totes up the number of dead directly resulting from the incident itself. With Katrina, I believe that total was somewhere in the neighborhood of 1,900. Now, the M^4 approach looks at the long term impact that these deaths will have on the population over time, in a holistic way, as it were." The professor paused in his singsong preface for a moment before continuing.

"Let's assume that the average couple in an advanced industrial or post industrial country, like the U.S., will have an average of 1.8 children, and that a generation is measured as about thirty years. I don't think anyone would seriously quibble with these facts, except perhaps at the margins. We also make the assumption that thirty-five million years will elapse before the next catastrophic die off. These occur about every hundred million years on average, and the last one was sixty-five million years ago. So statistically we have another thirty-five million to go in this cycle. Some, of course, say that the earth's increasingly sophisticated technology base may well protect us from some of these periodic disturbances. This may indeed be the case but for argument's sake we will keep the hundred million year cycle intact.

"So let's plug the numbers into the formula you see

displayed on your screens."

$$Mt = f[(Di.Br)\ (Eg\ /G)).\ Rp]0.0075)$$

Mt of course represents the total fatalities over time for any given event. This is arrived at as a function of the following inputs: Di or the immediate death toll from a disaster, times the constant birthrate, Br of 1.8. This product is in turn multiplied by Eg, the elapsed time of thirty-five million years before the next die out of the dominant species. This in turn is divided by G the constant span of time for each generation or thirty years. The product of the first half of the equation is in turn multiplied by the variable Rp which is the average constant of the population in a given area or region that is capable of reproducing over a given time, or 0.35. Finally we multiply these variables with a rather complex probability factor of 0.0075. Now let's plug in the numbers from a disaster with one hundred known dead and see what we come up with:

$$551,250 = [(100 \times 2.0) \times (35,000,000 /30) \times (0.35)\ ]$$
$$0.0075$$

In this case, Mt equals a total of 551,250 over time for the 100 immediate fatalities, this total equates to 5,512 dead per each immediate death, over the span of thirty-five million years. Admittedly, not an exact figure but nevertheless an important heuristic breakthrough on this timely subject." Merkulus looked squarely into the camera and smiled broadly in anticipation that everyone fully appreciated the brilliance of his reasoning as much as he did.

In the beginning of the Professor's spiel, Charlie had been pondering whether and when to interrupt him, so as to help the man cut to the chase, but as he rattled on Charlie became increasingly enchanted by the academic lunacy of his computations, and so let the good professor run his game. "Fascinating indeed, Professor Merkulus, so, in other words, the three known deaths from this storm really should be more accurately calculated as 16,536; am I right in this?"

"Yes, that is correct. Please understand that an exact outcome is impossible to predict at this time from the raw death totals. It is only after a disaster is over that a detailed analysis of the demographic damage can be accurately made. Both the Rp constant of 0.35 and the probability factor, which appears as 0.0075 are liable to change by some degree once an analysis of the actual dead takes place. I have used these set numbers to simplify the mathematics for your audience. In point of fact, both factors are likely to be altered to take into account the ages, sexual orientation and related disease factors of the deceased, with their corresponding effects on reproduction capacity of their respective groups. Because at this time most of the damage and deaths caused by the storm have centered over sparsely populated areas of the country, and that these regions traditionally have an older population mix than the population as a whole, this would result in a lower percentage for the fertility constant, Rp. Now of course if the storm maintains its lethal pattern as it proceeds to the more populated areas of the Midwest and Lakes regions, demographic mixes will change as the storm enters a more youth rich environment. This will naturally result in a higher metric." Once the Professor had gotten to the meat of his topic and was able to spin out the products of his feverish mental labors, he became more animated and collegial. He resembled in some ways a technically minded neighbor demonstrating a recently discovered technique for cleaning second story gutters without the need of a ladder or special hose.

Charles looked upon Merkulus as one would a narrowly precocious child, appreciative wonder mixed with amusement moving across his face. "Professor, I have just been handed an update on the latest fatalities associated with the storm. From what we can determine the death toll now stands at seventy-three, one of whom is our own Stan Kelokowski, who died so bravely this morning. Taking your mortality metric of 5,512 and applying it to the 73 known dead, I come up with a total death toll or factor of 402,376; is that correct, professor?"

Before Charlie could ask the next leading question, Professor Merkulus had interrupted and started his extrapolations. "Since a storm of this size could easily kill up to between 1,500 and 3,000 people, a Merkulus Metric can quickly render the historic death metric in the 8.3 million to 16.5 million range."

Just before the camera turned to him, Charlie nodded to the Anne Sessions, the producer, a wordless command. "Thank you, Professor, very interesting, if not unsettling. We're going to pause now for a break, but our show will continue with our other guests in just 60 seconds."

In less than a minute, the Internet was carrying Professor Merkulus's theoretical speculations as if they were sworn fact, on the same level as the distance of the earth to the sun. NBC, CBS, FOX, ABC and CNN all broke into their regular scheduled programming to zealously announce the grim news of the projected death tolls reaching upwards of twenty million people. At WEBCO the operators were deluged with thousands of panic stricken viewers attempting to determine if their daughter Jenny in Denver, or brother Mike from Durango should be written off.

"Well, let me say before continuing with our next guest, Nightingale Starkweather, that we have been receiving quite a number of calls concerning our discussion with Dr. Merkulus. Let me assure you that we will return to his thought-provoking topic of M^4 in a few moments, but now Ms. Starkweather.

"How nice of you to be with us this evening. I understand that the Earth League has, over the last twenty-four hours, been attempting to communicate with Earth, or as you prefer to term it, Gaia. Have you made any progress in that direction?" Charles steeled himself to deliver his questions with the same impartial and authoritative demeanor that he had used in interviewing the Professor. Yet it was difficult to keep the riveting gaze and craggy composure of an Edward R. Morrow when confronting the doughy and slightly cross-eyed representative of the Earth League.

"Only indirectly, Charles, there can be little doubt that Mother Gaia is trying to warn us that humankind's total disregard for her wellbeing is causing her great distress, but this is not new in and of itself. What she is really saying at this junction remains to be determined, however. I must say that our inability to communicate is not unusual given the current conditions. When the Mother is actively engaged in demonstrating her displeasure it is difficult to make contact. It is as if all her energies are being directed to the task at hand. It is only after the crisis has abated, and things have returned to normal, that we can hope to establish a link, and categorically determine what her intentions really were."

"Is it safe to say, Ms. Starkweather, that the more severe and prolonged the storm, the more important her message is, and consequently the greater urgency to make contact?" Charles smiled to himself as to the slick way he was giving her more rope. As with Professor Merkulus, Charles was going to give the Sister every opportunity to allow her words to make the fool.

"Yes, I think that can safely be assumed, but it is not necessarily a hard and fast rule. Over the course of the last twenty years or so the world has increasingly witnessed even more severe meteorological, seismic, and extraterrestrial activity. This increase is indicative of a profound paradigm shift." "Bingo," said Charlie to himself; the fatuous, tired-out phrase, "paradigm shift", told him that the discussion was about to enter into a realm acceptable to the chattering classes, bestowing on the charade a degree of bona fides, heretofore lacking. "In our relationship to the Mother, or should I say her relationship to us, she very well may be saying that our time on the planet is over, and she is in the early stages of sloughing off humankind for all time."

Charlie caught the eye of the news operations chief and signaled him to disseminate Starkweather's none-too comforting words to the greater world.

"One and two and fire," said Anne in the same firm and measured voice she used to start the show. Her fingers then set about launching on to the WEBCO web site the newest blockbuster coming out of the panel – "Earth Mother Mad – Our Time is Up" followed by the actual transcript of the discussion with Starkweather. In an instant, Anne's fingers furiously sent out over one hundred email bulletins to news organizations all over the world proclaiming that the end was indeed nigh.

"Ladies and Gentlemen, Charles Leuven here with our guests, Professor Conrad Merkulus of Marquette University, Nightingale Starkweather of the Earth League, and Dr. Milton Hough of the University of Wisconsin. Before going to our next guest, Dr. Hough, who has for thirty years been studying the behavioral effects of major disasters on advanced species, I must alert our viewers that the President will be speaking to the nation at 6:00 pm, Eastern Standard

Time, immediately following our present program. The subject of his address is understandably the great storm system that is continuing to build as it moves eastward. WEBCO will of course be carrying the President's remarks live and in their entirety." Charlie swung his stool in the direction of Dr. Hough, and in a more relaxed manner, began the interview.

"Dr. Hough what kinds of behavioral changes can we expect to see as a result of this current storm? And do you feel they will be of a permanent, or merely a temporary alteration from the norm?"

If Professor Merkulus conformed to the stereotypical image of the tweedy and voluble enthusiast from academia, and Ms. Starkweather was an MIA lost in a miasmic orb whirling around the planet, Dr. Hough could not be so neatly pigeonholed. He was a bit of a cipher, unprepossessing, starkly dull and so bland as to be a candidate-model of some sort of academic subspecies.

The doctor from Madison put his elbows down on the high table and leaned forward into the camera, his middle finger adjusting his glasses up the bridge of his nose. He began his discourse in a nasal Midwestern accent. "At this point, I very much doubt that any of the changes we are witnessing, or will witness, can be characterized as permanent. Behavior is a conditioned response to long-lived environmental stimuli. What we will likely see, however, are some unusual ad hoc survival strategies that will come to the fore due to the great stress this type of event causes. Before coming on camera, I was talking to a colleague in Moose Jaw, Saskatchewan. He was relating to me a number of reports concerning wolverines massing in the vicinity of isolated farms and hamlets in his province as well as in neighboring Manitoba. In fact, there had been more than one or two unconfirmed stories of people being dragged into the woods by these animals. Not a very satisfying way to go, Charles, but those are the reports I've been receiving."

"This phenomenon of animals massing to inflict harm on humans, don't you find that behavior highly unusual, doctor?" asked Charlie, in an effort to keep the interview moving along.

"I certainly do, yes, of course. But again, behavior like that is easily attributable to the stresses caused by the storm. Wolverines are basically solitary creatures. It is very unusual for them to band together unless conditions are truly appalling. I am confident that we will hear more stories about stranded motorists, lost snowmobilers and other unfortunates falling prey to these tough customers as well as to wolves, and even bull moose. Regardless, attacks on humans will still be isolated cases to be sure. More worrisome to me may be the breakdown in human behavior should this storm last a long time, and result in delays in rescuing the stranded."

"Please explain, doctor."

"Yes, the very condition of being isolated and cut off from one's normal support system tends to breed panic in those not used to such conditions. Let's take for example a small village, buried under ten feet of snow, electricity out, phones down, food low. It doesn't take much imagination to see revenge killings, mass suicides and even cannibalism breaking out once the social fabric is frayed to its utmost, and routine and supportive behavior norms are overwhelmed."

Seeing a juicy link with Metric Merkulus, Charlie jumped

in. "Professor, if such events come to pass, and we all pray that this is not the case," interjected Charlie piously, "won't that have noticeable repercussions on the outcome of the Mortality Metrics model?"

"Yes, of course, and in direct proportion to the number of deaths resulting by such means. I must honestly say that I did not figure that this type of behavior would be statistically significant, but I am beginning to change my mind," Merkulus studiously remarked.

"If I may interject," piped in Dr. Hough, "the real question about mortality may come later, if this storm continues into the Plains and the North Central area of the country. If cannibalistic fervor breaks out in a large swath of the country, we are at risk of losing the agricultural expertise that resides in these isolated hamlets and farmsteads. Should this country lose say twenty to twenty-five percent of its farming population, not only the U.S., but the entire world, may face famine, and severe economic contraction to a degree unknown during the modern age. This in turn will no doubt result in cataclysmic social and political dislocations with the attendant outbreaks of wars and civil wars. I think that Dr. Merkulus's M^4 theorem would be sorely put to the test if all these things transpire," concluded Hough evenly.

The camera swung to Merkulus who was busy entering data into a smart phone calculator. Sensing that he was being observed, he looked up with a stunned and frightened expression. "Quite right; it would alter things more than a tad."

"I think it's safe to say that the type of aberrant behavior that the doctor is describing comes from an awareness people develop when they finally realize they have indeed contributed to the Mother's state of hurt and rage. I think cannibalism and mass suicide will only be one vehicle in helping us to dispel our collective guilt," said Starkweather matter-of-factly.

Charlie saw his chance to show who "really cared the most". He pounced and took the cheap shot he sensed would instantly endear him to an audience collectively praying for someone to tip a bucket of boiling water on the head of Sister Starkweather. "Are you saying that the poor people trapped and abandoned are the ones directly responsible for this storm? Isn't this an attempt to blame the real victims of the disaster?" There, Charlie had triumphed. He was in fact now considered "one of us", a true champion of the voiceless majority that made up the country, a defender of common sense and fairness.

Unfazed, Nightingale Starkweather continued her hermetic defense. "What I am saying, Mr. Leuven, is that Mother Earth is the true victim in all of this, and the type of human behavior as described is merely the result of the Earth putting a mirror to the face of these parasites and letting them see what they have done to her for all these centuries," the Sister said with a voice like cold steel.

"There are many Native Americans living in these areas. Are you saying they are perpetrators against the Mother as well? I mean the National Weather Service did name this storm after a Native American deity after all." Before she could respond Charlie got the wrap up signal from Anna that the show was going to break. Charlie lowering his head in silent acceptance of the having the office of Tribune of the People granted him by an invisible but no doubt adoring mob. Then looking up into the camera's eye, Charlie signed off.

"That concludes our panel discussion for this evening.

I want to thank my guests, Professor Merkulus, Nightingale Starkweather and Dr. Hough for a very stimulating if not always uplifting exchange. This is Charles Leuven of WEBCO, where we bring America the weather as it was, as it is and how it will be."

Taking off his microphone, Charles turned to his three guests and cheerfully said, "I would love to talk with you a little more, but I have to get back and see how this storm is coming along. I want to thank you again for coming in, and for your patience regarding all the delays you were forced to endure. I really would like to have you back for a follow up show after things have settled down a little." Merkulus and Hough signaled their interest, asking to be included if some sort of reunion were to be considered for the future. Starkweather huffily expressed little interest, still miffed at Charlie for his set-up toward the show's conclusion.

Chapter 13

"...ONLY DIFFERENT KINDS OF GOOD WEATHER." John Ruskin

Upset after her talk with Charlotte, Sam was in no mood for doing much of anything. She decided the best course of action was to just hang around the sterile motel room until she was more collected. Failing to get into her book, Samantha started to pace, trying to come up with some workable solution on getting out of the personal and professional bind she had managed to get herself into. After half an hour of unproductive stomping around in a vague circle, and with no grand fix presenting itself, Sam decided to seek solace in the TV. The only program on at that time in the morning, besides cartoons, featured an insipid tale about sugar beet farming in the Red River Valley. Samantha quickly turned the machine off in disgust and decided at last to look for a good reporting location for the afternoon broadcast.

In a few minutes she was skirting along the icy roads outside of Warroad, eventually reaching the boat ramp where a myriad of car and light truck tracks fanned off onto the lake. Taking the plunge, Samantha left the frozen land for the frozen lake, and headed northeast on a deeply rutted track stretching out to the steel grey horizon. Norm had said the Angle could be easily reached from the landing, but her map told her otherwise. It showed a short jut of land that was clearly Canadian between the landing and her destination. It was obvious that she was going to have to swing further out into the lake than she had anticipated. The detour would add additional time to what was meant to have been a short out-and-back jaunt. It was only 2:00, still plenty of time to reach the Angle and find a good spot to file her report. She would be high tailing it back to town long before nightfall, if everything worked out nicely. It would simply be a matter of following the lights back into Warroad.

After a few minutes of driving, Samantha began to relax a little; it wasn't really so different than driving on the rutted paths on her uncle's farm in Lincolnshire. She soon became bored of the routine bumping and jostling, and looked to the radio for some company. After twisting the dials for a while, she finally discovered a radio station out of Kenora, Ontario. It played mostly country-western music, spiced up by an occasional pop offering, along with some incredibly bad local advertising.

About thirty minutes out from town, the trail seemed to flatten out and the ruts became shallower. It was difficult to tell whether she was keeping to the main path, or had veered off onto a secondary one that hadn't been used in a while. As Sam was attempting to get her bearings, the SUV's front tire abruptly grabbed hard to the left, causing the entire vehicle to lurch violently and then stop altogether. The smell of burning rubber seeped into the Explorer's interior, prompting Samantha to survey the extent of the damage. The left wheel had fallen into a large crack in the ice, where two ice sheets had once converged and then separated again. The tire was firmly wedged in deep enough to cause her to worry about extracting it quickly. After familiarizing herself with the peculiarities of the four-wheel-drive gear settings, Samantha was finally able to free her listing Explorer, minus a good deal of chewed-up tread and sidewall, and proceed on.

By then, however, a deck of thick, heavy clouds had moved in from the northwest; their dark color and brooding progress across the horizon did not foretell happy times ahead. There was no snow yet, although she spied a lower cloud formation dipping down below the main deck. These might be producing some snow squalls, outliers of the main system, thought Samantha. She now could feel the temperature begin to drop as frost started to build-up on the edges of the windshield and on the front windows. Strengthening winds buffeted the Explorer hard in one direction and then in the other as the light prepared to disappear from the sky.

Sam at this point didn't regret her decision to press on. After freeing the tire from the ice, she had thought about turning around and heading back to Warroad. But then what would she do there? It was better to have at least one little adventure than to die of boredom in a cheap motel room. She would be all right, she convinced herself; all she needed to do was confirm the tracks with the compass heading, and be a little patient. As it became darker and she moved further out on the lake, the trail became less and less well defined. Apparently not many ventured out as far as she had.

At last, just before she was going to revisit her decision to continue on, Sam caught sight of a dark form above the lake floor, perhaps a tree line on the shore. Letting out an unashamed shout of relief, she knew it was only a matter of a few minutes before she would be on dry land. "I've gone about twenty miles from the landing, so this must be the Angle; Norm said it was only twenty miles; I've made it," she said, letting out a deep sigh.

Her relief only increased when she saw a weak shaft of light coming out from the shore. In the next fifteen minutes Samantha was able to make out a large fallen evergreen and a boulder resting on the shoreline. It was then she noticed the light beginning to move in a small circular pattern, then it blinked on and off in short intervals, before returning as a steady beacon. Obviously, someone was directing her in; she was no longer alone.

Within just thirty yards of the shore, she could see what appeared to be a suitable landing spot, immediately below the beckoning light. "Thank God and thank you my guardian angel, whoever you may be," she whispered, surprising herself by her demonstration of religious gratitude. It was now time for the SUV to do its bit, and with a minimum of grinding and sliding it was able to handily take on the low but steep incline, popping up on level ground as easily as if it were climbing up over a curb. Appearing in full view, just off to the side, was a lone figure, the face obscured by the hood of a thick parka, tightly secured under the chin. The person moved slowly to the driver's side in a slow shuffling walk.

As the figure came close enough to knock on the driver's window, Samantha's sense of renewed optimism gave way to some trepidation concerning the identity of her "guardian angel". When the stranger opened his hood wide enough to reveal a face, Samantha's fears vanished. It was Norm Knutson! "What a gentleman to come out all this way, and in this weather, to give me a boost," thought Samantha, as she let out an audible sigh of relief. "Norm, thank you so much for coming out here; you are beyond sweet for doing all this, get in," she said quickly as her face began to go numb from the windy cold.

"That's OK, Samantha, I'm used to this. There's a small cabin a little ways down the road, just beyond the curve, off to the right. You'll be safe there for the evening. I'll meet you there in a few minutes."

The mental strain exacted by the drive, coupled with the exhilaration she felt upon reaching a place of safety, had dulled Samantha's normally acute sense of self-preservation. Her forgetfulness in posing the pertinent question of why a middle-aged man would leave the warmth of his home, and travel over twenty miles over land in front of a threatening storm, just to lend a hand to reporter, would soon come home to haunt her.

Sam's lapse into the land of the naïve banished quickly enough when she pulled up to the weather beaten shack to find Norm there shouldering a double bladed axe, staring at her with glaring eyes the size of hubcaps.

Over the years Samantha had seen enough slasher movies with their homicidal villains to recognize when a prime example of the genre appeared before her in the flesh. Perhaps her parents had been right after all: America was just a big criminal insane asylum, housing millions of lunatics ready to pounce on anyone displaying the slightest sign of weakness or vulnerability. Shaking off her shock and acting on impulse alone, Sam squarely aimed her big vehicle at the maniac called Norm. Sam struck her would-be assailant squarely in the legs just below the knees, but with too little momentum to knock him down and run him over. The blow was enough though to cause Norm to drop his axe and cry out in pained anger.

"You bitch! you think you can stop me! I'm coming after you, and when I get you I'll chop you up in a million pieces, you whore of Satan!" raged a limping Norm as he made his way to his pickup parked left of the hovel. On hearing these tidings, Samantha tried to put the SUV in reverse but found that she had wedged the thing too close to a tree and was unable to turn it away without digging a deeper rut in the icy snow pack. Realizing she didn't have the time to fiddle around with the gears, Samantha jumped out of the cab and ran into the cabin, making sure to pick up the axe on her way. A rusty kerosene lamp hung from the main rafter, its feeble, yellow glow barely reaching the far corners of the room. Bolting the door, Samantha next moved to drag the rough, heavy table up against the entrance, tipping it on its side, and propping it with one of the bunk beds she had managed to topple over.

While Norm was deciding on his next plan of attack, Samantha quickly surveyed her new refuge. The cabin was the size of an average room in a house, fifteen by twenty, she thought. There was a small pantry off to the left in the back. The permanent furnishings consisted of three sets of bunk beds, the table, and four cheap miscellaneous chairs. There were two windows flanking the front door, another in the back and one on the right wall as you entered the place. Spying what she thought were tools spilling out of a small backpack on one of the bunks, Samantha ran to it in hopes it might contain a pistol. She was disappointed to find that there was only an assortment of women's make up, and some combs and brushes. Just as she was wondering how this stuff had ended up in cabin in the middle of nowhere, a shot crashed through the door. Reflexively cringing at the sound, Samantha scurried on all fours behind one of the upright bunks. A second shot went through one of the front windows, blowing out three adjoining panes of the upper sash. Despite the noise, and the mental trauma of realizing that things were really as bad as they seemed, Samantha displayed remarkable poise. Not long now, she thought, better to go out with a bullet between the eyes than get hewed up by this drooling psycho.

"Prepare to die, Norm!" Samantha shouted with bordering on the brazen. She went over to the door, axe in hand. Her plan, if it could be called that, was to stand against the wall nearest the entrance and to do the first chopping when Norm burst in. Samantha stood frozen against the thin-planked wall, too afraid even to breathe, but still able to think about what a strange life she had already lived. Then another shot went off, and then another, but the sounds were traveling away from the cabin, as if they were being fired into the woods.

"Why did they fight so," Norm whined in a childlike voice as he inspected the handy work of his first two discharges. He knew she had the axe but she was just a strip of a gal and couldn't present too much of a threat. His leg still smarted from its run in with the bumper but he could tell nothing was broken; the cold would prevent the pain from getting too severe before he finished his work. "The best thing now is just to wait, and allow her to make the next move," he whispered to himself. "Her fear will betray her, and she'll make a stupid mistake. They always did make that one stupid mistake. In the end they all seemed to want to die. In a way they all just give up."

His thoughts concerning his quarry were interrupted by something darting from one tree to another, just outside of the light cast by the truck's headlights. Out of curiosity Norm turned away from the cabin and glanced into the black woods.

Shooting in the direction of the wraith, Norm stopped breathing as he listened to the cracking sound of the 30x30 Winchester echoing across the lake. For good measure he fired off another round. After the shots rumbled away, he thought he heard something further out on his left; he turned but saw nothing. "Time to get back to work," chuckled Norm. He turned to face the cabin. A good time to reload, he told himself, putting four more rounds in the rifle. Just as he was dropping in the last cartridge, Norm heard something snarl behind him. He lowered his body and, pivoting around on his good leg, came face-to-face with something that looked to be a cross between a small bear and a huge raccoon. Baring its sharp teeth, the creature stared into Norm's eyes, gauging the nature of its adversary. Unsettled, Norm instinctively let fly with a poorly aimed shot that went high and wide. The beast remained motionless; it did not blink or indicate that it was impressed in any way by the man standing just a few feet away.

As the two remain fixated on one another, Norm felt something grip down firmly on his right on the Achilles tendon. In a second, razor sharp canines had driven through the leggings and boot, piercing his ankle before lodging themselves into the joint between the leg and foot.

Norm moved backward and tumbled down on his back; he was finally conscious of a fiery pain shooting up from his foot to his groin. He instinctively kicked at his attacker while, at the same time, struggling to find his lost gun. Just as he thought his fingers had run across the gun's stock, the first wolverine now made its play. Leaping on his chest in one bound, the big male went straight for the fleshy exposed face, and with one swipe of its huge, clawed paw, sliced off Norm's left cheek.

Overwhelmed by pain, Norm managed to call on the last reserves of strength to kick off the big fifty pound male. In a flash his hand returned to where he thought he had touched the gun before half his face had been removed. It was there! Shoveling it up and slowly rising up on his good leg, Norm hobbled off toward the cabin. He knew he was up against it now; he simply hadn't counted on these things being around here. It wasn't his fault that they had come out of nowhere. He couldn't think of everything. Where was that no good Harlan? He was doing the best he could, but he needed a little help just now.

Inside the cabin, Sam steeled herself for Norm's second assault. Even though Norm, or whoever he was, was on his last legs, she would need to be ruthless if she was going to walk out of this nightmare in one piece. From what she had seen so far, the Nor'west Angle was not the land of second chances.

As he reached the shack, Norm could feel his strength noticeably weaken. Norm made a desperate, limping rush at the door, flinging his upper body into the planked door as hard as he could. The force was enough to shatter the framing holding the rusted hinges, but he hadn't enough strength to leverage his body to propel himself completely inside. His battered and hemorrhaging body stood betwixt two worlds. His head and shoulders were barely inside the cabin, hanging over the edge of the upturned table that Sam had placed as a barricade only a few minutes earlier. Outside, his legs flayed about in the frigid night, trying to gain traction for one last push, while feebly attempting to kick off the voracious wolverines that had resumed their attack, and were bent on filleting his calves to the bone.

In the dim light all Samantha could see was Norm's grotesquely lacerated face bobbing up and down above the table. In his physical pain and psychotic rage, Norm had all but forgotten about Samantha Hewitt; his only thought was to get inside and away from those devils. He could deal with her anytime.

The falling axe smashed through the left collarbone, coming to rest in the thick muscles at the base of his neck. Norm screamed out in soul-destroying agony. In contrast, Samantha had

160

become galvanized into a Boadicea of the north woods. Quickly pulling the axe out of Norm's body, she threw it back above her head, not hesitating even when the floating light from the lamp exposed again Norm's hideously mutilated face. The Briton was determined that the second strike would be the last. With one mad scream, and with all her strength, she let the axe come down. Blood from arteries and veins shot out from the wide, deep gash. Norm's broken body jerked spasmodically before slumping down between the doorjamb and the makeshift barricade.

Samantha would have stopped then and there if she hadn't spotted her forest allies gnawing on what was left of Norm's splayed legs. "Let's finish this business and give my friends something to tide them over on this long winter's night," Samantha said to herself, her frame of mind somewhere between shock and mild hysteria. It took just two more lusty whacks to remove Norm's head and right shoulder. She quickly shoved the severed parts onto the porch toward her warily admiring woodland friends, and, just in case their alliance became frayed by next morning, gingerly picking up Norm's 30x30 for safe keeping.

Exhausted and elated, Samantha at last felt safe. She knew she still had to deal with the storm until at least next morning, but compared to the preternatural malevolence of the likes of a Norm Knutson, what was a little snow? Despite her relief, she still felt that things were not quite right, that someone or something was lurking about out in the woods. She shined the large magniflex flashlight out into the dark from each of the windows. Nothing stirred except one of the wolverines, which was busy gnawing on the lower part of what was left of Norm. A gentle snow was beginning to fall, the lights from pickup made it seem like the flakes were dancing to-and-fro in a jerky minuet as the woods returned to a state of relaxed watchfulness.

Harlan Zinter knew what Samantha was doing; he even knew what she was thinking. He could see the dull light shining from the front windows, and then the stronger beam of the flashlight shooting out onto the ground and through the trees. So much for Norm's obsession with the English girl, Harlan, from the very beginning, had a bad feeling about Carl's crazy plan. It was too risky, too complex, too many things to go wrong. And now Norm had paid for it.

Only forty-five minutes had elapsed from the time Norm had first signaled the Explorer from the bluff. He had watched the whole thing from the pickup truck: the girl's arrival, Norm getting slammed by the SUV, the animal attack, and finally Norm's messy end. "I wonder what he was thinking right before he died. It must have been of such rageful hate that it was heard all the way down in Hell," he mused silently. Harlan realized that he was finally on his own, free of Carl/Norm. It was time. Carl had served many purposes in his life: teacher, friend, guide, but he had gotten old. He stopped being open to new ideas and techniques. His whole approach to things had become stale and predictable. It had been clear to Harlan since the first day of their escape that poor Carl wasn't going to be able to make the transition. There was more to freedom then just killing school marms. Now, he, Harlan Zinter, was ready to take another tack, one that spoke to the heart of the human dilemma. In many ways he had been preparing for this moment since he was first sent up to Mendota. But could he avoid making the same mistakes that Carl had made, becoming too obsessed with something? Would he be able to handle himself in the real world any better? Time would tell, best now to wait out the storm in the truck and deal with tomorrow when it came.

~

Roger Gartner did not like flying under the best of conditions and these were decidedly not the best of conditions. The pilots of the Gulf Stream-3 warned him, and his increasingly cantankerous father, that it was going to be a bumpy ride, and they might not make it all the way if the weather worsened. Stephan Gartner dismissed the pilots' misgivings with a wave of his shaky hand, sending a timorous Roger to relay his father's command to "damn the torpedoes" to the waiting crew. That was at 6:00 pm, a scant four hours behind the optimum departure time.

As Roger feared, the meeting at Bryce Leuven's townhouse went on forever. He couldn't believe that Leuven had asked for a get-together right before their flight to Minneapolis was scheduled. It was rude and discourteous. The simple financial questions and tax matters Bryce had mentioned on the phone were anything but simple; they were numerous and knotty, and required the services of a squadron of tax attorneys and lawyers to properly sort out. On top of that, Bryce insisted on plying Dad with one drink after another until he was completely inebriated. After a while it was obvious that Leuven wanted to delay their departure; but why? It must be something to do with Charlie and his gang in Milwaukee. Were they trying to put a deal together now that WEBCO was hot?

And hot was the word. The formerly unknown WEBCO had become literally golden overnight. People throughout the eastern seaboard were feverishly trying to locate WEBCO through their cable and dish providers, and if that failed, turning to their computers to bring in live webcasts. Even in New York people were taking notice. WEBCO's early announcement of the storm's ferocity, brought starkly into focus by the bracing death of Kelokowski, now something of a national hero, was making the once ignored weather channel a major news source for the national media. Byron Hale and Reggie Chevis were being quoted frequently, even at the expense of the major's own weather teams. All of this was helping to create the right buzz for a future IPO or an outright sale. Again, Charlie was getting all the glory, while neglected Roger was relegated to the status of a mere onlooker.

The business portion of the visit was concluded within the first forty minutes of the visit, when it was determined that Bunny's concerns were beyond the competence of those present, and would have to be referred to special committees for proper analysis. In frustrated wonderment, Roger watched as his crazy old man and the southern blowhard played game after game of checkers, and then tried their hands at some video game Leuven had set up for his grand kids. Try as he might to convince his Dad that they should be pushing off, Roger's warnings fell on stony ground, ignored or brushed off by a well-chosen repost from one of the elders. Roger thought they would be able to make their escape once they agreed to give up on the video game; but then Bunny pulled out a DVD containing the fabulous exploits of the third season of Bay Watch. It was Stephan's favorite when he was thoroughly potted. He watched, mesmerized by the voluptuous hard bodies in red cantering into the surf to save yet another errant surfer. As a result of this amusement the stay at Bunny's lasted another hour.

Finally at a little before 5:00, Leuven and Roger managed to half escort, half drag his father down the stairs to the front door, and on to the waiting car. As they were about to drive away, Roger looked up and caught sight of Bunny's face. His expression made Roger shudder. The older man's lips were curled in a self-satisfied and venomous smirk. His gaze shot down on the pair with the deep intensity of merciless lasers. Roger was convinced it was going to burn right through the car's roof, and then on down to its occupants before leaving it, and them, just one big immolated piece of slag.

"Dad, can we knock off the booze?" Roger asked, finally gathering up the courage to confront his father, after an hour and a half into the flight, and halfway to the bottom of the first fifth of Glenlivet.

"What? Oh, the spirits, that's what's bothering you, is it? Leave me the fuck alone, would you. Where in the hell are we?" Stephan slurred as he rubbed the window trying to see out through the pitch-black night. He glanced down at his watch, made a few inebriated calculations and decided that they were over Lake Michigan, and that within the next hour they would be on the ground in Minneapolis.

"Go ask the pilots were the hell we are. I think I know but I am curious just the same."

Roger leaped out of his seat, glad of anything that took him away from this unpleasant man. In minutes he was back with the grim news that he was sure would cause his father apoplexy. "Dad, the pilot was just informed that the airport in Minneapolis has been closed to all GA traffic, and we've been diverted to Eau Claire…"

Before he could finish, Gartner Senior exploded in a woozy torrent of expletive abuse, "We will never go to Illinois! It is not in my nature to turn around and run with my tail between my legs, just because of a little snow. God damn it, tell those jumped up bus drivers to take me directly to St. Paul, fuck the land of Lincoln!"

"Dad, Dad, they're talking about Eau Claire, Wisconsin, not O'Hare airport. It's only a few miles east of St. Paul. We can get a four wheel drive and still get there by midnight with some luck; I'll have the pilot get a car out to the airport so we can leave as soon as we get there. I think that's our best bet, Dad."

Stephan nodded drunkenly and was raising his half empty class of scotch to his lips when the plane suddenly dropped straight out of the sky. An icy tingle of fear shot through Roger's entire body; a scream from his father's direction only reinforced his panic. Looking over to his right he saw the almost unrecognizable face of his father, blood was gushing out of his mouth and nose. Roger, despite the heavy turbulence, made his way across the aisle to his father's seat. The wound was far worse than he had first feared. Gartner Senior had virtually devoured the entire highball glass, save for its solid glass base. He could see the half severed tongue wagging around in a bloody stew of gore and saliva, as the wounds gushed blood in such quantities as to make it difficult for the owner of WEBCO to breath. What Roger did not know, however, was that two of the longer shards had gone up through the soft palate of the man's mouth where they found lodging in the underbelly of his Temporal Lobe. After extracting bits of glass that were swimming in the open wound which had once been a mouth, Roger was able to stuff in pieces of a small hand towel to serve as a temporary bandage. His duty done, he headed up to the cockpit for help, trying not to vomit on the way forward.

"Ice," shouted the co-pilot to Roger as he stuck his head

into the cockpit. "It's on the tail; we're going to bring her down now. We have clearance at Green Bay airport. Please get back to your seat sir; this is going to be a close one."

"My Dad has been badly hurt; he's bleeding profusely from his mouth. We got to get to get him to a hospital!" Roger shouted back.

"Fifteen minutes on the outside; please return to your seat and do what you can for him. I'll call for an ambulance."

There was nothing for it except to return to the bloody leather seats and try to make the old shit as comfortable as possible. As Roger made his way back to the rear of the plane, he could see his father's eyes looking dumbly ahead, fixed on the forward bulkhead. For once there was neither anger nor calculation expressed on the dying man's face, only a vapid, glazed expression of surprise. Roger picked up Stephan's limp hand; it was still warm. He thought he could feel it trying to grip his but the attempt, if there was one, was very feeble.

The Gulfstream once again seemed to fall almost directly out of the sky as it tried to set down onto the snow-covered runway. It bounced down hard, repeating the dreadful bone jarring motion three times before finally coming to a noisy, swerving stop. The noise of the brakes and the shifting of the cabin's contents covered up the sound of Stephan Gartner's painful gurgling. The glass shards that had barely entered the underside of his brain were, thanks to the sloppy landing, given the opportunity to thrust up further into the cranium, effectively severing the old man's Hippocampus. On seeing the lights of the approaching ambulance, Roger carefully removed the bloody towel from his father's mouth. For his efforts he was enveloped by a gush of blood shooting out of the ripped cavity of his father's mouth. Then, like a spigot being turned off, it simply stopped.

Chapter 14

NEWS OF THE DAY

"The 7:00 O'clock Evening Weather Update with Byron Hale," the streamer announced as it trotted slowly across the lower third of the screen. Byron Hale, appearing as vital and committed as he had at 8:00 in the morning, greeted his viewers with a terse smile. "Good evening, America. 'The Great Storm Windigo', as it is being called, continues to move slowly across the midsection of the country, bringing to all in its deadly path life threatening cold, record snow falls and sustained gale force winds." As the camera moved from a close up of Byron to a wider shot, the public could see a large digital meter identified in bold type as simply M^4. The death tally according to the Professor Merkulus's equation had risen to 711,048 confirmed fatalities, and was ticking up at the rate of 5,512 every other minute or so. Besides Stan Kelokowski and one snowmobiler, most of the other one hundred and twenty-nine real-time deaths were traceable to three main causes: car accidents, small isolated avalanches, and heart attacks. The M^4 was Charlie Leuven's idea, and he was anxious to learn how the public would react to it.

Another addition to the Network's newly acquired batch of learning aids was a new listing of cities, organized by regions. Across from each city were four rows, listing from left to right the previous record low temperature, the new record low, followed by the previous all time heaviest snowfall, and finishing up with the confirmed snowfall from the current storm. The font types and sizing were similar to those on the M^4 meter. Except for two cases, all the new lows were at least twenty-five degrees below the previous records, and the snowfalls bested the old marks by between two and six feet.

"The President at 6:00 this evening," continued Hale, his voice increasingly taking on an added edge, so as to better compete in sanctimonious gravity with the official pronouncement coming out of the White House, "announced mobilization of units of the 101 Airborne and the 10th Mountain Divisions to assist in search and rescue missions throughout the stricken areas. The President has ordered special attention to be focused on small, isolated towns and rural areas. It is hoped that this direct assistance will stave off any threat to the nation's food supplies and diminished future agricultural capabilities. In addition, the President has ordered FEMA, and other units from the Department of Home Land Security, to bring to bear all their resources in providing emergency assistance to those locations directly impacted by the Storm. Governors in at least twenty-five states have mobilized elements of their National Guard forces or have issued stand-by orders. A spokesperson from the Red Cross issued a statement that all available emergency units are being mobilized and will be dispatched to sites designated by local and state officials.

"As of 7:00 pm Eastern Time, today, the FAA has closed all air traffic in and out of the following major airports: Albuquerque, Dallas, Denver, Kansas City, Omaha, St. Louis, Des Moines, Minneapolis/St. Paul, Oklahoma City, Tulsa, and Little Rock.

"In light of the situation, NFL officials have decided to postpone this year's Super Bowl in Minneapolis. The big game will take place exactly one week from this Sunday. NFL officials reluctantly made this decision in the interest of public safety, as a result of the increasingly deadly nature of the storm."

"Now for an in-depth analysis of the current weather situation and the outlook for the next forty-eight hours, we turn to Dr. Reginald Chevis, WEBCO's Chief Meteorologist and Climatologist," concluded Hale's unadorned reading.

"Thank you Byron," nodded Reggie succinctly. "Before turning it over to our local bureaus and reporters for up-close analysis of local conditions, I want to give our viewers an idea as to where the major weather systems are currently located and how they are interacting with one another." Chevis tried presenting the ongoing cataclysm with a sense of balance, avoiding comparisons with the last major Ice Age of 15,000 BC that Byron Hale, and other anchors, were so fond of bandying about. Reggie instead, while not downplaying the seriousness of events, attempted to comfort the audience with his relaxed presence, aided by the flowing lilt of his island voice.

"The three Pacific systems that came ashore yesterday morning have essentially merged into one massive front, which is currently situated along a north-south line fifty miles east of Bismarck, North Dakota, stretching south through Pierre, South Dakota. This massive front continues on to just west of Wichita, Kansas, down through Oklahoma City, ending up fifty miles south of the Dallas-Ft. Worth area. This system is moving east at an overall speed of fifteen miles per hour, though it is expected to slow somewhat as night falls.

"Snowfalls between the eastern slope of the Rockies and

the Central Plaines have been tremendous. Cheyenne, Wyoming, as of 4:00 pm Mountain Time, has already recorded snowfalls of over ninety inches, or nearly eight feet. That compares to an annual average snowfall of only sixty inches or five feet for an entire season! The snow is still falling there, so they can expect another two to three feet of snow before it is all over. The low temperature in Cody also hit a record of 58 degrees below zero. Denver is coming in at minus 49.5 degrees, easily surpassing its old 1875 record low of minus 29 degrees.

"And, I want to remind everyone these are absolute temperatures; when wind and humidity levels are factored in, wind chills are well below one hundred degrees in the higher elevations. Compounding these problems have, of course, been gale force and higher winds. These winds have reached seventy-five miles an hour on the high plains of central and eastern Montana and Wyoming. Naturally, they have caused whiteout and near whiteout conditions, and enormous drifting over wide areas. In Boulder, north of Denver, snow drifts as high as nineteen feet have been reported. Almost all roads, including the interstates, are closed from the eastern Rockies to Lincoln, Nebraska.

"The Jet Stream has dipped further south and east in front of the advancing low. Compounding things is a significant high coming down from Canada, currently centered between Omaha, Nebraska and Des Moines, Iowa. I expect this cold air to extend as far south as Jackson, Mississippi, running eastward to Montgomery, Alabama by the weekend. People in these areas can expect lows in the low twenties this evening, dipping down to as low as negative ten degrees by tomorrow night.

The third element of this great confluence is the large upper-level tropical depression coming up from the Gulf of

Mexico. The center of this system is tracking north-by-northeast at twenty-five miles per hour. It is currently one hundred miles south of Lake Charles, Louisiana. We're predicting it will make landfall around eleven tonight, in the Lafayette area. This depression will bring a great deal of moisture to the mix by Saturday morning as it continues northward. I expect it will follow the Mississippi River Valley north, before veering off toward the east, around the Memphis area."

Chevis silently caught his breath and stepped away from the screen. "After this important message we will be back, and I will give you my extended forecast for the nation over the next several days."

Charlie had been half watching, half listening to Reggie from the back of the control booth. The other part of his mind, aided by lack of sleep and an overdose of stress, was taking a casual stroll over a wide swath of what made his present mental state of being.

Charlie's foremost preoccupation was – what was the underlying meaning of the Storm-Windigo, if in fact it had an underlying purpose? Ancillary to that conundrum was – what part, if any, had he played in bringing it to life in the first place? He was forced to confess that whatever meaning "Windigo" may or may not have, would be a moot point until after it had run its course, and blown itself out into the Atlantic. Even after that it would remain a question that could never categorically be answered, like, the sound of the tree falling in the forest when no one's there, and all that BS. If directly asked what it all was really about Charlie would have to say that it was just a storm but much bigger and deadlier than most; a half-assed conclusion to be sure, given everything going on, but an honest one, nevertheless.

Charlie placed little truck with the claims being bandied around the blogosphere and the talk shows, that the blizzard was a harbinger of things even more profoundly catastrophic – the final death knell for the order of all being. Christ, had he put that idea into everyone's head via the good offices of that mad woman Starkweather? It had been meant as a cheap ploy to garner ratings and attention, and man had it worked! Just like that M^4 nonsense, and all the farmers going insane and making stews of one another. My God don't people think anymore? Where's their fucking sense of humor gone to? Is everyone merely part of a herd of politically-correct lemmings just sitting around, waiting for their marching orders? Sure, the earth's temperature might be getting warmer, probably was, but that didn't mean all that much, it had been far warmer in the past, and not that long ago in climatic terms, and the human race had pulled through. Granted this time there're more of us, so there might be a bit of a die off, but that alone didn't portend the end of the human race. Get a grip, things change. The whole planet wasn't set up solely for our amusement.

Charlie was equally dismissive concerning the fallout resulting from WEBCO's own hype, especially after it became clear that it was for real. Yeah, perhaps just a little too much – all that M^4 meter stuff, and all the other nonsense, a tad too flippant in light of what was going on outside the studio, but, again, it was not intended to be taken so seriously, a bit of offbeat fun that had just sprung out of Charlie's overactive and undisciplined imagination. Regardless of the brewing controversy, Charlie firmly believed that he and WEBCO would come out of it smelling like a rose. Whatever remaining clucking there might be as to his original motivations would be shortly cast aside by the acknowledgement that they had been the first to ring the alarm bells.

What had been Charlie's original motivations in spring the "Great Storm" on an unsuspecting public, and right before Super Bowl weekend! His motivations couldn't have been more narcissistic and selfish, all that was a given, certainly. His hope, his gamble that a disaster, man-made or otherwise would spring him from his rut of three years seemed to be happening. Yet, except for a little luck and some crazy on-air stunts, he had done absolutely nothing to bring it about, nor could he have. He thought of the little boy who sat in a corner after being punished, wishing horrible things to happen to his disciplinarian only to find the next day that person had been run over by a garbage truck. Was just thinking you wanted something to happen tantamount to causing it to happen? Charlie, for all his self-centered tendencies, could never accept that type of bald causality, any more than he could accept a PMS'ing Gaia pulling the world down about her. It was just like his dad had said – the big things are easy – too easy perhaps.

Then Charlie's mind left the world of weather behind, as it detoured to a subject he hadn't thought for a while – the first time he had seen Sam in the buff. Now, that was worthy of deep and languid consideration! It had been at her apartment on North Prospect; it had been in July and the weather had been sultry, a thunderstorm was moving across the lake, and the curtains on the open windows blew and floated around. She was the first girl with real auburn hair he had ever seen nude. She had an absolutely smashing body, almost intimidating. It was round but also taut. Her breasts were of a rare perfect size, firm and soft at the same time. Sam's legs, while perhaps a little thin, were well toned.

Her ass was also perfection, the over-used word pert jumped into Charlie's mind, as he concluded his revelry with a deep sigh. At the first sight of her naked perfection, he prayed that her physical transcendence would be transformed into sort of true spiritual "pal-ship", and damn quickly. What a fucking fool he had been to screw all that up.

"I would like to tell you what the forecast will be over the next couple of days." Chevis›s rounding voice gently nudged Charlie back to the more prosaic if bleaker present. "On Saturday morning the main low from the west will be advancing into the Ohio River Valley. At the same time a high coming out of Alberta will be bringing extremely cold temperatures to the Great Lakes region. The storm will be picking up moisture from the low coming in from the Gulf; as a result snow falls will be heavy right across the east central part of the nation – Kentucky, Tennessee and parts of West Virginia – and eventually the northeast as well. We are predicting dangerous amounts of lake effect snow for Michigan, eastern Ohio, western Pennsylvania and western New York. The one piece of good news is that we expect the gale force winds we've seen in the west and Midwest taper off by Saturday night. They will still be strong but instead of fifty to sixty miles an hour, we can expect wind speeds to max out in the low forties. Snow accumulations by tomorrow night will be between six and seven feet in Minnesota, Iowa and Wisconsin, northern Illinois and parts of Michigan. Further east of the Mississippi, in Kentucky, Tennessee and southern Indiana and Ohio, snow falls will be in the five to six foot range, thanks to all the moisture coming up from the Gulf. Below Memphis folks will be preparing for some nasty ice storms and gusty winds. Temperatures will, however, rise into the high thirties on Sunday.

"Now the Southeast and the eastern seaboard south of Philadelphia are going to be walloped not only from the weather coming out of the Ohio and Tennessee Valleys but also the extra cyclonic storm moving north from Florida. So Sunday you folks in the Southeast, especially east of the Appalachians, will be caught between four systems: the remnants of the massive low coming from the Plains, the Alberta High, the tropical depression that came up from the Gulf, and a new low coming up from Florida. So expect heavy snowfalls from Atlanta up through Baltimore. They may be as high as five feet, with wind gusts as high as 50 miles an hour in the Carolinas. Virginia, West Virginia and Maryland will have temperatures in the teens during the day as the cold from the Ohio River Valley cascades over the mountains.

"I wish I could report to you that the storm will be on its way out over the Atlantic by Sunday night, but we do have a very intense low developing in the North Atlantic two hundred miles northeast of Newfoundland. If it decides to retrograde into the Canadian Maritimes and New England, the main part of the storm will become stalled over New York and Connecticut. I wish to caution our viewers in the Northeast that it is still too early to determine precisely the track of this potential Nor'easter but we are on it and will keep you advised.

"Turning it back to you, Byron," Chevis's tone the same as if it had been a perfect day in May.

"Masterful, Dr. Chevis, very informative. After the break Courtney will give us an update on the eastern Rockies and the upper Great Plains."

As Courtney Wilcox was getting ready for the spotlight,

Charlie stretched his arms above his head and yawned. It was getting on to eight, should he stay here or go home for a few hours? The sofa in his office was comfortable enough but not that comfortable. It was only a short walk across the park. He could be back in fifteen minutes if anything happened; besides, things weren't supposed to get interesting until Saturday morning.

Chapter 15

UP ON THE MOUNTAIN FOR THE REST OF MY LIFE

The smell of dank, stale earth told Stan Kelokowski he might not be dead after all. The second indicator of his continued livelihood was two sets of yellow eyes drilling into his own. The four orbs were patiently menacing yet curious. They were not far away but somehow distant, as if signifying an unbridgeable gap between observers and observed. The final sign of his vitality was the throbbing pain on the left side of his head, and the dull aching in his upper chest.

After a few minutes of agonizing stillness, Stan's attention was drawn again to the two pairs of unblinking eyes that hadn't broken their gaze since he awoke. He came to the conclusion that eventually he would have to move about, and that these changes would have to be done slowly so as not alarm his two minders. But as he attempted to bring himself up on his right elbow, Stan was overcome with an all-encompassing pain. He let out a clenched cry; falling down on the cot, he cupped his face with his hands in a futile attempt to ease the hammering in his skull. The cry startled the beasts, but instead of lunging forward in attack, their tongues, as wide as cricket bats and the length of a man's forearm, caressed Stan's fisted hands. The oblations were quickly followed by the wafting of a putrefying odor emitted from the beast's muzzles, a smell like a stew of fish heads and boiled cabbage. Relieved and a little grossed-out, Stan moved his hands toward one of the two massive heads. Sensing friendly overture, the two animals decided on further intimacies, the one at the foot of the cot stretched out his front paw in salutation. His partner, less formal, leaped up and placed his front legs and head squarely across Stan's chest, bestowing as he did several slobbery licks. The pressure of the considerable weight made it difficult for Stan to breathe; it also sent another shot of pain through Stan's upper body. But the animals' friendliness was reassuring, more than compensating for the renewed discomfort.

After a while Stan tried to sit up again. This time the pain was not as bad as before and he was able to swing his feet over and rest them on the floor, while bringing his upper body into a sitting position. Casting off the heavy wool blanket, he started to inspect his wounds. There was a large swelling on the left side of his head, at the part line. The gash had been roughly stitched by sutures that had the plasticity of thin, nylon fishing line. As crude as the work was it seemed to have done the job. Moving on down to his side, he felt a number of bands of tightly wound tape, moving up from the bottom of his rib cage to the pectorals.

Satisfied that his wounds were not life threatening, Stan reached out like a blind man to see if he could find something substantial enough to steady himself as he attempted to stand up. His knuckles eventually scraped across something he thought might be a large piece of furniture. Hoping for the best, he steeled himself before launching up to a standing position, the dogs scurrying about yelping encouragement. In the midst of trying to steady himself for this first steps, a door at the end of the room banged open, and a beam from a flashlight shot straight out at the cot before landing on Stan's face.

"Steady, mister, you've had a bad time of it this morning.

No sense in making things worse by waltzing around before you're ready," came the gruff voice from the other end of the flashlight. Stan could not tell if it was the voice of a man or an older woman. Either way, it had about it that western twang he remembered from the westerns he watched as a kid.

"Hi, my name is-"

"I know who you are, Mr. Kelokowski; you think I can't read a driver's license? You sit down now for a moment, and I'll come back with some coffee, lukewarm, I'm afraid, but coffee all the same. My name is Hannie, Hannie Monrieth; these two are Blossom and Toro."

Stan reluctantly decided his new landlady might be onto something and slowly sat back down on the cot. While waiting the wolf-like dogs renewed their attentions, vying with one another as to who could demonstrate the most affection in the shortest amount of time. Blossom and Toro were huge mongrels; their square heads had the look of a mastiff, attached to the low, supple body of a wolf. Within a minute, Stan was rejoined by Hannie; this time she held a mug of coffee and a large battery-powered lantern.

Resting the lantern on a hook on the side of the beat up hutch, Hannie latched on to Stan's jaw with one hand, unapologetically twisting his head one way then the next. "Looks like those stitches are holding, not much blood from the wound. I don't know what hit you but it came at you pretty hard; same for your ribs, at least three busted, but I doubt if they poked into any of your vitals. You'll live from this fleabite, that's for sure, now we got other worries. If you're ready, I'll introduce you to some of the gang."

Hannie appeared to be in her late sixties; she was of

average height, thin as a rail with long salt and pepper hair parted down the middle and set in two braids. Her face was nutmeg brown, like her small flinty eyes, and heavily creased by the perpetual winds that blew through the local canyons of northern Wyoming.

Lead by the dogs, the pair slowly made their way to the far doors. As they crossed the room which was a combination root cellar and storage area, Stan caught sight of his camera and other gear neatly stacked by a rack holding jars of preserves. The walls of the long corridor were of hard packed earth, the ceiling supported by thick posts and beams every five feet or so. Stan felt he was moving gradually higher; as he shuffled along, his breathing slowly becoming more even.

The passageway opened onto a kitchen and large eating area, dominated by a large round oak table. Around it sat seven people in five chairs, four of which were women of various ages, an old man, and two squirming children of between three or four. The adults all wore tired, pensive expressions on their faces, the old man and one of the younger women dumbly nodded in Stan's direction but no one spoke to him. The kitchen was dark except for another battery powered lantern hanging from the permanent light above the table, and a couple of flickering candles in the kitchen; all were fighting a losing battle to illuminate the room. On the wall behind the table hung a large, rectangular Navajotype rug; the hands on the clock above the door going off into the other part of the house were pointed to 2:00 o'clock, presumably a.m. Hannie, forgetting her promise, didn't introduce Stan, but marched him through the kitchen into the next room, where she invited him sit down on an old leather chair.

"How you doin', mister?" she asked more out of politeness

than real interest. To Hannie it didn't matter how her guest was doing. There wasn't anything more she could do for him so the answer better be "fine, I'm doin' fine" otherwise it didn't matter very much. "We're in a bit of a state, I can tell you. This here storm has dumped more snow on us than I can remember, and I go back some. The wind has sent the drifts clear across the compound. That plowing and scrapping you hear up there are the boys trying to dig through so as to get us some air before we all suffocate. Even when we break through, and get some more oxygen down here, we'll still have to worry about getting the snow off the roof. All that weight can come crashing down on us if we don't get a move on, especially if it warms up and the melt turns back again to ice during the night. We built these places pretty good, but they have their limits."

Stan listened to Hannie without comment. As he allowed Hannie's litany of woe to seep into his battered skull, he became perplexed by the sudden recent changes in his own life. A few hours ago he had only a few weeks to live, then he learned of his reprieve, and now it was back to square one, only a few hours to live. He also realized that he hadn't thought of his family or even the storm that caused him to be here in the first place. Had it slammed into Milwaukee by this time? Was his family all right? What the hell was going on out there? It didn't seem very real to him, none of it did but apparently it was. After these thoughts came and went, Stan became aware for the first time of what sounded like shoveling and the muffled conversations of the men who labored above the house.

"Where are they digging from?" He blandly asked as his ears finally caught sounds coming from above.

"Down at the far end of the house, beyond this room

here, that's where the door is, the side door; that's where they started." Hannie, nodding her head in the direction of her words. "Problem is where to put the snow."

Stan nodded too. "We'll let's hope for the best. Is there anything I can do for you?"

Hannie was surprised by the question. Her guest looked pretty beat up, but she was not going to let his offer go by without some thought as to the type of weight he might be able to pull. "My daughter and niece could use a break from those two kids, are you up for some babysittin'?"

In a short while Stan assumed the duties of nanny for Jake and Emily; they were two good-natured children. Stan enlisted Blossom and Toro in the fun, as he created a questing fantasy wherein the two kids rode on their mighty steeds in search of the magic sword whose wielder would bring peace and justice to the shire. The game seemed to go on for hours since Jake and Emily were keen on adding permutations and additions to the basic story line. Then the children became lethargic, and then sleepy. Was this the beginning of the end or just naptime?

He placed the two on the couch, and was about to start back to the dining room to see what state the elders were in when a tired, low shout of elation rang from the area of the side door. Stopping automatically, Stan turned in the direction of the voices coming from the far end of the house. As he slowly proceeded down the corridor, a gentle whisk of cold air ran across his face, followed by a big man, snow-covered from head to foot. "We made it. We got air, man!" Then the man removed his cap and stared hard at Stan. "Who are you?" Before Stan could respond Hannie was at his side.

"This here is Mr. Kelokowski, the fella that Keith found

this morning; can't you remember anything, Marvin?" Sheepishly, Marvin extended his hand. Stan took it and tried to shake it firmly but felt his grip was not very impressive compared to the thick-callused hand that engulfed his.

"Well, we're through, Keith or Art just punched on through about a minute ago, still blowing and snowing like hell though. Don't look like it's going to let up this morning, so we still got to work on it but the worst is over," Marvin exclaimed triumphantly.

"Good work boys. When you go back up there tell them to start working on getting the snow off the roof. We don't want to wind up as flat as a pancake. How many feet of snow is there up there?" Hannie asked, a more relaxed expression began to smooth out some of the deep lines on her face.

"I reckon a good eight feet on the north face but a lot less on the south, but it's hard to say for certain" replied Marvin.

"That's about what I figured. Why I figured it to be that much I can't say though." Hannie muttered, half to them and half to herself, as she made her way back to the kitchen to rouse the somnolent distaff members of the establishment. "Wake up and get going, you need to help out here before we're all crushed to death." She repeated this refrain to each of the five women whose heads now rested on the table. Slowly they came to and began to recognize where they were.

After the shifts had been changed over, and the four men had sacked out in the living room, Hannie called Stan over to the table and sat him down. "Let me tell you, Stan, we got a lot a work ahead of us here and it's going to take some time. I think it's only fair to warn you that it's going to be a while before anyone comes and inquires how we're fairin'. We're off the main road about three miles and when things get bad the town folks have a habit of forgetting about us, until they first get everything ship shape in the valley. So don't expect to be able to call home tomorrow. You're going to have to wait it out like everybody else. Do I make myself understood?"

"Yes ma'am, I understand," responded Stan to Hannie's "let me tell you how it is" speech. "I think I can help, I'm feeling better, my headache is mostly gone and I'm breathing better, too. If I can get up topside I might be able to move some snow for you."

"I appreciate the offer, I don't need no permanent invalid on my hands but if you think you can help out a little go ask the boys where they can use you," a skeptical Hannie responded.

Stan got up and made for the tunnel that led to the roof. It went straight up from just outside the doorway. The boys had notched out small ledges every eighteen inches or so to act as a makeshift ladder. Despite his condition, Stan quickly picked up the knack of shimming himself up, using the notches like rungs to keep him from sliding down.

It was still snowing when he raised his head out of the tunnel. The wind was still brisk but no longer fearsome. Looking out, Stan could see that a trail from the opening of the tunnel across a large section of the roof had already been engineered. A line of old doors and planks had been laid to prevent whoever was shoveling from being consumed by the soft, fine snow. The three-woman crew was already making some headway in getting snow off the roof, but progress was still slow due to the height of the drifts surrounding the house, making it hard to find a clear place to deposit the snow from the roof.

As dawn was peeking over the low hills to the east, Keith,

Hannie's eldest son, appeared by Stan's side and pointed out where he had come upon Stan nearly twenty hours ago. Even as the grey daylight strengthened, Stan could find no trace of the road he had been taking to Greybull. For that matter, there was no sign of Greybull, not even its lights.

Closer at hand, Stan gazed down a buried open yard and building compound. The oblong open space was around three acres. Circled around it were four other buildings standing off on the edge of some woods. Three of the four houses were covered on their west and north faces by huge mounds of pristine snow. Only the last house, a smallish cabin at the far west end of the little settlement had escaped burial by a combination of the inexplicable vagaries of snow and wind. The roof of the cabin displayed only a light, snowy dusting, and anyone walking out of the front door could have made a circumference of fifteen feet all around without getting snow in his boot.

As the light became stronger, Stan spotted two humans and three dogs emerging from the log cabin. He could also begin to make out the tracks that went over to the nearest house. Judging by the width and depth of the path, it wasn't the first time these people had be up and about. A few minutes later, he could make out a tunnel from the clearing to the next house. Near it people were crawling on all fours out of the tunnel entrance and onto the clear area of ground next to the front door.

Later in the afternoon, Stan made another visit topside. This time the sun was shining so brightly he had to put on the sunglasses that Marvin handed him before going up. The wind had died down to little better than a wisp. The eerie stillness caught Stan by surprise. As he looked out over the hills, he thought he must be atop a huge glacier, sailing inexorably across the northern hemisphere toward some far off destination. All the small vales and dips had been filled up and smoothed over to create one huge plateau floating among distant hills to the northwest.

Just before nightfall, Keith Monrieth, the oldest of Hannie's children came over and took a seat between Stan and the old man, Douglas Dunbar, Hannie's father. Old Douglas was deaf and didn't speak much, otherwise he seemed alert, a sly smile permanently creased on his withered face. "For a sick man you seem to be able to carry your weight all right," Keith offered. Stan, who was beginning to learn the laconic ways of the West, turned and nodded in Keith's direction. "I guess you're wondering who we are, and why we're here. You landed into a den of thieves and no accounts called the Monrieth/Drummond clan." He said good-naturedly. "We've been in these parts as long as any white man, so early that we're half Indian, Crow and Shoshoni mostly. Over twenty-five of us live up her when we're all assembled. Most of the men work in the gas and oil fields, and are away a good deal, the others work in Greybull at the rail yards. Marvin, my cousin, and me work at the yards. I was coming back from the night shift when I ran across you, me and my two pooches, that is."

Stan nodded again and thanked Keith for saving his life before going to tell him a little about himself and why he was out in northern Wyoming. Keith shook his head in wonder of the ways of media. "You hear that Ma? Stan said he was going to Greybull to do some weather reporting. Is that crazy enough for ya?"

"Of course he was. What do you think he was doin' with all that camera stuff," Hannie replied, sometimes amazed by the dimness of even her smartest child.

"It's just a bad storm, worse than most but just a storm,"

offered Linda, the wife of Keith's absent brother, Sid, violently flipping her head back to force her long black hair from her face.

"A storm yes, but it isn't a local one, it's ripping all across the nation. WEBCO, my company, was the first to sound the alarm," the pride in Stan's voice barely suppressed. "This thing is a really big one, and all you folks have taken the first blast of it, you've sort of become a part of history."

"Great, I knew we were going to make history," Hannie said as she put on another pot of coffee.

Keith said nothing for a few seconds; finally after stroking his short, red beard a number of times, he spoke. "Stan we realize that we're not the typical bunch of Americans; maybe people living in the cities and suburbs might be interested in how we live out here, and how we're dealing with this storm. Now I rescued your camera and all, and seeing you're not fit for much heavy work, maybe you could make a movie about us, you know a documentary? We might be able to make some money, and go to Hollywood for one of those reward ceremonies. I hear there're a lot of them."

Stan remembered being startled by the request. Why would these people who lived an unspoiled life in the mountains want to go to Hollywood? Had the rot of the celebrity culture somehow oozed out to places as far off the beaten track as this place? But then he thought for a moment more. If he had some money he could move out to Montana or someplace like it and get a few acres on the side of a hill…. Yes, he, Stan Kelokowski, the nowhere man of WEBCO. Inconspicuous Stan – who had lucked out of a bogus cancer diagnosis, survived an historic blizzard, and so on – was now ready for a new life. "OK, sure, why not, let's give it a shot."

188

Chapter 16

COMMUNICATIONS ARE NOW OPEN

Outside there was little sign of the storm that was scheduled to rampage through Milwaukee the next morning. A brisk wind and some light snow skirting the sidewalks were the only impediments to Charlie as he walked the short distance between the office and his condo. The peacefulness of the streets and park was a welcome relief from the none-stop craziness of the station. He was at last able to reflect a little on what had transpired over the course of the last few hours. To a large extent Charlie was pleased with the performance of his staff. They had pulled off a significant coup, or rather a series of coups: the first being the declaration of an unofficial national weather emergency. They had also been first to bring the harrowing footage of Stan's last moments to the attention of the American public, not to mention a host of other exciting stories from various outposts throughout WEBCO's rickety empire. The panel interview was undoubtedly a tour de force. As bizarre as it would have seemed in normal times, it managed to have struck the right note for the time – a kind of disaster fantasy in a chat show format. WEBCO was the talk of the US, and it would remain so for quite a while longer if Charlie could keep all the knives up in the air a little longer.

Still there were some things that troubled him. The "Escape to Redoubt Alpha" might be judged as a piece of contrived theatre, if not handled right. Reggie had assured him more than once that Milwaukee would be taking it in the teeth by no later than mid-morning. It simply wouldn't do to be seen running around helter-skelter in a giant snowmobile unless there was a good reason. Nevertheless, Charles remained skeptical; he would not feel better until the winds howled like banshees, the snow fell like ash from Vesuvius, and the temperatures dropped to absolute zero. Only then would he feel right about moving the show to Ice Station Zebra.

The second thing that was bugging Charles was the whereabouts of Stephan and Roger. Just after 8:00, he had received a nearly incoherent call from Roger saying that his father was in critical condition at a Green Bay hospital. Once he was stabilized, Roger had emphatically stated, he was going to make a dash down 143 to pay a visit before the End of Time. "Christ, that's all I need is that idiot jumping around in my face just as we need to get out of Dodge. I'll pray to God that he is too stupid to find his way to the station. I didn't know that creep even has a license," Charles continued muttering to himself as he entered the elevator. He was surprised to see it full. While nodding to the crowd inside, he noticed that more than one occupant had a champagne bottle in hand. Apparently, end of the world parties were going to be the happening thing in Brew Town this evening. He was too tired to care, sighing with relief when the last of the exuberant occupants had exited.

But what was really worrying Charlie was whether Sam was all right. The last anyone had heard from her was late morning. She hadn't called in after that and her scheduled airtime had come and gone without her making an appearance. Was she hurt, dead or was she just making fools of them while hiding out in some doss house in the woods until the storm cleared?

Deep down he knew that if anything were to happen to her he would feel terrible. Never mind what a second death in the WEBCO correspondence corps would do to his reputation as a network executive. It would be like Cynthia all over again. "There's nothing I can do now; she's off on her own. I should have gotten her off that flight when I first discovered what she was up to. Christ was I an idiot," was the last fully formed thought Charles had before his head hit the pillow and he fell into a blank sleep.

A phone call woke him from his serial nightmare. It was almost the exact same dream as he had the night before. This time, however, Cynthia had been replaced by Samantha and the dream ended not in hospital but as the Aston Martin became airborne. Charlie was speculating whether this new twist to the dream was a good thing or not as he groggily reached for the phone.

"Yes, hello," he answered in a voice that conveyed a more alert mind than the one he possessed; he turned the digital clock around to catch the time, 7:05 a.m. according to the blue digits.

"Chief, its Jimmy, you wanted a call if things changed. Here's the scoop. Old man Gartner is dead. That fuck face son of his is trying to make it down here before the glaciers pay us a visit; says he wants a complete report prepared before he gets here."

"I'm not surprised, it sounded bad. Did you get any more details as to what happened?" Charles asked.

"Only that the plane hit some god awful turbulence over Lake Michigan, and the old man ended up munching on a glass of scotch. That's what my new friend at the Green Bay city morgue claims. Anyway, you owe me two hundred clams for that tidbit, and I don't want you to pony up with dinners at some kraut restaurant. Got it?" Jimmy concluded with just the right amount of intimidation in his voice to make Charlie know he was serious.

"Do you know when Roger left?"

"Best I can gather is about 6:30 give or take. That is if he scrammed from his bedside vigil after the old man kicked at 6:00. If he split earlier, who knows?"

"Right, OK; are you at the office?"

"Yeah."

"I'm going to clean myself up and head down there as soon as I can. Is Reggie around?"

"Somewhere, I saw him just before I called you. I'll get him on the line."

Within half a minute Charlie was talking to his chief meteorologist. "How are things shaping up? Are we going to need to put our doomsday plan into action?"

"Let me say this, Charlie, you won't be looking like a complete fool if you do. The storm has come out of its stall and has gained some speed; its center is pretty much right over the Mississippi. We're going to get hit around eleven, give or take a half hour," Reggie ended, no outward sign of distress or alarm in his voice.

"I see. How come northern Wisconsin got clobbered during the night?"

"That wasn't the main event, Charlie. Storms of this size and intensity can create sizeable disturbances far out in front of the main show. I think what happened to the Gartner's was that they hit a tight squall line coming out of the northwest, just the luck of the draw, so to speak."

"I see. I'll be back over in forty minutes."

~

Keith Marlow and Janice Berg were anchoring the early morning show as Charlie passed by the studio on the way to his office. "Hey Chief, we just got a text message from Sam. She says that she will be able to go on air for the 8:00 am show," announced Tad Shultz excitedly.

Surprising even himself, Charlie lowered his head for a short prayer of thanks before verbally acknowledging the news. "Do you know where she is?" he asked the assistant producer in a relieved voice.

"It said the Nor'west Angle of Minnesota. I'll have to look that one up, never heard of it."

"Somewhere up in northwest Minnesota, I suspect," Charles replied without irony. "Before she goes on air, tell her I want to speak with her." Now that this burden had been lifted, he made his way to his office as if floating on a blue-green wave, telling everyone he ran across that Sam had been located and she was all right.

The light was flashing on his phone the moment he entered. He picked it up and was connected to Mary Barber, "Yes, Mary, What's up?"

"Your father called from New York just before you got in. He says he wants to talk with you as soon as possible."

"OK, I will. You should be getting home or up to the Lincoln Park office before much longer. I think we have some big SUV's scheduled to leave around 9:00," Charles said with genuine solicitousness.

"Got it covered, Chief, I'll be riding shot gun on the 9:00

to Paducah."

"Great, I'll see you up there by mid-afternoon." Charlie immediately speed dialed New York. "Dad, it's Charlie; what do you need?" Charles asked unemotionally.

"Well son, I assume you learned about Stephan? As much as I grew to dislike the man in the last year or two, it was, nevertheless, a nasty way to go," Bunny Leuven answered evenly. "Dad, I thought down deep you liked him. You were in business together long enough; what happened for you to turn on him?"

"I didn't turn on him, Charlie. He simply couldn't go any further, that's all. After Cynthia's death he became a complete alcoholic. You know all this, don't you? It was very distasteful, that's all, a man that can't hold his liquor."

"Why did you invite him over for a meeting when you knew he had to leave before the storm?" asked Charlie, guessing at the answer.

"Oh that, I guess I was lonesome that afternoon. A moment of weakness, that's all. You do know I'm getting old; increasingly feeling compelled to tie up any loose ends, just in case I suddenly drop dead."

"I see, Dad. I can't say that I'm sorry to see him out of the picture."

"Damn right, you better not be sorry. He was going to mess everything up in a few months. I think he knew it too; at least that's what I guessed from his hang dog manner. The old guy didn't have much life in him from what I could see yesterday, just an old drunk. The thing now is that fool Roger."

"Yeah, I hear he's coming down to pay us a visit along with a full review of operations. He's as nuts as his dad, and ten times more stupid."

"Stupid he is son but I'm afraid that's what makes him dangerous. He's grieving for his dead daddy, who he probably loved and hated in equal measure. He also hates you. Fortunately, there are clauses in the corporate by-laws concerning succession and corporate governance that all but preclude the poor bastard from ever running World Media. So in a word, Roger is out. I haven't told you this until now because there was no reason to. But I have a hunch that Roger knows about it, and that's another reason for him to hate you, and for you to be on guard. I know he carries a gun with him wherever he goes. Now you tell your man, Jimmy, what is going on and he'll look after you; that's all for now. Oh, and remember what I told you last Christmas, the big things are easy. So see it through and don't sweat it. By this evening everything will be clear sailing. Say, should I wax my cross country skis?" Bunny's voice now turned jocular, replacing the hard, world-weary tone he used to describe the situation with the Gartners.

Taken a little aback by what he had just heard, Charlie was slow in replying. "I see, Dad, all this is very interesting; thanks for clueing me in. I'll be sure to tell Jimmy; though I have a feeling he already might know." Charlie could almost see a sly smile forming across the hawkish face of his father. "And, yes, Dad, I think the skis will come in handy in the next couple of days. I'll talk to you tomorrow. And thanks again."

Charlie lowered the receiver and looked out the window. He couldn't see much from his office chair, just a swirling mass of grey-white static, like on a TV that's lost its picture. He got up and moved nearer the window. Staring down, he thought he could make out the outline of the Milwaukee Art Museum and its brilliant Calatrava designed Quadracci Pavilion. The gracefully soaring glass and white steel frame appeared as an ethereal sailing ship sundered from its earthly moorings, gamely trying to reach port through a hurricane of screaming whiteness.

~

The small cabin shuddered when the latest blast of wind shot through the rafters. The wooden shelves on the walls had long ago been divested of their fishing tackle, matches and men's magazines from the previous summer. The suspended kerosene lamp swayed from the rafters, empty and flameless now after being left on all night. Samantha stiffly moved out of the goose down sleeping bag and reached for her flashlight. Somehow she had survived the night with little more to show for it than a few bruises and some numbing on her face and hands.

Almost inured to the cold after her first night in the north woods, Sam sat up, and promptly got out of the bag. She was surprised that she didn't feel colder once she was out of it. She kept her parka open during the night and now the simple act of zipping it up seemed to keep her as warm as the bag had during the endless night. She lit the Coleman stove hoping that it would give off a little heat but it was too weak, and the cabin too drafty, for it to gain on the cold. Using the last remaining bottle of water she had, Sam mixed up some dry noodles to make breakfast.

The fact that a large pool of Carl Troutmann's congealed blood was just a foot or so from her makeshift kitchen did not disturb Sam in the least. It had been a fair fight and she had won – simple as that. Any possible guilt she might have had for the taking of another human's life was completely assuaged by the fact that old Norm had started the raucous in the first place.

However, Sam couldn't help wondering from time to time what the story was behind Troutmann's craziness, and which corner of hell he had crawled out of. She looked at her watch, 6:45. Plenty of time before her 8:00 report, but first some breakfast.

After eating, she packed up her gear and prepared to make her exit from hell's half acre. She soon found out that this was easier said than done. Beginning at about 10:30 last night, long after she had conked out from all the excitement, the West Angle was visited by the full brunt of the front. Blizzard conditions had blown the soft snow up to the mid roof of the cabin's front façade. The two vehicles had vanished from sight, transformed into rounded moguls. Sam made her way to the opposite side of the shack, where she managed to open the small window in the rear after a couple of hard tugs. To her relief barely six inches of snow had piled on leeside of the hovel. Thankfully there was no sign of the small, vicious creatures that had besieged the cabin and eaten half of Norm.

~

"Chief, we have Sam on the phone, do you want me to patch her over?" asked Tad from the office entrance, only his head visible from where Charlie stood.

"Yes, thanks," said Charlie as he pivoted on his heels and made for the phone. "What the hell am I going to say to her," he wondered as he picked up the receiver.

"Sam, are you all right? I've been worried about you," tumbled the words from an increasingly nervous Charles Leuven.

"Fine, just fine; you know cooling my heels until air

197

time," Samantha's voice was as cold as the frigid air of northern Minnesota.

Charlie got the distinct impression that if he had been in the same room with her, Sam would have gone for his jugular. He decided for once to ignore his natural confrontational impulses and let things play out on their own accord. "Sam, I understand that you're up in the Nor'west Angle; is that right?"

"Yes, I am."

God, this is going to be a hard slog, thought Charlie. She's really going to make me work for it. "Do you need anything? Can you get out on your own or will you need some help? Let us know, and we'll be there for you," pathetic, thought Charlie, is the best he could do?

"I'm fine, I'm going to do my report and then return to Warroad," Sam said matter of factly, doing the best to conceal her concern for the real fix she was in. It'll probably take me a couple of days to get back to the station."

"I see, well if there is anything we, I, can do just let me know, we're all pulling for you," ended Charlie in a defeated tone. "I'll send you back to Tad now."

"Shit, I blew that big time," swore Charlie loudly, hitting his forehead with his fist. At that moment Allison entered the office; Charlie motioned her frantically to sit down. "I just got off the phone with Sam; she says she's fine but something is wrong, and she doesn't seem to be in the mood to tell me what it is."

"Gee, I wonder why that is," Allison mockingly replied in an unaccustomed display of solidarity with a fellow sister.

"OK, OK, it's no big secret what happened between us; but I need you and Tad to find out what exactly is going on up there, and if she needs help in getting out. Is that fair enough?"

"Fair enough, Charlie," she said, already making for the door.

"And now over to our mid-day anchor, Samantha Hewitt, who has been doing yeoman's work as a field reporter in the front lines of Storm Windigo," intoned Keith Marlow from the anchor chair. "Samantha, how are you doing up there in northwestern Minnesota, and have conditions improved since last night?"

"Thank you, Keith. Well as you can see, we are experiencing a very sunny morning here. I can see almost entirely across Lake of the Woods. The downside is that the temperature is only around 20 below now, we'll be lucky to see a high of zero today. On the plus side the winds have died down to only ten miles an hour, and if you stay in the sun, something I'm doing now, the temperature goes up a good ten to fifteen degrees, so it is tolerable." Sam's reporting was professional, yet informal and chatty; if someone had lost contact with the world for a week and just tuned in they would have thought that she was reporting from outside a rural Midwest Wal-Mart.

"I understand that last night was pretty rough," asked Keith.

Having fallen asleep before the big show, Samantha had no idea what conditions had been at 3:00 in the morning. Compounding the need for rest after her ordeal, she had also made the mistake of taking her instrument meters into the sleeping bag with her. Undeterred, Samantha put the best face on the situation and lied. "Yes it was, temperatures reached almost sixty below, winds were gusting to 52 miles per hour and the snow fell exceedingly hard. I'm going to pan the camera over to the cabin where I spent the night." The camera slowly picked up the side of the shack. "When I got here yesterday evening, there was only about a foot of icy snow on the ground, but, as you can see the snow is up to the roof line in places. So it was pretty rough indeed," concluded Sam with a game smile on her face.

Keith was going to ask the next question, when across from a small clearing behind the cabin, two large animals came bounding threw the deep snow. "God what are those things?" demanded Charlie who, with Reggie and Charlotte, were in the control booth watching Sam give her report. "Can you zoom in? Tell Keith to queue Sam about those critters."

"Here's the zoom, Chief," the director said calmly. The two animals were now seen in a tug of war, each holding in their mouths a large object.

"What are those things?" asked Reggie with genuine curiosity.

"I think they're wolverines; God they're much bigger than the ones I've seen in zoos," replied Charlie carefully. "Is that a head in the left one's mouth?"

The answer to that question became an emphatic yes when the two frisky rascals, as if on cue, turned their heads to the camera to reveal a human head gripped firmly in the wide jaws of the slightly bigger animal, the two upper canines neatly dug into Norm's lifeless eye sockets. His mate in the morning's hijinks had a more tenuous hold, pulling as it did on what was left of the right arm.

Sam then reappeared in the picture. She now held Carl's Winchester and was aiming it at the pair. The shot went wide, but it was close enough for the wolverine holding the arm to let go and scamper off, followed by his buddy who took the opportunity to run back into the woods along with the raggedy remains of Norm's head. "I'll see you later, I've got to get into the cabin, there's a lot of this around here," Sam said hurriedly just before she turned off the camera to conclude the satellite feed.

There was silence in the control booth. Charlie moved towards the door, already pressing the numbers on his cell phone to get in touch with Jimmy.

Chapter 17

RETREAT TO REDOUBT ALPHA

At 1:37 in the afternoon an icy gust of wind, clocking in at just under ninety four miles per hour, snapped one of the four steel tethers keeping WEBCO's main antenna aloof on top of the US Bank Corp. building. The three story pinnacle received its coup de grace moments later when a quick series of sharp gusts roared over the top of the building, taking out two more of the three inch thick support stays, causing the whole tower to quiver and topple over. A fourth cable held fast, allowing the antenna to smash into the lakeside of the building, between the thirty-seventh and thirty-four floors. There it remained, skidding along the face of the tower in a forty-degree arc, bumping and scraping along the façade, until an especially violent burst of wind sent it down to the deserted street below.

The noise of the falling antennae echoed throughout the upper stories of the building. Cal Thornquist had a pretty good idea as to its cause, but hoped, against hope, that his suspicions were baseless. "Ed, grab your coat and come with me. We need to check out what happened," ordered Cal Thornquist to his assistant, Eddie Smoltz, who happily complied. "Finally a chance for a little action," he thought.

Upon opening the door to the roof the pair was met by a dark gray wall of stinging snow and chaotic winds. Struggling for balance, Cal warily took the lead, fearful that one or more of the cables might still be flaying about in the wind. Barely able to see even a few feet in front of them, they moved along on all fours as they inspected the state of the four large dish antennas. The dishes were as important to the functioning of WEBCO as the now defunct antenna. It didn't take long for Cal to write off any possibility of salvaging them. The whipping cables had done their work, leaving two of the dishes completely gutted. The mounting brackets of the remaining two dishes had been casually ripped out from their poured concrete bases, like so many unwanted weeds. Wobbling around on what was left of their anchorings, they emitted a nerve eviscerating sound as they scratched back and forth on their specially built platforms. Like dancers engaged in an archaic quadrille, the two disks came face-to-face, only to promptly take their leave and fall back to their designated places as the wind shifted or abated.

Cal motioned to Eddie that he had seen enough and to retreat back to the door. Even if it had been on a clear day in June, no amount of jury rigging would ever get this bunch of scrap metal up and running.

On hearing what Cal was up to, Charlie made his way to the landing just below the final flight of stairs to the roof. It was there that he met the two. "Chief, we're fucked," shouted Cal as his feet came down on the last step. "It's all smashed to shit; we'll never get it up and running."

"OK, any sense in sticking around here then?" Charlie shouted back.

"I think Operation Retreat with Dignity should be put into effect immediately sir," a saluting Thornquist answered in mock military precision.

My God a display of irony coming from flat

top Thornquist, will wonders never cease, Charlie smiled to himself. "Right, well let's do it then. I'll call Jimmy to have the Cat brought up from wherever he's hiding it. Let's meet in the lobby in thirty minutes," said Charlie glumly. He felt like an admiral leaving a stricken flagship in the heat of battle. Would meteorological history view his acceptance of the tactical situation as heroic or cowardly? Charlie didn't much care. He didn't have the energy anymore to romanticize every little conundrum by associating it with some historic event. Events were succeeding in grinding down even Charlie's grandiosity as he gradually came to accept that things were what they were, and nothing more.

It took longer than expected to assemble everyone in the entrance hall, but eventually the final nine were gathered together, as their rescue vessel loomed up and out of the blinding snow, as if on cue.

What appeared before them was nothing like what they thought a snow-grooming vehicle should look like. Instead of a Hummer-like cab riding upon a twin track under carriage, what they beheld was an egg-shaped contraption reminiscent of a World War I tank, except instead of the tracks being on the side of the iron box they were underneath it. "My God," said someone, "it's an old Bombardier D-12; this is going to be a real thrill. Where did Jimmy get that crate?"

And a crate it was. Nine evacuees crammed themselves into the bright red cab; Susan and Ed, Milwaukee natives, shared the front seat with Jimmy, and were assigned the role of navigators and lookouts. Charlie sat behind Susan, sharing the middle seat with three others. The remaining three were stuffed in the low and narrow back seat. "Everyone on board?" asked Jimmy, glancing back into the cab at his uncomfortable cargo. "The heater isn't working too good, but I figure our body heat will keep us from freezing. We need to go about eight miles, so it's going to take us about an hour before we get up there." To the sound of grinding gears, and accompanying squeals of delight from the nine refugees, the cat lurched and sputtered away from the stricken headquarters.

The D-12 was noisy, uncomfortable and, despite the collective body temperature of its ten adult occupants, extremely cold. Their destination was the old WEBCO building station just north of the city limits. The nondescript, one-story brick building was located in the northeast corner of Lincoln Park, just a stone's throw from the Milwaukee River. "OK, listen up; some of you haven't been up to the old place, so I'm going to give you our route up there. It's pretty straightforward, up I 43 to the Hampton Street exit then over to North Milwaukee, River Parkway and then right again. How's that?" Jimmy asked rhetorically, not particularly caring about the response of his passengers.

The downtown that greeted the travelers wore a grieving and abandoned face. Its radical transformation made it feel unreal; more of a movie set than a real downtown. Save for the constant howl of wind ripping between the ice-encrusted buildings, the center was eerily placid. Drifts on the windward side of the street were already reaching for the second story in some cases.

Like so many scattered carcasses from a winter's death march, cars, small trucks, even city buses were left abandoned where they had ground to a halt, often enough in the middle of the street. Only one person was spotted in the mile or so distance from the east end of the downtown core to the freeway entrance, a hunched over man darting into a small office building off of Wells Street. Jimmy's unfamiliarity with the operational characteristics of the

Canadian-made contraption, especially the pivoting capabilities of the tracks made for slow going. It wasn't until they reached the entrance ramp to the freeway that he discovered some of the neat tricks the Bomb-12 was capable of. Unfortunately, the cost of reaching this milestone was at the expense of more than fifteen vehicles having their side panels scraped clean or their bumpers ripped off.

Once on the freeway the Cat was able to pick up a little speed. They had been on the empty road for only a few minutes when two small shapes zoomed past them, the high-pitched whine of their engines filling the cabin with an irritating foreboding. "Christ, what or who was that," shouted Charlie from the middle seat.

"I think that was Hub Wagner and a camera man. He said he wanted to get some footage of the move up to Redoubt Alpha. It is Redoubt Alpha right?" Cal asked from the other end of the middle seat.

"Yeah, yeah it's Redoubt Alpha, but why on earth are they screwing around in this type of weather?" retorted an annoyed Charlie.

Susan piped up, "Reggie thought that some video of our retreat from Moscow might play well on the evening broadcast."

Before Charlie could respond, a fireball erupted two hundred feet ahead of the plodding Bombardier. One of the snowmobiles had slammed straight into an overpass abutment, sending flame and smoke spiraling high into the air. "God, I hope that guy had the sense to jump off, but if it was Hub that may be a problem," offered Cal, as the big Cat churned its way up to the crash site.

"There he is, off to the right, ten feet in front of us,"

shouted Susan.

It turned out that it was indeed Hub, and he fortunately did have the foresight to leap clear of the runaway iron dog, just before it kissed the bridge's concrete base. While his thinking was quick, it was not quick enough to escape injury entirely. The momentum of the snowmobile had carried Hub's body along with it, sending his head rolling into the wall, knocking him out flat.

Like a good vicar taking care of an errant member of his flock, Cal had been the first out of the D- 12, leading the rescue efforts on behalf of his knuckleheaded assistant. "He's alive, all right. Help me get him into the Cat!" shouted Cal back to the mother ship. Charlie and Keith helped him drag Hub through the snow and into the cab. The interior was now more cramped than ever, making the next half hour almost unbearable. The accompanying snowmobile carrying the cameraman, now sufficiently chastened by the fate that had befallen Hub, obediently fell in behind the Cat.

~

An aging Ford Explorer was making equally slow progress in navigating the drifts and abandoned vehicles littering the highway south of Green Bay. The crazed looking driver hunched his head forward over the wheel, his face nearly up to the windshield. After many a false start and unexpected delays, Roger Gartner was finally getting the hang of driving in a place that had all the characteristics of the North Pole. His adaptation to local conditions was decidedly slower than Jimmy's, but then again, Roger, though in possession of a New York State driver's license, had never bothered to learn how to drive beyond the basic requirements of getting himself back and forth from New York to the Hamptons. He certainly had never experienced anything like the conditions that confronted him on this endless track of featureless Wisconsin roadway.

By the time he had found the entrance ramp to the freeway, Roger was beginning to become irretrievably unhinged. The strength he mustered to continue on was derived solely from his appointed mission of bringing Charles Duquesne Leuven II down, down to a subterranean depth from where he could never re-merge. Roger's deep-seated inadequacies had finally rushed in the moment the doctors at the hospital had pronounced his father dead. Self-absorption quickly morphed into something far beyond neurotic preoccupation or simple self-hatred. His daemons roared into his consciousness from some long undetected grotto, filling up every crevice and corner of his soul - their triumph rapid, complete and permanent.

Roger was now bereft of hope, alone in a black world surrounded by swirling whiteness. He would now have to forge on through life as best he could, no longer buttressed by the continual denunciations and diminutions of his acidic father. There would be no one to belittle and berate him now, except himself. And with Roger alone with only his scorched psyche for company, he'd never know any mercy. There would be no pause from the constant drumbeat of a cosmic choir attesting to his eternal loathsomeness.

But it was not these disjointed mental ramblings that made Roger insane. It was rather a competing mania that told him that with his father's death he had been finally set free. All the hurt and humiliation he had endured over the years were now to cease, becoming as insubstantial as the dancing snow. Roger's twisted belief that his father's death would somehow released him from the very things that were overwhelming him was the real source of his lunacy.

Refusing to accept this unrelenting and ferocious dichotomy running at large in his mind, Roger devolved into a singularity of misery. The only constant in his chaotic mental world was his obsession to crush Charles Leuven down to the subatomic level. Once that labor was concluded he would be able at last to take full possession of his father's legacy. It had been Charlie who from the start had worked to doom him to irrelevancy. It had always been Charlie, and his evil father Bunny who, from the first, had set out to destroy the good family Gartner. Now they would know what it was like to suffer as he had for all these years.

Early last night, Roger believed his father had died in the plane as it landed in Green Bay. He would have, but for the efficiency of the paramedics who, upon detecting a slight pulse in the old fellow, undertook all the heroic measures in their bag of tricks to keep him going for another ten hours. While accompanying his father to the hospital, Roger began to design his plan for revenge against Charlie, the true killer of his wonderful, horrible father. A host of alternatives crossed Roger's mind on how to deal with his rival. After discarding all those who could demonstrate a modicum of restraint and Machiavellian maturity, Roger opted for the straightforward. Confusing simplicity with elegance, Roger would simply drive down to Milwaukee, find Charlie, and shoot him dead.

He always carried a gun when traveling; for this trip he had packed a modest snub-nosed 38 Smith and Wesson. He had a vague idea of how to get to Milwaukee. The only thing he needed was a means of covering the hundred and twenty miles that separated him from his prey. While dedicated doctors and interns pretending to be brain surgeons carved up what was left of Gartner Senior, Roger started calling all the rental car agencies in town. Not surprisingly, given the time of night and the worsening weather, they were all closed. Next he bought a copy of the Green Bay Press Gazette and thumped through the used car listings. He was trying to find a late model SUV, or anything that had a chance of getting him to Milwaukee in one piece. His briefcase contained thirty-five thousand dollars in cash, once intended for call girls, blow and all the other accouterments for a fun Super Bowl weekend. Unfortunately, the sellers were not as receptive as he had thought they should be. Even the allure of a fifty percent bump over the asking price was not enough to bring them out on a bad night. They suggested he wait for the storm to pass, and then they could deal. A more persuasive person might have been able to coax one or more of them to brave the elements and drive the few miles to the hospital to do the deal. Roger, however, when initially thwarted responded with sarcasm and whining, an inevitable non-starter with the stolid German locals. In the end, they all hung up on him, some concluding their conversation with thick oaths and slurs.

At about two in the morning the doctors announced that they had been unsuccessful in stopping the bleeding, and offered their opinion that he most likely wouldn't make it 'till sunrise. Roger went into the ICU and looked down on a face that was unrecognizable beneath the swelling, drainage tubes and bandages. He felt nothing for the wreck of a human lying in the bed. In Roger's way of thinking his father had died on the plane, and what happened after the landing was only a sordid joke.

He, nevertheless, stood by the bedside for some minutes before turning and heading back to the waiting room.

He was now becoming frantic; his plan to kill Charles looked like it would fall victim to the need for observing the proprieties of his father's death vigil, and the realities of the worsening weather. Frustrated and dead tired, Roger decided to lay himself out on one of the waiting room sofas.

Just as he was trying to make himself comfortable on the vinyl and aluminum settee, a voice came to him from across the room. "Mister, I couldn't help but hearing; you need a car?" The speaker was a short man outfitted in gray-green kakis and a matching long sleeve shirt. He was around fifty or so, but his thinning slicked back hair made him appear older. "I got a '01 Explorer I was thinking of selling. I could let you have it at a good price," he said softly.

Roger was sitting up now, expectantly taking in the words of this heaven sent vendor. "Great, is it here, I mean can I see it now?" He asked hurriedly.

"Sure, grab your coat, it's out in the lot, I'll bring it around," the little man replied, in a low voice that seemed to swallow the last syllable of each word.

Roger, who knew nothing about cars, looked at the rusted out door panels and the cheap bondo job as if the heap was something heaven sent. To him it had the same lines and styling as a prewar Mercedes limo. The tires still had some tread on them, at least the front two, and the engine revved smoothly. Back inside the hospital, Roger opened his brief case, took out four stacks of wrapped bills, and handed them to the seller. "Here's twenty thousand, take it or leave it. I'm not dicking around on this," Roger said in a manly and authoritative way. The little man also decided not to dick around and blurted out "deal" before Roger stopped talking.

"I don't have the title and the transfer form, that's the only thing."

"Here's my card, send the documents to me as soon as you can, OK?"

"You can trust me, sir," said the custodian, looking Roger straight in the eye and wondering if all New Yorkers were such fools.

Stephan Gartner died at 6:03am on Saturday morning. Roger signed the necessary papers, promising to contact a funeral home to make arrangements for the body to be flown back to New York. By 6:45 he was inching out of the driveway of the hospital parking lot and on to Airport Drive headed to the freeway.

The Explorer, despite its years, drove fairly well, but several minor mishaps and wrong turns prevented Roger from reaching the entrance ramp to I 43 until well after 7:20. From there on things went fairly well, if slowly, until the exit ramp to Kiel and Cleveland. Two eighteen wheelers had jacked-knifed, blocking the two southbound lanes. The delay soon caused Roger to become hysterical; for over an hour and half he screamed at the top of lungs, slammed his fists down on the steering wheel and dashboard, stomped his feet until they nearly went through the floor boards. At one point in his tirade he put his gun to his head, and was about to shoot himself when he caught sight of a trucker staring down on him from the cab of his rig. Exhausted in mind and body, Roger finally collapsed, falling asleep with his head on the wheel.

A polite but firm rapping on the Explorer's driver window

woke Roger at 3:00 in the afternoon. "Sir, are you all right? Please proceed if you can; the road is open now but I advise you to stay off the interstate until things clear up," came a faceless voice from a hooded parka.

Roger signaled the officer that he was fine, and put the car into gear. It had been idling for hours, slowly sucking the gas tank down below the half-full mark, but at least the heater had kept him from freezing. "What type of people would come out in a blizzard to rescue some stupid truckers," wondered Roger as he slowly accelerated.

Near the Port Washington exit, he decided to give WEBCO a call. The phone rang three times before a recorded message announced that due to damage sustained in the storm, studio personnel had temporarily evacuated to an alternate site in order to continue operations. He decided against calling the number on the recording. "Why give them a warning?" But where was the new, or old office? "Shit, shit, where the fuck are they, those bastards? Think, think, that other place, you were there once, near a river, north of town." He was able to visualize the site of a nondescript office building by the river. Next out of his memory emerged the street name Hampton. Then he remembered he had his iPhone; that would do the rest. He would find it, and he would find Charles. "I've got him now!" screamed Roger as he put his foot firmly on the accelerator and saw the speedometer rocket to 15 mph.

As chance would have it, the two opposing forces arrived at the half buried station only minutes apart. Team Bombardier arrived first, as the last light of afternoon was beginning to dim, and unloaded its cargo of cramped and bitching passengers at the front door. Hub, who was by now conscious, was more or less able to walk under his own steam. Everyone except Charlie and Jimmy Dasimmi immediately scurried into the shelter of the building. Charles needed to talk alone to his go-to-man, and the two climbed back into the Cat and held their brief meeting. By the time it had concluded and the two occupants were getting out again, the lights of a large vehicle skirted across the parking lot until they fixed themselves on the rear of the Cat.

It's not unusual that impending confrontations that have enjoyed years to fester have their denouement in a manner of seconds. This was certainly the case with the one between Roger and Charlie. Shouting obscenities, Roger jumped out of the Explorer and remorselessly headed toward the Bombardier, pistol in hand. Charlie and Jimmy, hearing Roger's strained voice, jumped back into the front seat of the Cat. Sensing a bad situation, the ex-cop shifted the gears into reverse and floored the engine. Poor Roger's body was thrown back onto the front end of the recently acquired Explorer, his upper back and head forced back onto the hood, as the Bombardier's left track rode up and crushed the would-be avenger. Entering a new dimension of agony, Roger screamed and fired the gun into the underside of the CAT as the track slowly moved up on his body, smashing the life from out of his chest and head. Final obliteration came when Jimmy put the Bombardier D-12 into drive. The tracks stuttered for a moment before going forward. The hesitation resulted in them flicking and scraping Roger's upper teeth and nose high into the sheltering pines in the front of the building.

"Jesus Christ, Jimmy, we don't need this," stammered Charlie as he jumped out of the cab. The sight of Roger's scrambled head and crushed body were a little too real for him after everything else that day.

Jimmy joined him at the front of the Ford. "You're right, Chief, we don't need this, but neither did old Roger. You better let me take care of this, looks like police work to me," the ex-cop said as he bent down to retrieve the fallen revolver. He then pulled Roger's body off the front of the Explorer and dragged it off to the side of the building, trusting that the falling snow would soon cover it before daybreak. "I'm taken this ride down to the hood; someone won't resist a jack with the keys in it and all." With that he disappeared into the front seat and drove south toward Capitol.

Charles stood stunned: first, Cynthia, and then Stephan, now Roger. I guess he really did hate me after all, they all did, except for Cynthia. He turned back towards the entrance, a deep shudder went through his entire body as he appreciated how utterly disquieting life could be at times.

Chapter 18

LITTLE PRINCE TO THE RESCUE

"Get up fly boy, it's time to go." Jimmy Dasimmi's square bulk loomed over Charlie's cot in the nondescript room that served as his temporary office.

Aroused from a deep sleep, Charlie tried to ignore Jimmy's insistent prodding, "Huh, what time is it? God, it's only 4:30, what is this?" he wailed as he attempted to cover his head with the top of the sleeping bag.

"No dice, Chief; Reggie says that there's going to be a break in the storm at about 6:00, and it's only going to last for an hour or so before we get another batch of bad weather. So you got to go now, or sit here and listen to all this weather voodoo until Monday. What's it going to be? Oh, yeah, why don't you try to remember poor Sam out there in the middle of nowhere fighting off all those hyenas while you get an extra forty winks."

Ah, yes Sam; I must go and rescue her, that's the only way I'm going to redeem myself and make this mess whole again, Charlie thought as he sprang from the cot and reached for his shoes.

By now Charlie was sick of all the weather talk, and all the family intrigue nonsense. He was beginning to feel that a quick death earned by crashing a light plane into a frozen lake had some appeal to it. Charlotte barged into the room, wordlessly handing a mug of coffee to Jimmy, who in turn passed it on to the woozy Leuven. He thanked the human conveyor belt with a nod and then moved over to the small desk to look at the flight charts he had poured over until midnight. Sinking into the chair, Charlie took a long pull on the mug. Like electricity coursing through a maze of circuitry, Charlie's neural grid spasmodically flickered and then gave off a low wattage buzz as it powered up. His brain started to grind out all the rout calculations necessary to start a new day, finally his head jerked to the side; Charlie was ready to save Samantha.

He was glad he was getting out of town. Yesterday hadn't been great, starting with the collapse of the antenna and the smash-up of the dishes, closely followed by Wagner's stupid snowmobile showboating. The final topper was Roger's noir ending, complements of the Cat. He was sick of the whole thing, even the fake dramatic hype. He didn't care anymore about racing fronts, colliding weather systems and farmers eating their babies. All he needed to do was find Sam and bring her back, and then everything would be great.

The Bombardier D-12 crawled through the early dawn to Timmerman Airport, a small general aviation field, a few miles west of the studio. Technically, like all airports in Wisconsin, it was closed to all nonemergency flights, but that hadn't stopped Jimmy from getting everything ready. The big Chicagoan could be convincing when he needed to be, especially when he had Charlie's money to throw around. After over twenty phone calls on Friday he eventually found a person, one Walter Evans of Kettle Moraine, who was willing to pick up some quick cash. For $25,000 a day plus fuel charges, plus the placement of $1.5

million surety bond in an escrow account in case fortune frowned on the enterprise, Mr. Evans was willing to charter out his beloved Otter to Charlie Leuven. It was a rather steep price. However, not completely unfair considering Evans was agreeing to lend out his baby to someone he didn't know, and for purposes that seemed rather vaguely sketched out, all this in the aftermath of a huge, crippling storm.

When the Bombardier arrived, the gates to the hanger section of the airport were unlocked, but it took both Jimmy and Charlie ten minutes to clear the snow away on one side of the double wide, chain-linked gate before it would swing free. Once in, Jimmy made for a small hanger at the end of a row of unremarkable structures. Charlie got out and knocked on the side door; in a few seconds it was swung open by a tall, lean man in coveralls and a down vest.

"Perfect timing, she's been all checked out and she's ready to go. My name is Stu Leland, I'm the mechanic. Walter couldn't make it for obvious reasons," said Stu as he proudly pointed to the De Havilland Otter- DHC 3 parked expectantly in front of the large hanger doors.

"Stu, a pleasure to meet you; my name is Charlie Leuven," he said in a relieved tone as he extended his hand to the mechanic.

"Fair enough, Charlie. Let me show you around this beauty, they don't make'em like this anymore, that's one thing I can tell you. This plane has been everywhere and done everything in its long life. It'll get you in and out of places you wouldn't believe. Say, how many hours do you have under your belt, Sonny?" asked the lean man abruptly.

"Something close to six hundred; I'm rated ATP for two engine", said Charlie as he stared up at the Otter. The big radial engine gave it a stocky, redoubtable appearance when viewed from the front end; it was only when the plane was approached from the side that Charlie realized how big and long it was, far larger than he really needed for this trip. Just behind the engine the name the "Marmot's Whelp" was painted on the front fuselage in bright red, scripted lettering. The more he looked at the Otter the better Charlie felt. It was a tough looking bird, with an all business sense about itself that spoke of adventures in distant and undisturbed places.

"Sounds good to me, have you landed and taken off with a ski rig?" asked Stu while acknowledging Jimmy's entrance from the side door. "No, I'm rated for seaplanes but I've never flown with skis before. Give me some pointers about what to expect."

Satisfied that the stranger wasn't some suburban know-it-all, Stu grunted and smiled. He gently took Charlie by the arm and led him around the plane explaining its idiosyncrasies and flying characteristics. The mechanic then opened the pilot's side door, motioning for Charlie to climb in as he went around and limberly hopped up into the copilot's seat. Charlie followed, taking the pilot's seat on the left, as Stu excitedly acquainted him with the peculiarities of the plane's gauges, switches, wheel, and sticks, pride underlining every word that came from his mouth.

While Charlie was occupied with Stu, Jimmy quickly stowed away the luggage, dumping two small overnight bags on the rear passenger seats; a coffee thermos and some sandwiches filling a small knapsack were deposited next to the pilot's seat. Finally, Jimmy lugged two duffle bags and placed them in the floor behind where the mechanic was sitting. Shortly after Charlie and Stu concluded their run-through, the big twin doors of the hanger rolled open to reveal a wide path cleared of snow. Charlie started the engine, and then ran through his checklist again before putting the Otter into gear and then cautiously taxiing out of the hanger.

A few minutes after reaching climbing altitude, Charlie stared out at the soft, still landscape below. There were no signs that there was any living thing in the city; no cars were moving, no trucks or planes or even trains could be seen. The city, and all the cities from Denver to Cleveland, was in the same state of lockdown, suffocating under the same heavy tarp of snow and ice. The pale sun was preparing to fight for preeminence with a contesting line of low ceiling, cumulus-stratus clouds coming out of the Southwest. Thinking it was a site he might not see again, Charlie hurriedly took a few snaps from his iPhone camera.

Once up to the eight thousand foot cruising altitude, Leuven checked the compass heading. The night before, he had plotted a course that would take him north-northwest over Appleton and Wausau, Wisconsin; and then up to the western end of Lake Superior, just east of the Apostle Islands. Once across the lake at Two Harbors, he would change course to the west-northwest and head straight to Sam and her wolverine buddies. As best as Charlie could figure the jaunt was about five hundred and fifty miles up to the Angle and then another two hundred plus miles back to Duluth, the easternmost city in the region that had a real airport and medical facilities. The plan was to get to the Angle between 2:00 and 3:00, pick up Samantha and get to Duluth before sundown. By flying at a conservative hundred and twenty knots, he calculated he should safely get there and back with fuel to spare. Charlie was counting on only two things: that the high westerly's would be less than forty miles per hour, and a clearing in the cloud deck, predicted by Reggie, would materialize once he reached northwestern Wisconsin.

He was not used to flying in complete silence. There were no passengers to ask silly questions or flight instructions being issued by distant towers in the arcane numerology of flight-speak. Today there was only the drone of the Pratt and Whitney-Wasp1, and the occasional weak gusts that gently buffeted the old work horse from side to side. She had a firm, steady feel to her, with the tendency to hunker down and firmly hold a heading. Yet, at the same time, she was willing and agile. After setting the automatic pilot, Charlie decided that he would catch up on his reading and took out his Kindle and found the Eric Ambler novel he had started a few days ago. Before delving into it, he remembered that he needed to "tweet" his loyal followers about his daring mission to save Samantha from death's clutches. He had been told by Hale that, ever since the panel discussion on Thursday, the number of people following his Twitter missives had skyrocketed, and now easily numbered into the hundreds of thousands. Satisfied after a few lines of abbreviations, Charlie sat back and started reading.

As Reggie predicted, the sun emerged just south of Ashland. It was strong but not as glaring as it had been on Thursday at the Milwaukee airport. Was it only three days ago that all this craziness had started in earnest? Charlie put his book down and peered out the side window. He could just make out the first batch of the Apostle Islands dead ahead; soon it would be time to get to work.

Lake Superior was frozen white to the southwest – all the way down to Duluth, however, east and north of the islands there was nothing but the cobalt blue of cold, open water. The January thaw coupled with churning winds had forestalled any hopes of turning the inland sea into one big ice rink. Catching Charlie's attention were the huge, crystalline ramparts that the northwesterly winds had piled up along the windward side of the islands. Resembling the shoreline of Antarctica, the jagged escarpments stretched for mile after glittering mile along the low-lying coast, a testament to the ferocity of the recent storm.

Charlie took the Otter down to five thousand feet, slowing the plane to seventy knots. Extricating himself from the pilot's seat, he moved to the rear where the duffle bags had been stowed. He had expected just one bag: a little unnerved by the thought of what Jimmy must have been up to late the previous night, Charlie passed on investigating the bags' contents. Despite the thick canvas he could tell the body (or parts thereof) was still mostly frozen. A night out in the snow, and Charlie's decision to keep the plane's heater down to forty-five degrees had prevented any serious defrosting of his would-be assassin. Charlie began the struggle of getting them out of the door for their final send off.

What a sorry end my friend, thought Charlie. He realized he had never truly hated Roger. He had known him too long and too well for that. In many respects they had grown up together, and if never friends, the majority of their early lives where spent in reasonable harmony. It was only after Roger turned fourteen that Charlie began to recognize that something was off. His mother ignored him nearly altogether in favor of her handsome "do no wrong" James. Stephan, of course, had paid too much negative attention to him in a farcical and futile attempt to turn him into a replica of their ever-absent wonder boy. If either parent had had any insight and compassion, they would have found a sinecure for the poor fellow in one of their firms and left him alone to reach his own level. But they didn't, and Roger

222

wouldn't or couldn't accept the fact that he was only an average guy born into a family of assholes. And, so this was the result, a lonely, bleak ending in the middle of nowhere.

Charlie wasn't a fatalist but he couldn't help observing that once a life hits the skids inexorable forces seem to create a critical mass that, barring a miracle, can't be denied. Life for those unfortunates becomes almost predestined. Roger, the poor slob, was finished once he decided to play his father's game and take the old man's advice of what he should do, think, and behave; from then on he was dead meat. Charlie hadn't felt so sad since Cynthia's death but what could be done now?

He pushed the door far enough open so the duffle bags were half inside and half outside the plane, then with two great shoves of his booted foot gave his childhood comrade one last ignominious send-off. In honor of Roger, Charlie sharply banked the plane around and dipped the wings in the direction of the splash down. In all that cold blue, the dark, mangled remains of Roger Gartner hardly made a dent as they entered the waters with the smallest of splashes. If Charlie felt sad, he also felt exceedingly grateful that his own life, for whatever reason, had been lived absent the pain and disappointment that had dogged Roger's.

~

Ron Stensgaard banged open the door to his brother Don's room and announced at 10:15 that conditions were ideal for a snowmobile romp across Lake of the Woods. "Yeah for sure it's cold but there must be almost five feet of new snow on the Lake; we can go forever!" Ron exclaimed in exasperation over his brother's protests concerning the hour.

"Just get up now and I'll call Siggy; he's been dying to get that new Polaris job his uncle left him out on the lake for a real spin. I know he'll be up for it, and hey once you're up try pouring those two bottles of peach schnapps into a thermos. It'll go down real good out there come lunch time." Don nodded warily, resigned to the fact that once his older brother got an idea in his head, no matter how crazy, he was destined to tag along.

Because of the weather, Ron was longer than expected in getting the two old Arctic Cat snowmobiles up and going. Things always took longer in the winter. Intense cold slowed everything down, seizing up physical movement and mental processes alike, often to the extent that they seemed to operate as slow motion hallucinations of their normal selves.

The Stensgaard modest ranch house was about a mile from the lake and almost exactly equidistant between Warroad and the town of Baudette. Siggy Abrahamsen would be coming west from Baudette to their usual rendezvous point, a small feeder creek to the lake. He would be more or less on time since his snowmobile was parked in a heated garage, helping to make for quick and easy starts. The Stensgaards didn't have that luxury, they kept the pickup and snowmobiles in an old shed out back. The two machines each had their own heaters that were plugged into the house's electrical system by a series of long extension cords. The current would be enough to keep the oil from seizing up during nights of extreme cold. By the time Ron had the old wool blankets off the machines, Don was making his way out of the house with two knap sacks filled with beef jerky, various types of booze and two tins of snus.

By 1:30 all three snowmobilers had left the shore and were racing around in the lower bay, testing out the snow and the machines before heading out toward the Angle. Siggy was riding high on his big blue Polaris 800cc. Ron and Don had to be content with their 500cc "dogs". Ron's machine was red and Don's was blue. They weren't really theirs; their dad, Buck Stensgaard, had bought them a number of years ago for him and his wife, Lois. Since retirement, however, Buck and Lois spent the winters in a Nevada trailer park outside of Reno, leaving the ancient machines to the tender mercies of their sons.

Ron wished he had a new and bigger machine so he could better keep up with Siggy's Polaris. Today, like all days, he and Don would have to be content to take up the rear, straining so as not to be left behind. To give them the illusion that they were part of some impressive vanguard, the brothers Stensgaard would normally spread out and act as distant flankers behind the big black Polaris. It was all worth it though. In the end their underpowered machines really didn't matter much. Being out there in the bright snow and cold always brought Ron to life. On the old Cat he could forget about his boring job at the window factory, about his stupid and chronically unfaithful girlfriend with the big tits. He could forget about everything but the roar of the engine and the bounding of the machine across the frozen wastes heading off toward a shoreline that doubled as a cloud bank in the far distance.

~

The sun had started its slow descent by the time the Marmot's Whelp's deep drone was heard over Lake of the Woods. Samantha checked her watch once she heard the throaty bass of the big engine. What day was it? Sunday, it must be

225

Sunday, she thought as she stiffly got out of her sleeping bag again and made it over to the back window of the shack. She couldn't see anything except the white expanse of ice on the lake. She moved away and looked around at the cluttered room. In the corner the last of the freeze-dried noodle packets was sticking out of a grease-stained paper bag. The portable Coleman stove remained unlit; two expended fuel canisters littered the floor. It was all a sorry mess, not a place to starve to death in, that was certain.

Then the hum of a plane's engine returned, this time closer. Sam ran to the rear window and saw a plane off to the northeast; then she remembered the GPS locator. She had turned it off during the worst of the storm to save on the batteries; hopefully it hadn't gone all phooey in the deep freezer of the cabin. Eventually, she located it at the bottom of her sleeping bag; nervously, she switched it on. After an eternity the thing lit up and Sam squealed with relief. "Just maybe that plane is looking for me," she prayed.

Charlie was flying at only seven hundred feet as he made his first approach to the stark and uninviting peninsula. There were a number of cabins scattered around, but none appeared to be inhabited. Nevertheless, the coordinates, as picked up on Saturday morning, pointed to the tip of the Angle as the location from where Sam had made her last report. Then in the middle of his first approach his locator picked up a steady beeping signal. This has to be the place, thought Charlie, swiftly banking the Otter around to make a second, lower pass.

This time he could make out two mounds next to a snow-covered cabin and what looked like a trail leading down to the shore. Around the shelter were at least three stocky animals. They

226

were mostly dark brown but each had patches and crescents of ginger brown fur on their chests or shoulders. Off in the distance, they amiably circled around the trees, not much concerned with anything in particular.   They must be our wolverine friends, thought Charlie. On the side of the cabin facing the lake, Charlie saw something like a piece of red cloth waving jerkily from a window. She was there! Time to get this thing down and play his part of a lifetime, Charlie mused as he let out a big sigh of relief. He edged the Otter up and banked to the south in preparation of his final approach. As he did, he saw out of the corner of his eye, a few miles off, three shapes moving at considerable speed in Sam's direction. Were they wolves bounding across the drifts to feast on the last morsels of ready meat for miles around or something else entirely? No, they were moving too fast for animals. They must be human's on snowmobiles racing over the wastes towards his beloved.

Lack of sleep over the last few days had dulled Charlie's capacity for analytical thinking. Instead of sizing up the three as possible good-hearted rescuers or just a bunch guys out for a joy ride, Charlie's mind immediately concluded that the three were harbingers of Conrad Merkulus's direst predictions – cannibals out on a killing spree! Or, just as bad, comrades of the maniac who had befriended Sam only to turn on her once she was vulnerable. Whoever they were, they no doubt had been in deep cover, along the frozen creeks and fens, just waiting for their time to strike. And who could really blame Charlie for his outlandish conclusions based on the slimmest of circumstantial evidence? Hadn't all the events since Tuesday been based on just that – the flimsiest and most tortured of speculative and self-serving forecasts, and hadn't they all turned out to be more or less on target?

Charlie knew he didn't have much time; the three amigos were within a couple of miles of the cabin. He quickly grabbed the bag behind his seat and extricated from it one of his favorite toys – a MP5 with a telescopic sight, the hobbyist's sniper rifle. He attached the stock to the gun and then proceeded to bring the plane parallel to the three bouncing wraiths. He figured that all he needed to do was to knock out the lead driver by disabling his engine. Hopefully, then, the two remaining outriders would break-off in order to rescue their stricken comrade. Once the three had sized up the situation they would probably high tail it back to their hideout on the shore. If, however, they proceeded on, confirming Charlie's direst suspicions, he then would have the right to blast these backwoods ghouls all the way up to Hudson Bay.

"OK, you god damn yellow hammers prepare to eat lead," breathed Charlie slowly trying to establish a rhythm as he flew low and to the right of the lead rider. He quickly closed the gap between the Otter and his target until there was only a football field distance between them. Steadying the MP5 on the open window frame, he carefully aimed as he tried to synchronize the looping movement of the snowmobile with the gentle rolling of the plane. But it was all a bit too much to get right. He simply couldn't get a steady head on the big black machine long enough to let off a shot that stood any chance of being successful. He would have to change tactics. Banking off to the north, Charlie made a tight turn back again. Zooming down just a few hundred feet in front and a hundred feet above the now bunched trio, Charlie fired off a full clip just a few yards in advance of them. The noise in the cockpit was deafening but Charlie's gambit seemed to do

228

the trick. Fearing that a plane flying so low and so close was up to no good, the three eased up on their throttles even before the first shoots rained down, splashing up like little geysers. Without even signaling one another, the three simultaneously changed course and accelerating to the south.

"Well thank God that worked," Charlie said, not displeased with his performance, "now let's get Sam."

Samantha Hewitt, who had become worried for a few moments when the plane suddenly veered south, quickly reclaimed her composure when it banked around again, to land only a short distance from the shore. Now, she didn't know whether to laugh or cry as she saw her rescuer emerge from the big bush plane. The tall man was bedecked in a thick parka that appeared to be made out of crudely stitched together hides and pelts. The hood's edges were lined with some type of fur, and on his feet was a pair of magnificent, knee high leather boots. The topping touches were the two ammunition belts that crisscrossed his chest, from which hung two holsters each containing a very large revolver. The character was dressed like someone out of a Jack London novel; all he needed by his side was a barking sled dog.

"Who was he?" wondered Samantha. It couldn't be Leuven; he wouldn't walk across the street for her. But he might have paid someone to come up here and do his dirty work for him. She decided not to wait for a letter of introduction. Snatching up the rifle and quickly slipping the last four cartridges into the clip, she headed out the back window. In her rush, Sam miscalculated the force she needed to clear the ledge, landing head first in the low drift. Once on her feet again, Sam quickly glanced around; hoping that no one witnessed her clumsiness, she proceeded to fire off two shots, as if daring anyone to make a smart comment.

The man waved his arms back and forth in acknowledgement and then pulled out a huge gun from his left holster. The .44 Magnum let out a terrible roar, ripping and rolling across the lake for miles. The racket startled the wolverines; they instinctively cowered, not sure of what to do; finally, deciding that discretion might be the better part of valor, the three scampered off behind a small hillock, there to observe humans from a relatively safer vantage point.

The parka-encapsulated figures increased their respective speeds as they moved closer to one another. Samantha, tumbling down from the bank to the lake, righted herself and was now lumbering and tripping along. "It must be Charlie, who else would dress up like that and fly a bush plane in the middle of a blizzard? It must be him, who else?" she whispered to herself as she slogged forward forcing her way through the heavy snow.

The question mark in Charlie's head was simple. "Is this what love is? Do I really love her?" Then for a second, Charlie stopped thinking and the last few months flashed by in an instant, the romance, the breakup, the Storm, the flight, the fact he was here in the middle of nowhere in an old plane with man eating wolverines lurking about, the fact that she was running as fast as she could to him, the fact that if this wasn't love then it didn't exist.

They collided into one other; the bulkiness of their clothing buffered their embrace, causing them to fall back for a second until Charlie lifted her up and pulled her towards him all in one sweeping motion. They fell into the snow in a heap and rolled around hugging and kissing each other for a long, long time before realizing their furry friends on the shore had taken a renewed interest in them.

The two were working to regain their footing when Samantha hauled off and soundly slugged Charlie in the arm, causing him to fall down on one knee. "You are a complete shit, you know. I've had an absolutely horrid time of it here while you've been playing at bush pilot of the Yukon. It simply isn't fair. Charlie Leuven, you are the worst human being I've ever met. My father was absolutely right about you Yanks, a bunch of spoiled cowboys, the lot of you…" exhausted by this tirade and all the things she had endured in the last few days, Sam burst into tears, and would have dropped to her knees if Charlie hadn't caught her.

"It's over, Samantha; let's get the hell out of here. Do you have anything you want to take with you?" He said gently, caressing her head that rested on his chest.

"No, let' go. I hate this place," She said through heaving sobs.

They arrived in Duluth shortly after 5:30, the sun having just reached the horizon when the skis scraped along the half plowed runway. Samantha spoke hardly at all once she was buckled into the front seat. Soon after takeoff, she ravenously devoured two sandwiches, and a little later in mid-sentence of some unimportant detail concerning her recent trails, she fell dead away, and stayed asleep throughout the rest of the flight.

As they flew over International Falls, Charlie called WEBCO and talked with Reggie and Cal. According to their reports the city was still in the throes of a nearly universal paralysis. There was, however, the first appearance of detectable signs of life re-emerging in the old town. Some of the main streets were said to be partially open for emergency vehicles and the airport authorities said they would have at least one runway open for regular commercial flights by Tuesday morning. The big news came from the East, where the nor'easter had slid down from Canada colliding with the fronts coming out of the Great Lakes and the Ohio Valley. Cities from Boston on down to Washington were getting clobbered, and it wouldn't be until late tomorrow before the worst of it was over. Charlie wondered if his Dad was out skiing in the Park.

Reggie said he would alert the Duluth affiliate of their expected arrival and obligingly jotted down the news flash that Charlie wanted sent out to the media. Cal broke the bad news that the antennas on the bank building couldn't be replaced for at least sixty days but they could utilize feeds from other sources to make WEBCO look like a reasonably respectable weather outfit. Charlie, prior to preparing for landing, took a few moments to tweet some of the details of the rescue to his multitude of "followers" throughout the vast reaches of the Ethernet.

The pair was greeted at the Duluth Airport by a squad of reporters and a small medical corps. Before Sam was whisked off to the hospital, accompanied by Charlie, the president of WEBCO gave the assembled reporters a brief synopsis of the day's events, lauding Sam's bravery and tenacity in the face of a host of life threatening traumas. He also dropped the name of Norm Knutson, as the identity of the assailant whose head was briefly featured in a tug of war between the two wolverines, who some wags had already dubbed, White Fang and Black Tooth.

The resulting story became front-page news throughout the Great Lakes region and then the nation as a whole. Headlines trumpeted the heroic rescue as something harkening back to another era of true romance and daring-do. Typical was the byline in one Chicago paper, "WEBCO Exec. Braves Legions of Wolverines" and "Frozen Wilderness in Death Defying Fly-in Rescue of Cub Reporter." Another read, "WEBCO Reporter Battles Wolverines, Storm and Homicidal Maniac in Far North." A smaller article on page nine of the Milwaukee Sentinel announced that authorities now speculated that the individual who attacked WEBCO reporter Samantha Hewitt on the Nor'west Angle was probably Carl Troutmann, a recent escapee from the Mendota State Mental Hospital, in Madison, Wisconsin. The story went on to detail Mr. Troutmann's four year reign of terror and the string of grisly murders in northern Wisconsin during the 70's. For some reason the paper neglected to mention Harlan Zinter, Troutmann's cousin, and fellow escapee.

But Charlie and Samantha didn't care what the media reported or didn't report. Once she was released from the hospital later that night, they went to a suite at the local Radisson Hotel overlooking the port; there they stayed for the next twenty-four hours under of mounds of snowy white sheets and down filled duvets.

233

Chapter 19

THE HEROES RETURN

On Tuesday morning Charlie and Samantha flew back to Milwaukee aboard the redoubtable "Marmot's Whelp." Still emotionally drained from the crazy mishmash of events of the past few days, neither said much during the uneventful flight. Occasionally, Charlie would take Sam's hand in his and give it a squeeze or bring it up to his mouth for a gentle kiss. Other than these modest displays of affection, the trip over the silent forests and farmlands of northern Wisconsin proved strangely dreamlike for the two travelers.

As they crossed the northern part of Lake Winnebago signs of life became more apparent. A train was spotted making its way west. Sam pointed out several trucks on a four-lane highway heading off in the general direction of Chicago. There was little car traffic, however, until they reached the Milwaukee suburbs. Near Timmerman Field the pulse of activity quickened a little – when up to two vehicles could be seen standing at a traffic light. Slowly, the return to normalcy was in the ascendance, replacing the fear and chaos of the last few days.

While in Duluth, Charlie had the good sense to have the skis removed from the landing gears, helping to make for a relatively smooth landing for the old Otter on the partially cleared runway. The plane jauntily taxied over to the hanger where just over forty-eight hours ago it had departed on its mission of mercy. A large crowd of media people, ranging from network reporters, on down to the local news stations and papers, were waiting impatiently just inside the hanger. Charlie was gratified that Susan Brownell had been able to drum up this type of reception during what must still have been a busy news cycle. But on reflection, he decided it was only their due; through dint of their individual and collective acts of daring, he and Sam had become at least minor celebrities. It was only proper that the media lavish some attention on them. Certainly they were perfectly cast for their assigned roles – young, rich, beautiful, intelligent and well bred. How could anyone miss?

Sam, on the other hand, thought it rather overdone, and was not shy in communicating her distain to Charlie about what she considered to be "unwarranted attention and fanfare." As the plane was pulled into the hanger by Stu Leland and a fellow mechanic, Samantha blurted out to Charlie, "I've had it with this stupid business. In a country ravaged by blizzards and all sorts of natural disasters, the best allocation of news talent these idiotic producers could manage is to send all these reporters to greet us? What a bunch of vain and narcissist assholes," she said heatedly.

Charlie shrugged and smiled a knowing smile. "Don't be so priggish, Sam. This is America, after all, and here we do not live by the laws of scarce resource allocation alone but by every transient whim of an insatiable media ever longing for something new, bold and amusing." He then turned his head and waved, still smiling, to the cameras.

Once out of the plane, and standing near the rear of the fuselage, Charlie and Samantha agreeably answered the reporter's inane questions. To Samantha – "Did you ever give

235

up hope?" "When did you suspect that Carl Troutmann was a madman?" "Did you kill him or did the wild animals?" "Will you be returning to WEBCO's morning anchor position?" "Were you ever personally attacked by the wolverines?" And lastly, "When are you two getting hitched?"

The questions put to Charlie had less to do with the rescue than about the accolades now being showered on WEBCO for its numerous examples of gutsy reporting. The future of WEBCO as an independent network was the concern of a local business reporter. The last question shouted out came from an anonymous reporter from Chicago, "Have you been in contact with Roger Gartner, and do you know his whereabouts?"

Naively, Charlie hadn't expected news concerning Roger to be of interest to anyone outside of WEBCO and the two families. Had something taken place during his absence to get the question onto the media's radar? Looking out over the attentive faces, he spied Jimmy Dasimmi leaning against the wall. Jimmy's square face was an opaque mask, a look that Charlie immediately interpreted as a warning to be careful.

Turning to the reporters, he blandly constructed an answered to the unwelcomed question. "The last time we heard from Roger was Saturday morning. He called us to say that his father, Stephan Gartner, had died tragically in a plane mishap, and that he would be driving to Milwaukee later in the day. When he didn't arrive everyone assumed that he had been prevented from joining us by the weather and he had probably taken refuge somewhere?" Charlie then halted his remarks before attempting to wrap up his show of feigned ignorance. "From your question, I must assume that his whereabouts are in question. If true, this naturally causes me great concern, both on a personal and professional level. Once I return to my office I will give it my full attention." Charlie hoped this would hold them for a while until he was able to better craft a fuller explanation, one that anticipated all the angles and loose ends to this low voltage mystery. He, however, couldn't help but notice Sam casting a quizzical gaze in his direction.

"I'm afraid that we have to go now, Ms. Hewitt and I want to thank you all for coming out here. It was a great homecoming and we are truly touched, but it's time for us to get back to work," Charlie said smiling.

Jimmy pulled the black SUV up to the side door of the hanger and quickly made for the airport's exit. Hampton Avenue and the other main thoroughfares had enjoyed at least one quick plowing since Sunday morning, enough to create serviceable, almost subterranean, causeways between mountainous piles of plowed snow. In what were formally the medium strips or left hand turn lanes, huge mounds rose up making it impossible to see oncoming traffic. Making driving more treacherous was the foot deep pack of snow and ice that now served as the streets' pavement. Side roads weren't so lucky. They had been completely abandoned to the elements, and were still impassable after three days. In that time blowing winds had sculpted a landscape of rolling hillocks and crested snow waves untouched by man or machine. As compensation for their municipal neglect, these neighborhoods had a certain purity about them, as if they had been hidden away in some far off country meadow waiting to be stumbled upon by some appreciative of nature or photographer.

Jimmy drove slowly; he spoke little outside the necessary recounting of what had happened around the studio and in the city since Sunday morning. The black Yukon pulled up to the double glass front doors of WEBCO's temporary headquarters. Most of the staff were gathered on the small porch; they gave out a collective and hearty cheer when the doors opened, and out popped the heroes of the hour. Charlie and Samantha were hurriedly rushed inside to the main foyer where a table laden with bottles and glasses stood at the ready. In typical Midwest fashion, the women gathered around Samantha and the men surrounded Charlie. After a few toasts to the quick and the dead, the two foci of attention flung their respective orbits and satellites yet further apart from one another, spiraling out into separate reaches of the building. There were many exclamations of wonder, horror and admiration as the two recounted their respective ordeals in the northern wastelands. In an hour the groupings started gradually thinning out, as either a sense of professional obligation or boredom eventually triumphed. While Samantha was content to enjoy her reign as long as possible, Charlie was itching to get to somewhere private in order to get a rundown from Jimmy regarding what had happened in his absence. Pleading important calls to New York as his excuse, Charlie managed to extricate himself from his admirers. Once in his office, he quickly came to the point. "Jimmy, have the cops been sniffing around?"

"If you mean whether representatives of the local constabulary have made inquiries pertinent to the disappearance of a one Roger Gartner of New York City, the answer is no," Jimmy stated with mock formality, " at least not in a serious way. They called late Sunday afternoon, just to ask whether Mr. Weasel Face had contacted us."

"What about his SUV, anything on that?" Charlie asked pensively.

"I don't think that is a problem; I went back to it yesterday night and adjusted the plates and vehicle ID. I don't think they will track it for a while. I'll run it down to a compacting yard I know of outside of Chicago as soon as things clear up. So don't worry on that score."

"OK, OK, I'll leave it in your all too capable hands," concluded Charlie, a little more relieved now that he knew Jimmy was still paying attention to the details.

"Any problems with the dump?" asked Jimmy casually.

"No. Roger went straight down into the big sea waters and Kitchi-gummi gratefully received another soul." Slighted disturbed by his own glibness, Charlie's face fell into a frown. Just talking about Roger and the car had made him uneasy. He wanted to grab Samantha and head back to New York as fast as possible. He had had it with the Midwest, the Storm and WEBCO. Despite his tired exasperation, curiosity got the better of him; and after Jimmy exited; Charlie turned on the lone TV in the office.

While they were in Duluth, he and Sam tried to avoid watching much TV, limiting their viewing to a few minutes each day. That was plenty to get the general idea of what was going on. The big thing by Monday was the Nor'easter rampaging down from New England. As with most of the big stories concerning the Storm, WEBCO had scoped its competitors, and was the first to warn the East Coast to take cover. Now back in his office he wanted to get caught up on everything he had missed since he left town. Each network had variations of a theme – the Eastern Seaboard, from Portland, Maine to Wilmington, Delaware, had sustained a body blow. Snow and ice along with winds of nearly ninety miles an hour had taken down large chunks of the electrical grid, leaving millions without lights and heat. Snows of up to sixty inches had crippled all coastal air and ground transportation.

239

Literally hundreds of old buildings saw their roofs collapse under the weight of the unprecedented snowfalls. The toll was especially high from Cape Cod on down to Long Island. Hundreds, if not thousands, were either injured, dead or missing. The President had called out additional units of the US Army to assist the National Guard to help restore basic services and help the afflicted.

Yet in all the mayhem there were a few oddly uplifting things. There were a series of stunning photographs, soon to be iconic, of an iced over Manhattan. One, due to the interplay of brilliant sunshine and ice, featured a glistening string of icy filaments appearing to join the Empire State to the Chrysler Building. In another, the San Remo, the Belvedere and the Majestic on Central Park West had become huge, glistening ice palaces forming a protective rampart from the east winds. But on a decidedly sadder note, there was the haunting photograph of the Rodriquez family of Boulder, Colorado. After their car careened off the road and into a pond, the five had managed to climb out of their vehicle only to freeze on the side of the highway. The picture captured them encased in ice; each holding another's outstretched hand, in a single unbroken line. Something in the resigned, beseeching figures, was reminiscent of the gaunt faces in Rodin's sculpture The Burghers of Calais.

Despite these wonders, Charlie was more interested in spin than photography; he whipped out the formulae for M^4 and after some quick calculations, based on the media's best current estimate of 6,500 dead or missing, came up with the impressive figure of 35.8 million dead as a result of the "Great Storm". "Pretty grim stuff," whistled Charlie, "clearly impressive figures though, and directly in proportion to all the bother we went through."

Taking the M^4 total as the actual death rate for a moment, Charlie remembered that his family still lived in New York. His anxiety mounting, Charlie decided to check in on his dad to see if anyone was all right. After several unsuccessful attempts to get through he finally heard his father's voice. "Dad, it's Charlie; how are you fairing?"

"Ah, Charlie, good to hear from you; we're all right; just came in from outside. I tried to do some skiing but everything was too iced up; beautiful though, I must say. It is getting a bit cold, we have heat but the oil is getting low and we've had to turn down the thermostat to conserve. Otherwise, things are fine. You and Sam, how are you doing? I saw the footage from Duluth. It reminded me of Errol Flynn and Olivia de Havilland, or better yet Steward Granger and Deborah Kerr, great stuff son, great stuff."

Glad to hear that everything was fine on the home front, Charlie brought his father up to date before getting to the underlying purpose of his call. "I understand Roger is still missing. Have you been in touch with Mrs. Gartner about him and Stephan?"

"Well, I talked to Eleanor on Saturday concerning Stephan. Frankly, son she sounded somewhat relieved about it. He must have been impossible to live with during the last year. Now, you say Roger is missing. I haven't heard anything from Eleanor about that. I guess I better give her a jingle. What have you heard in Wisconsin?"

"Only that he was going to be driving down to Milwaukee from Green Bay on Saturday," replied Charlie, anxious not to reveal any more information than absolutely necessary.

"I see; I suppose we must remain hopeful that he will turn

up in a day or so, one way or another. You know son, it's funny how things and people can just suddenly disappear not to be seen or heard of ever again. On the other hand, sometimes folks who you might think are dead and gone pop up out of nowhere, life's funny like that. Vanishing off the face of the earth does happen once in a while, you know. It's as if they walk off into a different dimension or something. I'm sure he's fine where ever he is, so don't worry yourself about him."

"OK, Dad, I'll take your advice. I guess I need to get back to business here, there's still weather news that needs to get out." There was something in the nonchalant way his father spoke about Roger and his half-hearted attempts to learn more about his fate that bothered Charlie. He sensed what he had said came as no great surprise to Leuven Senior. Charlie was sure that his father knew more than he was letting on. His words were too carefully phrased and delivered to be off the cuff remarks. The drift into his deep Southern accent clinched Charlie's suspicions. But who was feeding him the information? It must be Jimmy, who else? Charlie could not escape the conclusion that they had conspired to delay the Gartner's flight on Friday in hopes that they would get caught up in the storm.

"Oh, son, one more thing; I think you and Sam may want to think about moving back to New York. We need someone to run World Media from here. I think that person should be you. We'll talk about it once things return to normal, whatever that is."

New York, New York, this whole thing had its genesis in Charlie wanting to get back home. Now that he could, now that he was being invited back with open arms he felt indifferent and let down somehow. Through all the nonsense that he had hyped for the last week, all the craziness, danger, heartache and tragedy

242

he had experienced or witnessed, it just didn't seem to matter that much now. He had gotten Sam back, and that was the only thing he really cared about. He could be happy in Milwaukee, Paris or Harrisburg, PA as long as she was with him.

"Right Dad, we'll talk in a few days. I've got to go mind the shop. Don't do anything too foolish." He always knew that too make it in New York from nothing, you had to be a real son of a bitch at times. Though the youngest and most sheltered of the Leuven siblings, Charlie was not so naïve as to be unable to detect that beneath his father's courtly manner lurked a steely resolve and ruthlessness. Did these usually well disguised qualities permit for the selective use of murder?

But was it murder? Had his dad merely intended to delay Stephan and Roger's flight as an annoyance to them and nothing more, cruel fate intervening to eventually polish the two off in due course? The death of Stephan, and even Roger, was certainly one of several desired outcomes if his father had really orchestrated a virtually untraceable conspiracy. Either way, Charlie had to admire the simple elegance of his Father's scheme. He was equally repelled by the fact that the man he so admired felt compelled to undertake it in the first place. No matter how clever, it still relied on violence to succeed. It was also indirectly a negative indictment of his own capabilities of handling the Gartners on his own. His Father was lucky that only the immediate targets of his malice were brought down, and the pilots and others were not killed as well. It was all very Sixteenth Century; Machiavelli, himself, might have nodded his appreciation. Perhaps old age was making his Father too impatient, pressing him to tie up all the loose ends of his business affairs so as to be able to hand them over to the next generation in neat and manageable bundles. If his Father was doing this for him, imagine what he might be up to on behalf of his older brothers and sister?

He sighed deeply, rummaging around in the lower drawer of his desk; he brought out the pint of White Horse he'd discovered on the first day he had taken over the office. He took a long pull. It was too warm and a little stale, but the flashing burn shooting down from his throat to his extremities revived him, helping to flush out of his system all the worries and doubts which had built up in him since Roger had arrived in Milwaukee, crazy to kill and crazy to be killed.

Chapter 20

NEW YORK REDUX

Autumn was coming to New York. The sky was enchantingly chaotic clouds, big and small tumbled and collided with one another releasing into the atmosphere a joyful and exuberant energy. Their shaded grays and whites were from time to time pierced by the rays of light from an unseen sun. The overall affect was a display of dense, tumultuous expectation as a new season was ready to come into ascendance. Up on the thirtieth floor intermittent breezes whirled and sputtered across the penthouse terrace causing a few desiccated leaves to scuttle here and there over the stone floor. Samantha found the slow change from summer to fall hopeful. The summer had been long and rainy, and the change to cooler, drier weather was welcome. There was, however, tentativeness about the change in seasons; the cool fall air had not quite supplanted the old warmth of summer. A kind of stylized but hopeless tug of war between the two contending intervals was required before the preordained winner could officially be declared, and then life could proceed with confidence.

One minute Samantha was chilled by the arriving autumnal winds only to feel the lingering warmth of the past season in the breath of the next breeze. Alternating between buttoning up her cardigan and taking it off entirely, she, in the end, resorted to undoing all the buttons and letting the sweater billow up around her. Satisfied with the compromise, Sam sat down and stared off across the park, losing herself amid the phalanx of great buildings along Central Park West: The Century, The Majestic, The San Remo and The Eldorado. There was a haunting grittiness about those brooding Art Deco masses that she never grew tired of, especially late at night when they were lit by a few scattered lights.

"Dear, may I join you?" asked Patty Hewitt, poking her head through the French doors.

"Why yes, of course, Mother, please do. I love it out her on mornings like this, just look at the view; I think it's absolutely marvelous," answered Samantha in a welcoming voice.

"Yes, it certainly is; London has nothing to match it. Here, I brought you some coffee. I thought it might go to warming you up." Patty Hewitt handed her daughter a large mug topped off with cream from a small tray before sitting down beside her. The base of the bright aluminum table, around which they sat, was sculpted in the form of a hand, the fingers outstretched forming a perch for the glass top.

"Thank you, I could certainly use some. Oh, I quite forgot, Lionel Vesey and Anne Blumenthal are coming into town tonight. They'll be staying here, of course." Sensing that the names did not register with her mother, Samantha went on. "You remember, from the wedding, Lionel, the man who was losing all that weight, a great raconteur on Hollywood, very droll, and, Anne Blumenthal very LA-ish but with a real heart. Father, if I recall, was quite smitten by her."

"Oh yes, now I remember, I didn't see much of the young lady but Lionel certainly held court in the grand style. He's some sort of director, isn't he."

"A screenwriter, actually,"

"Yes of course. Will Charlie be coming home early today? I haven't seen much of him since we arrived. I can't image what keeps him so busy now that WEBCO's been sold and that other company, whatever it's called, has been pretty much liquidated. What could there be for him to do?"

"Well there's a lot of money to be invested, and still one or two small assets that he's shopping around, the odds and sods of what remains of poor old World Media International. I also suspect he's cooking up something for us to do in the future. But to answer your question – yes, he promised to be home by two and take you down the street to the museum to see the Klimt's."

"Speaking of money dear, may I ask you a personal question, none of my business you understand but Cornelius has been pestering me about it since the we've come over."

"Of course, go ahead, I'll try but I'm not familiar with all of the Leuven's business dealings," replied Sam, curious that her mother would bring up the subject at all.

"Well the point is, on the flight over your father read an article in a magazine about New York real estate prices in which your own building was mentioned. I guess what I'm trying to say is can you really afford this place? I know the Leuven's are a wealthy family but, still," Mrs. Hewitt's voice trailed off into an embarrassed silence upon realizing that the state of her daughter's finances were none of her concern.

Sam gave out a short laugh, "Oh, mother, please don't worry. Charlie says we have oodles. Apparently, he was playing the commodities market and bet heavily on something or other and the bet turned out to be right. All very curious the timing right before the storm and all but apparently quite legit."

Mrs. Hewitt let out a relieved sign and decided to steer the subject of conversation back to the afternoon museum visit. "We are so looking forward to seeing those pictures, anything that smacks of Mittal Europa brings tears to Cornelius's eyes."

"The pictures really are exquisite, I hope I can join you but I do need to do a few hours on the party before I can get away. I think Charlie was right; we should have delayed it until the place was more finished. As it is now, I'll be lucky to have the living and dining rooms presentable. I guess I must chock up my impetuosity to new bride nerves. I just hope the guests keep their cruelest comments to themselves;" sighed Samantha as if mentally preparing for a frontal assault of critical articles in the society sections of the three dailies.

"Nonsense, dear, the place looks fine. You and the decorators have done miracles with it. People will know you've only been here a couple of months, and besides, from what you've told me, everyone coming will be relatives or old friends. I doubt if they will have their daggers out for you. Just having the place must make everyone quite envious, I understand from Bunny; how I like that name, Bunny, that places like this don't come on the market very often. You were lucky to swoop down and snag it," Mrs. Hewitt said encouragingly as her attention was caught by the clouds whipping over the Park.

"You can thank my new sister-in-law, Flavia, for learning that the place was coming on the market. She told Charlie in March and by the middle of April we were accepted by the board. That's record time for these things in New York; sometimes one's application is delayed for months, and then denied in the end on the filmiest of excuses. Fortunately, Bunny knew a couple of people on the board, that certainly helped, and then Charlie's status of world hero simply did the rest. The only bad thing is I will forever be indebted to Flavia for the tip. I don't think I've met anyone half as snobbish as that self-centered cow; she is simply ridiculous."

Before her mother could comment, Samantha abruptly steered the conversation in an entirely different direction. "How's Father doing with Bunny, are they getting along any better?" asked Samantha hesitantly, knowing how difficult her father could be when jostled out of his narrow comfort zone. And Bunny Leuven was certainly capable of doing considerable jostling if he was of a mind. "Never were two men from such opposite ends of the universe, they're completely different in everything: general interests, temperament, politics, mores, you name it" she ended with a rising note of frustration in her voice.

"Right you are darling, but what is one to do? I still thank God you weren't there at the dinner we gave at the faculty club, after you went on your honeymoon. I thought I would die of embarrassment when your father flung himself at poor Bunny merely for raising a good-natured toast to the Maggie Thatcher and Tony Blair. How could the poor boy know of Cornelius's odd political leanings? Anyone who believes Stalin was the apogee of progressive thinking obviously has no sense of humor about such things. Fortunately, the fish fork stuck in the chair to the left of Bunny's head. Naturally, once your father realized what a fool he had made of himself, he profusely apologized. The whole thing made for a rather sticky dessert course though, not too much gay banter there, I can assure you. Nevertheless, by the end of the evening, Bunny had begun to appreciate the odd sensibilities lurking behind Cornelius's rather alarming reaction.

"Now, to answer your question, I would have to declare

that I think they are actually getting along quite well, almost chums in a way. Bunny's strategy of plying Father with Bourbon and Branch every afternoon has had a most a salutary effect on their relationship. Last night, I even heard them laughing about something or other, what I couldn't say, as Cornelius was tight lipped afterward but I surmise that it was something to do with sex."

Samantha always wondered what a country woman like her mother saw in her cantankerous and pedantic father. They were an odd pair but for some reason, or reasons, they had managed to make a life together over the last thirty plus years. Perhaps it was because they had managed to carve out separate lives and careers for themselves which, though accessible to one another were also different enough to require that each come to acknowledge the dedication and sincerity of the other.

Sitting across from her mother that morning, Samantha consciously, for the first time, saw her as a woman who was more than the sum of her roles: wife, mother, grandmother, horticulturalist, and environmentalist. She was Patience Hewitt, and in her unassuming way, she managed to obtain from life most of what she wanted without making a big fuss about it. Samantha wondered if she possessed the same strength and equanimity of character to do the same.

Satisfied with her conclusion, Samantha's attentions were brought back to the physical realm. Looking across the table, she was struck by the ageless quality of her mother; at nearly seventy, she appeared very much as she did at fifty. Her high cheekbones and taut skin had done their job in banishing excessive wrinkling and sagging. Her hair had a few more strands of silver but the strawberry blond base was retreating in good order. I wonder if I shall age as well as she, thought Sam.

"Mother, you know as well as I that beneath the entire Socialist clap trap, Father remains a paternalist Victorian at heart. It's really quite amusing. I'm glad that Bunny saw through all his flannel," Samantha replied as she started to get up from the table. "It's getting on to 11:30 now, I must be seeing to hanging a picture or two, and all the whatnots one must remember for this type of thing, so please excuse me for a bit."

The two women as they were about to go inside stopped beside the stone balustrade, to gaze a few seconds in unconscious genuflection toward phalanx of towers on the far side of the Park Neither of them spotted a lone man standing under a tree on the other side of Fifth Avenue just below the lake-like reservoir. The little man, however, had been catching glimpses of them every time one or both had made their way to the edge of the terrace.

~

Charles Leuven sat at his desk in the modest paneled office, one of several in the family suite that he shared with his brothers Bryce and Putnam and his father when he had the inclination to make the trip to Midtown. Peering out the window at a perfect October day Charlie was grateful that he had agreed to escort Samantha's parents to the Neuve Gallerie in the afternoon; breaking off early would allow him to enjoy the first real day of autumn, especially as Saturday promised to be disagreeable.

Charlie was as at peace with himself as anyone; a hair's breath over thirty-two had a right to be. Since their decision to pare back public and social engagements to a bare minimum following their honeymoon, the new couple was finally able to catch their

251

breath and find relaxation in their new life together. Evidence of his new found piece of mind was detectable in how he carried himself, upright and broad shouldered. He now had about him an aire of informal dignity that, as he aged, might gracefully mutate into something approaching gravitas.

Family and friends commented on how much calmer and more mature he seemed, attributing the jettisoning of his boyish frenetic qualities to his marriage to Samantha. Others said he had come by it by his time spent in the stolid Midwest where quixotic notions and behaviors were frowned upon. While all these observations were correct in themselves, only Sam, and perhaps his father, really understood the cause for the change. It was no secret, really. Charles Leuven had done something in life; something, while perhaps a little absurd, was nonetheless momentous. He had played the game as a man, played it for keeps, and had won it in a big way. Granted his path to fame and riches was strewn with quite a few corpses, but they were all unintentional causalities in his youthful dash to "self-actualization". There had been, of course, the Gartners, and even the odious Carl Troutmann might be included as collateral damage; but such are the ways of the world when one plays in earnest; even if the play was originally an elaborate game of make believe.

Looking up from the open file, Charlie caught the face of his watch, it read 11:30; coinciding with the inspection of his timepiece a voice in the Brooklyn patois came across the intercom, "Mr. Dasimmi to see you for your 11:30 meeting, sir."

"Please send him in, Vicky, thank you."

Charlie was out of his chair and halfway to the door by the time Jimmy nonchalantly strode in. The two greeted one another warmly and then quickly sat down. "A little early, but would you like a drink?" asked Charlie, guessing at the answer.

"Sure, a weak Scotch and water, ice, if you've got it, my doctor says that I need to cut down a little on the proof, if you know what I mean, can't take the high octane stuff anymore," Jimmy commented blandly, looking around at the surprisingly Spartan office.

"Here you go. How's old Milwaukee?" asked Charlie out of politeness.

"Same old same old," shrugged Jimmy. "All your old friends at WEBCO say howdy. Charlotte's getting married to some lawyer and Hubertus Humperdinck of snowmobile fame has decided to move out to Denver to work with his brother, other than that no real news. Oh say, how could I forget? Stan's gone Hollywood."

"What?"

"Yeah seems like when he was hanging out with the Apaches in Wyoming he had nothing better to do than shoot a documentary about those mountain men who rescued him. Get this – Robert Redford is backing the thing. It's going to be featured at the Sundance Festival. Is that fucking amazing or what, Chief?"

"Incredible is what comes to mind, Stan. And shot on my dime, I'll have you know." The last sententious thought was accompanied by a wink. "Jimmy, wonders will never cease... never cease."

Jimmy nodded back and smiled. "Oh, one thing more; I think the cops have given up looking for our good bud Mr. Roger Gartner. A friend of mine on the force said that as of August they deep sixed the caper into the cold case file. No clues, no one pushing them to solve it. Even his grieving family doesn't

253

seem interested, so who cares, right? I guess that's that. But don't get too cocky, it's my experience that things like this have a habit of coming back to bite, so we still need to be careful."

"Don't worry; I'll take your advice to the grave. Every evening I pray that we put enough rocks in that duffel bag to keep him at the bottom of Superior until the next ice age," sighed Charlie before going on to the next topic. "Now have you decided on the family's offer to move to New York?"

"Yes, I have, it's a very generous offer but I just don't see me being that busy investigating companies and people to warrant a permanent move out here. But the job still sounds interesting and I want to do it. I've given it a lot of thought, and here's my idea. I stay in Milwaukee during the summer months and work from there, and during the winter I live in New York," Jimmy said in a tone of calculated indifference.

"That'll be more expensive, of course, but OK, I think that can be worked out provided you reconsider if the work load grows so that we need you here all the time," countered Charlie, trying not to hide his disappointment.

"Listen, Charlie we live in the modern age of email and iPhones, and big jet planes to fly us between distant cities, don't you think we can cut out this permanent move stuff from the start?"

"I suppose you're right. Let's leave it that you'll be bi-coastal for the foreseeable future," smiled Charlie.

"Bi-coastal, that's rich, Lake Michigan to the East River. I like it."

"Great, I have some work to do before I go home, so we're going to have to conclude our chat for now. I understand you're going to be picking up Dad and taking him over to my place tomorrow evening. So we'll see you then."

"Don't worry, I'll get him over safe and sound, and thanks for the invitation."

Jimmy was about to get up from his chair, when Charlie at last came around to what was really on his mind. "Jimmy, I almost forgot, before you go, I need to tell you something. I think my place is being watched... scoped out by someone. A couple of times, when I've been on the terrace, I've caught glimpses of this guy hiding out by the edge of the Park with a pair of high-powered binoculars. Didn't think much about it until yesterday when I spotted a weedy little guy wearing the same type of coat and hat as the man with the binoculars. This time, he was sitting on a bench along Fifth Avenue right across from my building; his head tilted as far back as it could go, just staring up toward the penthouse.

"I should have jumped out of the cab and beat the shit out of him but I was late to this meeting, and besides beating the hell out of some chump wouldn't look like such a good idea once it was spread all over The Post. Anyhow, I want you to check it out, and find out who he is, and whether he's dangerous," ordered Charlie, displaying more apprehension in his voice than he wanted to reveal.

"What time of day has he been skulking around?" Jimmy asked, retaking his seat, his eyes glued to Charlie's after realizing how serious his boss took the stalker.

"I've seen him in the mornings mostly, around 9:00 to 10:00, 10:30 sometimes. He's thin with longish hair, sort of a squirrely guy. That coat I've mentioned is a long brown tweed number, pretty stylish, really. The guy has this long far off look, as if he isn't quite all there. I've seen him at the southeast

255

end of the Reservoir, around 86th Street, right outside the little playground on the corner."

"I best be going, I'll check out the area now, just in the off chance he might still be around. My worry is he may have gotten wind of the party. I'll also check out the neighborhood tomorrow morning as well. I wouldn't worry too much. These types of creeps come with the territory, fame and money; you know how it is, Chief."

"Let's say I'm getting to know," sighed Charlie as he led Jimmy to the door.

About an hour after Jimmy had headed uptown, Charlie was strolling up to the cashier to pay for his lunch at his favorite diner. As he waited for his change, he heard the singsong voice of a man speaking to a boy, presumably his son. "See that gentleman at the cash register. Do you know who he is? That is Charles Leuven, the man who saved America during the Big Storm Windigo and rescued that girl up in Canada. Go now and ask him for his autograph, I am sure he will give it to you."

Charlie turned around to confront a black haired boy with large round, dark eyes. He might have been from India or Pakistan and was probably no more than nine or ten. The lad confidently held up a pad of paper and a ballpoint pen in his outstretched hands. Charlie smiled at the father, a man in his late thirties, wearing a blazer and a tieless striped shirt. Looking down at his eager beseecher, Charlie readily took the solemn offering, and after learning the boy's name, wrote on the paper in his sprawling hand: "To Saresh, Knowing you'll have worlds to save too. Charlie Leuven." "Here you go Saresh, I don't get many requests for autographs, but I'm always happy to oblige." The boy stood with his head held fully back, eyes beaming with a quizzical look on his face as if to ask, "who exactly was this Charlie Leuven, anyway?"

Nodding at the father and patting the boy's shoulder, Charlie turned and left the diner, entering the stream of pedestrian traffic on Madison Avenue as if walking on air. A long nurtured dream had just come to pass and Charlie Leuven felt on top of the world, bursting to tell Samantha about the happy incident. If his eyes had taken him to the back recesses of the diner he might have noticed, before leaving, a thin, nervous man with long brown hair sitting alone in a small booth.

~

Harlan Zinter loved New York with a child's devotion. This was true even though The City had disappointed him countless times. But to Harlan, the important thing was that it never rejected him out right, and for this single act of mercy, Harlan was eternally grateful. He figured that all the petty humiliations and slights were in themselves positive indications that the Big Town had at least noticed him, and was perhaps testing him for some important future mission. Because of this kind of backhanded attention, Harlan felt an obligatory duty to reciprocate by embracing New York with the fervor of a new convert.

The City's toleration of the little man was partially due to the newcomer's steadfast persistence; more fundamentally, however, it was the result of its monumental indifference to people with decidedly poor prospects in life. Nevertheless, in time, tolerance morphed into a grudging, off-handed acceptance of the dazed wanderer with his catch bag of pathetic pathologies and homicidal fascinations.

Something in The City's collective heart recognized Harlan's need to find a resting place, no matter how mean or obscure. And because of humbly demonstrating his yearnings for even the minimal amount of inclusion, The City had decided not to crush him outright, but instead shrugged aside its misgivings and made a place for him over in Long Island City. There was always room for one more - on a temporary basis.

Harlan profoundly needed the reassurance of being part of something more solid than himself, a quiet anchorage to sort out the events of the past few months. He had been able to piece together only bits and pieces of his life from the time of Carl Troutmann's death until his arrival in New York, but even now a coherent, linear narrative still eluded him. He remembered Carl's screaming agonies as he was ripped apart by the wild beasts, while simultaneously being hewed up by the pretty girl with the axe. He watched it all, first from Carl's truck and then, in the open somewhere between the vehicle and the tumbled down fishing shack. He remembered kneeling during the height of the blizzard, ghosts of Carl's death screams and curses swirling around, helter skelter with each violent gust. Then there was silence as his cousin's dark soul departed and his torn and broken body was swept off the cabin porch like a dead branch. These memories had only a dreamlike ring of truth to them; there was nothing more substantial, nothing emotionally connective about them, even in their collective horror to elicit anything more than a dull nod of hazy recollection.

Free of Carl, Harlan recalled shouting out into the maul of the storm his thanks and proclaiming his resolve to begin again on a new and purer course but the exact words he used in the oath were now lost to him. His next memory was of a man and a plane taking the pretty young woman up in the air, leaving Harlan alone in his redemptive isolation. Then he suddenly found himself in Fargo, North Dakota.

He was in a bar on the outskirts of the downtown area of Fargo when he came to; the saloon's TV was yakking on about the aftermath of the Big Storm, chattering incessantly about all the damage and loss of life and of the darlings of the hour, Charles Leuven and Samantha Hewitt. A discarded newspaper on the stool next to his was dated a little over a week after he drove across the lake with Carl. That was all. How he survived alone out there on the Angle, and then turned up in Fargo no worse for wear, he wasn't sure.

Later that day he found a boarding house on the north side of town, paid the old lady three months in advance, from the money that he discovered in one of Carl's small? Harlan then proceeded to hibernate until April, appearing occasionally to eat a small meal and watch a little TV.

One morning Harlan awoke to hear fears of the spring floods being endlessly discussed by the other residents of the clapboard house. The old landlady quickly assured him that there was no cause for alarm, and that the house was on high ground, and over a mile from the Red River. It had nicely escaped past floods, even the really bad one of 1997, the time when half the downtown burned to the water's edge. The news of a coming calamity, even though it might not affect him directly, was something Harlan wanted to avoid at all costs. The next day he packed up his meager belongings, settled his bill in cash, and proceeded to buy a bus ticket to Milwaukee.

On the ride across Minnesota, Harlan was once again confronted by the stark and hateful barrenness of the Plains. Many stretches along the endless route were still buried in blackened snow. Sitting there in the bus for hour upon hour, Harlan began to think of where all that money he had found in Carl's bag had come from. When he first opened it in Fargo, it contained $29,750 in fifties all neatly bundled. Was it the schoolteacher's, who Carl killed with the vacuum cleaner? Maybe it was in that Buick that they jacked outside of Rochester, the one driven by the guy who looked like a clerk. He had only spent eighteen hundred since the first of February. That wasn't much, but things would be different in a city like Milwaukee where everything cost a lot. He was lucky he had it. The money would be enough to support him in his quest to meet and win over Samantha Hewitt.

The bus at last made it to Minneapolis where there would be a two-hour layover before the next one left for Milwaukee. Fidgety after being cooped up in a bus for ten hours, Harlan decided to go out to the diner across the street. On his way he picked up a paper from a one armed man in the station's kiosk. Rummaging through the Star Tribune, between bites of toast and scrambled eggs, he came across a story about the sale of WEBCO to a large cable network operator in the South. The story went on to say that Reggie Chevis was being promoted to general manager and much of the current staff would be retained. An accompanying article trumpeted the news that Charles Leuven the CEO of World Media International, headquartered in New York, and former president of WEBCO, had announced his plans to wed Samantha Hewitt, a former WEBCO anchor, in early May. The site of the wedding would be in London. A picture of the smiling couple graced the article.

Harlan stopped reading, leaned back in the booth and decided to change his destination to New York. It was going to be a long trip, but he figured that buses were the safest way for him to travel. Cops were unlikely to still be hanging out in skuzzy Midwest stations trying to eyeball someone who was in all likelihood dead. He had spotted himself in the diner's wall sized mirror, and thought he looked pretty scruffy. His hair was too long, and he didn't like the scraggily beard and the torn parka. But he wasn't a bum, he had a small fortune of nearly thirty thousand dollars to his name, and best of all he was free of Carl and on his own. He had lost a good deal of weight since the Angle; with the right clothes and a decent haircut he would look pretty presentable. Maybe he would look good enough to appeal to Samantha Hewitt. He would rest up for a couple of days, buy some new clothes and a few portable luxuries, maybe take in a movie, before the long ride to New York.

During the somnolent months in Fargo, while lying in bed staring out the frosted window of his small room, visions of Samantha began to percolate in his tired, drab mind. By the end of March his preoccupation had turned into an obsession, controlling much of his waking thoughts. Yet he had only seen her three times in his life, barely over an hour in total. The first time was in the Warroad diner, the second in the woods by the cabin as she struggled through the snow to reach the cabin. The last time was when the man with the plane and the strange coat spirited her away from him. It was what he had not seen, that made the real difference in his estimation of Samantha' powers. The cleaving of Carl's head until it dangled by a single ligament was such wonderful malice! At a minimum, he must thank her for freeing him from Carl. That was a wonderful act in-and-of-itself, one he'd be grateful for the rest of his life. But he must do more than merely say "thanks." She was something to be worshipped; and he would worship her, not from afar, but right beside her. He would free her from that Charles Leuven, and anyone else who tried to prevent him from worshiping her.

Upon reaching New York Harlan's simple plan was immediately frustrated. He could not find his beloved amongst the towering stone and glass citadels. He spent half the first day in a panic. The city was huge, far bigger than Minneapolis or even the parts of Chicago he had seen from the bus. She wasn't listed in the phone book, and directory assistance didn't have any listing for her, or for that matter Charles Leuven. It seemed that she had disappeared, out of reach, as invisible to him as he was to himself. Which building could house her? It must be the best and biggest building; it probably was guarded, night and day, by a host of police and detectives whose sole mission was to prevent him from seeing her again. All through May and June Harlan frantically walked the neighborhood streets he came to identified as most suitable for her. Only the best, toniest areas were worth investigating, Fifth Avenue, Central Park West, the Upper East Side, Sutton Place; these became his stomping grounds.

Once, his fear and frustration grew so great he decided to spend a week's budget on a charter helicopter ride over Manhattan in hopes he might spy her walking the yard of some penthouse roof top, under the protective gaze of her minders. Back and forth, head bowed, she'd be walking, until looking up toward a fluttering sound overhead, she would at last see him and beckon him to fall from the heavens to return her favor of rescue. But the day he had decided on was cloudy, rain spattered the windshield, and air turbulence caused the machine to violently rise and plummet, making him sick, and forcing him to abandon this stratagem after only fifteen minutes.

His obsession over Samantha never left him; from the roof of his studio apartment in Long Island City, he'd strained to make some type of spiritual contact with his beloved. Nearly every evening Harlan would focus his mind in hopes of picking up some wave of psychic energy being emitted consciously or unconsciously from Samantha's pure soul. Like a radar beacon his mind would slowly but repeatedly scan all the buildings from Turtle Bay up to The TriBoro Bridge, listening carefully for a returning ping, a celestial chord ringing out from all the cityscape's profane and superficial chatter. Once or twice, he detected the weakest of sounds, a faded echo coming from the other side of Roosevelt Island, but by the second sweep of the area it had vanished.

While temporarily discouraged, Harlan reasoned that all great quests by their very nature must encounter dangers and vicissitudes in direct proportion to the sublimity of their objective. Although not close to despair, his money was beginning to run low, forcing him to look for work. After fruitlessly searching for three weeks, Harlan spotted a small sign in the window of a caterer off of Third Avenue in the Seventies, "Part Time Help Wanted, Inquire Within" was all it said, but it was enough, and by that afternoon he had been hired by the Mansfield and Longines Catering Company as a grunt loading and unloading vans at the freight elevators of New York's finest Coops and Town Houses.

The work was only part time at first but it paid well enough, twenty dollars an hour plus a small percentage of the gratuities. After four weeks he was put on full time. It was perfect – much of the work was in the evenings or weekends giving him his days to search for Samantha. It was during one of these scouting parties that he spotted Charles Leuven coming out of a building on Madison Avenue. He followed him for several blocks before his query hailed a cab and escaped uptown.

Soon after seeing Charlie the real thing happened. He was working at a charity function at the Whitney Museum when he spotted her across the main room. She was more beautiful than a human could possibly be, better than all the angels, and more distant than God. He froze instantly, his mind concentrating on one thing only – the sending of the right signal to make her aware he was so very near. All she needed to do was turn her head a little to the left, but Samantha didn't turn her head, she merely laughed and threw her head back in reaction to some apparent witticism of her companion, a little bald man wearing a small gardenia in his tuxedo lapel. Again and again he sent out the signal but she did not bother to acknowledge him. She moved off into the crowd, leaving him stranded behind the cash bar.

Harlan was crushed for the rest of the evening. After work he listlessly took the subway to the Broadway station in Long Island City and walked dejectedly back to his mean, little room. But as he reached the door of the four-story building he suddenly realized for the first time the true reason he had to make the connection with Samantha. It was not to thank her, or pledge his undying devotion to her beauty and goodness. He knew now that she was not another, not a separate, distinct and separate person. They were actually the same person mistakenly split-off from one another at conception. But they were more than twins, they were one. Only a merger, a melding of their souls and bodies, could displace their mutual deficiencies. At that time of perpetual union, the gnawing disquiet that continuously reminded them of their incompleteness would end at last.

Part of his epiphany on that bleak early morning was his appreciation that Samantha needed him as much, if not more, than he needed her. The relationship was not an unequal one after all. Their common purpose demanded a seamless spiritual amalgamation for both to flourish. First, they must obliterate their false selves; then they would pass into a new, refined and undifferentiated realm of pure knowing. The only problem was she was blind to her best interests, blind to her sordid incompleteness. Samantha, Harlan concluded, must be enveloped in some type of miasma that prevented her from realizing her true condition. It was as if she was surrounded by some sort of cloaking force that blocked her from detecting his longing psychic signals. Knowing that he had almost found her, he must devise a way to awaken her. Then there would be no Samantha and no Harlan; at that point there would only be a new soul, a single emergent life.

Exactly eleven days after the charity event, Harlan was in the backroom of Mansfield and Longines when he happened to see the work roster for the next two weeks. Listed as the last event was a dinner party at the Leuvens'! The address was neatly hand printed; as was the number of guests, eighty to ninety, and the names of the employees who would be assigned to it; listed last was Harlan Zinter.

Chapter 21

THE LITTLE THINGS

That same evening a chilling fog had begun seeping its way into the city, moving silently but steadily, filling every corner of the island with the kind of romantic atmospherics which made the mind recall more mysterious times. Through mists two men in black tie moved silently in slow, rough cadence with one another. Their large hats and long open coats were vaguely reminiscent of a pair of sinister characters out of fin de siècle London or Paris. One of them was tall and thin with shocks of long white hair escaping out from under his black hat; the other one was younger, shorter and dark. It wasn't until they had turned off of Madison Avenue and headed toward the Park that they began to exchange words.

"I understand you and Charlie reached some sort of deal concerning your continued association with us." The statement was offered only to break the silence; the details of the meeting had been conveyed to Bunny in a telephone conversation with Charlie the night before.

"Yeah, Chief, I think we worked everything out pretty well," replied Jimmy in a tight, non-committal voice.

"Excellent, you've done some good work for us over the last couple of years. Charlie and I would hate to lose you. You know, when he first told me, I knew he had come across someone we could work with. Whatever his faults back then, he was a good judge of talent. It's funny that after all those telephone calls between us before and after the storm, that this is the first time we've actually met one another," Bunny Leuven remarked in a regretful tone.

In his typical commanding manner Bunny Leuven continued, "I'm glad you're on board. Charlie's going to need someone to talk things over with now that I'm getting on in years, and I can't think of a better fellow than you to help him. Oh, by the way, during the times you're in New York you might as well stay at my place. There's plenty of room and Louisa is a darn good cook. I go a little daffy at times with no one around. Think about it for a day or so before deciding."

"Why thanks for the offer Chief, I certainly will. Sounds like you're thinking of retiring."

"Not exactly, but I'm almost eighty and my ticker is not as strong as the doctors would like, so you never know what might happen," came the matter of fact reply.

"Charlie seems like a new man from the time he got off the bus in Milwaukee; he's really come into his own, you must be proud of him. What do you think will be his next thing, you know business opportunity?"

"I don't know exactly; I only know that he's been exploring a lot of different things. He'll make up his mind eventually, and he's capable of coming up with anything. That's why I need you to help me steady him in case he gets a burr under the saddle. And, yes, yes I am proud of him. He's come a long way in the last couple of years; there's no denying it. I must admit that I had my doubts about him, and not too long ago. However, the way he handled himself with the storm, and more importantly his latching on to Samantha, has made all the difference. If I were to die tonight I would do so with the utmost assurance that Charlie was going to be OK. That takes a great burden off my shoulders, I can tell you." Bunny spoke with a mixture of relief and a dash of self-satisfaction in his behind the scenes contributions in Charlie's recent transformation.

"That Sam is a catch. She reeks of class, I gotta say. He couldn't do better if he looked for a million years."

"Yes Samantha is something all right. I wish my daughter would stop a minute and try to adopt some of the manners Samantha so effortlessly displays. She would be much more tolerable if she did, and a good deal happier," a note of resignation was detectable in the older man's voice.

"Kids, there's always something going on to make a parent worry."

"Yes there is Jimmy, yes there is."

The two fell silent for the remaining short blocks to Charlie's duplex, giving Jimmy the opportunity to reflect on the whirlwind of events that had recently shaped his life. "Christ is life strange or what? Here I am, an ex-flat foot from Chi being taken in by this family of lunatics. These folks play for keeps, and I like that, especially because they're smart enough to set things up just right so they can't get pinned for anything. Now, me, little Jimmy Dasimmi, is practically living on Park Avenue with cooks and maids and all for babysitting an over grown kid for a couple of weeks. Life is fucking strange. I can't wait until Charlie figures out his next move; it will be worth the ride, that's for sure."

Arriving at the building the men entered a private elevator to the penthouse apartment. They shared it with two youngish couples that Bunny vaguely recognized after a few polite remarks

268

mentioned Cornell and the crew team.

The door opened onto a marble foyer, large antique glass mirrors magnifying the effects of the maroon and white stone. Two maids took the group's coats and hats, and motioned them to the main salon. There, just before a step down to the main floor, stood Flavia Leuven Porter in a long gold silk gown that sought unsuccessfully to feature her matronly contours to the best advantage.

Upon seeing her father, she strode to greet him, placing a peck on an unoffered cheek. Ignoring the bulky figure of Jimmy Dasimmi, who she mistakenly took as a member of her father's protective escort, Flavia offered a few dour comments concerning the caterers. Bunny winced at her boorish tone and took pains to introduce Jimmy to her in a way that he hoped would convey to her the appropriateness of his presence. Unabashed, Flavia simply contorted her mouth from a grimace into something dissembling a smile.

Seeing an easy target for some amusement, Lionel Vesey, who had been sitting down on a lone chair near the living room entrance, noiselessly loomed up and began to monopolize Flavia's attentions, freeing Bunny and Jimmy to make their way to the bar. "Tell me my dear, Miss Flavia, where did you come by this miraculous gown?" Before she could reply, Flavia found herself sailing across the living room to a small alcove at the opposite end of the apartment. Her escort, now markedly thinner than when they had first met in London for the wedding, moved her with the newfound confidence of the newly svelte.

"I can only surmise," Lionel pattered on, "that your residence must be in the very heart of the fashionable demi-mode of this great metropolis. My guess it's in the Astoria or perhaps the Anthrop. There, in a vast complex of rooms circling the entire courtyard, you delve into the ancient oriental mysteries of some neglected cult. I see you surrounded by bevies of youth who, entranced by your hermetic knowledge, think solely of surviving your every desire."

Flavia held her hand up to her mouth and giggled, her face blushing a deep rose color. "I'm not familiar with those buildings, I'm an East Side person; although I now live in Greenwich, you know. I would never think of going across the park or downtown except to take the children to the Planetarium.

"Now, Mr. Vesey didn't we meet in London during my brother's wedding?" Flavia asked in the blandest of voices indicating she would no longer be a partner to Lionel's verbal flourishes, as it was now time to turn to more serious topics.

"Why, yes we did, and do you know that after the nuptials, I dashed over to Paris, and in a small shop off the Rue St. Honoré I purchased these enchanting lorgnettes from an old woman of grand and ancient lineage." He then took the eyewear out of his dinner jacket pocket, brandishing it before her before placing the antique glasses to his eyes; Lionel then bowed his head over Flavia's chest, inspecting her ample cleavage with intense scrutiny, and at such close range, as to leave two small red circles on the upper part of her right breast.

"Mr. Vesey what has come over you, have you no manners?" squawked Mrs. Porter as she moved away from her admirer. Before she could summon her husband Demo, who was droning on about bank reregulation in the next room, Anne Blumenthal, who had been observing the exchange after having come up silently behind Flavia, quickly pulled Lionel to his feet and moved out of the range of Flavia's contorted fist.

"Very funny, Lionel, but sometimes you take things a little too far," said Anne, trying control the gleeful expression on her face. "That poor idiot has no defenses against someone like you. You'd think she would be more hip growing up in this town but maybe not. Say, get me another drink, would you sweetie?"

"Of course my love, I just couldn't resist, that's all. Such exacting prudery, you don't come across that very often," Lionel replied as he scouted out which of the two bars was closest.

In a corner of the main room Cornelius Hewitt was being introduced to Jimmy Dasimmi by Bunny Leuven. The spare professor didn't quite know what to make of the solid, square man with the large noise and two tiny BB's sized eyes. When he learned that Jimmy had grown up in Chicago, he quickly surmised that he had been, or still was, a high-ranking member in a local Mafia clan. Knowing, from viewing several movies dealing with the Costa Nostra, that its members could be ticklish when outsiders began asking too many questions, the good professor decided to tread lightly. "Dasimmi, that's an Italian name, isn't?"

"You got it professor, I'm a Dago from the get go," replied Jimmy in a mockingly sinister tone as he looked up at the lanky, bespectacled man.

A little stunned by the forthright answer, Hewitt decided that the best course open to him was to forge straight ahead. "Did you grow up in Cicero by chance? I understand Al Capone recruited many of his most loyal lieutenants from that quarter. Very similar to the recruiting practices of the old Lithuanian royal family around Voruta during the 13th century, I suspect," he offered lamely, immediately suspecting his awkward attempts to form some type of bond, no matter how tenuous, may have gone astray.

271

"I remember my grandfather making a similar comparison's right before Frank Nitti had him rubbed out."

"Frank Nitti, yes he was Capone's successor, I believe. Oh, I say, quite sorry," said Professor Hewitt sheepishly, not knowing how to take Jimmy's last rejoinder.

"Don't mention it, Professor." Seeing from across the room the increasingly uneasy look on her father's face and fearing he was about to really step in it, Samantha grabbed Anne and Lionel from the bar and marched them over to reintroduce them to her father and Jimmy.

Well over ninety people, if not more, were scattered in the three oversized rooms adjacent to the terrace. It was the right size group for the dimensions of the main floor; there were neither too many as to make it uncomfortably crowded, nor too few as to give the gathering a desultory appearance. Off to the right of the large dining room was the main bar; manning it were two well-scrubbed college age kids. A third older man was assisting them to ensure that there were adequate stockpiles of all the various liquids, napkins, stirrers, lemons, limes and other things in ready proximity for the two bar keeps.

Harlan Zinter's job was not very taxing this evening; Mansfield and Longines had overstaffed for the occasion by bringing in a couple of extra hands, happily resulting in a lighter than normal work load for Harlan and his associates. This gave him the opportunity from time to time to unobtrusively observe the goings on from his vantage point beside a large potted palm. He could easily see Samantha Hewitt going through the motions of enjoying herself and being attentive to her guests, completely oblivious of her secret longing to merge her soul with his. Harlan could also observe Charlie Leuven moving around the place

272

as if he owned it, with his preening good looks and bogus air of authority. He came off as someone who was only capable of appreciating Samantha as some sort of door prize won at a raffle, just so much chattel to put on display for his friends. He would not miss her for long once he and Samantha were united. God, she was so ridiculously close but still too far to make his approach. He would wait patiently until his time came.

Like all parties, this one had its predictable rhythms and a predetermined life-cycle: from the initial, awkward stages of first greetings and sorting out of groups and individuals, to a more relaxed and convivial period when occasional happy outbursts and guffaws would rock one of the rooms. This stretch went on a bit longer than usual because there were so many old friends and family members in attendance. But inevitably the last innings were characterized by a more subdued atmosphere. At that time people would confess what was really on their minds; guests, weary of standing, took to the chairs, and the demand for drink would slacken off to be replaced by tea, coffee or water. It was during the beginning of this third stage that Harlan began to position himself for his final move. Quietly he opened the French doors behind the bar and slipped out on to the terrace to await the pre-ordained coming of Samantha Hewitt.

Around one o'clock a few adventurous souls, led by Charlie and Samantha, tired of the stuffy apartment, decided to make a break for the terrace. In the breezeless night isolated clouds and thin wisps of the once thick fog floated through the trees and under hazy street lamps. Off to the right, the large circular darkness of the reservoir seemed a void capable of absorbing any light that may fall within its circumference. Beyond the cautious luminescence of the event horizon along the jogging path was a perfect blackness from which nothing could escape.

At his vantage point at the north end of the terrace, Harlan made out the hosts and their friends. One of the men possessed a startling resemblance to Andrew Jackson, another, much burlier, struck Harlan as capable of violence. The last person in tow was the bitch who had ordered everyone around when they first arrived. She reminded him of the county social worker who discovered him and his sisters playing naked in the rented house next to a gas station outside of Rhinelander. It was the last time he had seen his sisters. That woman with her cheap sense of moral superiority had broken up his family, destroying what little chance he had of a normal life. Perhaps he should kill her after capturing Samantha's heart.

Harlan saw the little group scamper over to the wall, laughing and exchanging quips before stopping to take in the view. His plan was to wait until cool evening air began splintering off the coatless onlookers, forcing them to retreat inside or risk catching a chill. At that point he would make his grand declaration. The first to depart was a tall woman and a man with a strange pair of glasses. "Now", Harlan called to himself. "Do it now!" In an instant he had silently made his way to within a couple of feet of his intended. Like a large cat, Harlan swatted at Samantha's left arm, catching it near the wrist. Once sure of his hold, he went down on one knee, preparing to pledge his cosmic devotion to her. But the words did not come out as they were meant to, not like they did when he rehearsed them in front of his mirror in Long Island City. All he could hear himself say was "my imperishable longing" an interminable silent pause, and then "our destiny together demands no other recourse" followed by one or two similar stanzas which he had picked up from assorted books and old movies. He saw Samantha staring down at him with an expression of alarm mingled with shy amusement, as if to say "Oh you silly little man, how sweet of you to bother; now please go away." Knowing he had messed up his long sought for chance, Harlan felt an uncontrollable rage well up from that emotional desert that he called his soul.

He was now on his feet and looking straight at her, shrieking at the top of his lungs, "Don't you understand what this is about? Are you really so stupid not to realize your incompleteness, your ultimate futility without me?" Sensing that the men on the terrace were about to close in on him, Harlan began to feel the thing he wanted most in the world slipping away. Unless he acted quickly it would be lost to him forever.

Fortunately for Samantha, Harlan signaled his fragile hold on reality by a quick series of facial contortions that sweep across his face like jerky frames from a silent movie. Charlie, guessing that the little man must have been the stalker he had seen in the days before the party, fiercely unlocked Harlan's grip on Samantha's wrist and moved her back from the edge of the terrace wall.

In a mad effort to ensure the success of his psychic messaging, Harlan leaped upwards in an explosive fury. He hoped he would be able to grab Samantha's head and with it between his hands conduct some sort of mind-meld with her. But his timing had been set off by a matter of seconds when Charlie succeeded in moving her out of range. Instead of grasping Samantha's head, Harlan unwittingly wound up grasping Flavia's instead, as she, in an effort to better berate the unruly servant for his lése-majesté, had pushed her way into the place where a Samantha had stood only a second before.

His claw-like hands squarely dug into the flesh behind Flavia's ears and his small neat teeth gnashed at her left eyebrow, tugging and ripping it back and forth in an attempt to tear it off entirely. Unbalanced by Harlan's violent attack to her head, and the unsteadying weight of her assailant as his legs and arms wrapped around her upper body like a chimpanzee, Flavia lurched back and forth along the side of the wall. The pair would have both gone over then and there, if it hadn't been for Jimmy Dasimmi giving Harlan a solid punch to his left ear, momentarily stunning the madman, and giving Lionel enough time to snatch up Flavia's arm and pull her back from the brink.

But Harlan was not going to be denied by a single punch; he had come too far to simply call it a night. Screaming at his adversaries in some unintelligible gibberish, he jumped simian-like to the top of the wall, and then, still holding on to Mrs. Porter's chin and hair, quietly stepped back into the abyss of the damp night pulling an hysterically screeching Flavia along for the ride.

But the two did not fall far. Lionel hadn't entirely lost his grip, although after they went over the side, he found himself holding on to Flavia's ample calf rather than her arm. Then, in a flash, Jimmy was by his side, taking a hold of Flavia's other leg. Harlan, still ranting at the tops of his lungs, was able to place his feet on the side of the building's brick face. Like some kind of miniature King Kong holding on to dilapidated Fay Wray, Harlan attempted to run back and forth across its facade in a thirty degree arc while still clinging to Flavia.

Harlan was close to succeeding in his insane scheme of bringing them both to grief when a passing shower intervened. The light precipitation was sufficient enough to cause him to begin losing his footing on the side of the apartment building, as well as his grip on poor Flavia. Knowing that he could not hold on much longer, he could think of nothing better than to redouble his efforts to move the two of them back and forth like a lumpy, writhing pendulum. It was at this time that Flavia's neck discovered a small piece of rusted steel that had managed over the years to work its way out from the original brickwork. Though not particularly sharp, the emergent ironmongery had developed a wickedly serrated edge, sufficient to rip and cut Flavia's exposed neck.

Back and forth the two swayed, while above Flavia's family and friends were engaged in a valiant effort to hoist her back up to the terrace. Finally, the elements and the blood streaming down from Flavia's neck began to turn the tide. No longer able to hang on, Harlan decided to go for broke. Placing his toe on the top of the small pediment that circled the building for leverage, Harlan sprang upwards with all his might in the hopes that once he came back down the full force of his dead weight would free Flavia from her rescuers.

As Harlan propelled himself upwards, the momentary absence of his pressure on Flavia coincided exactly with Lionel, Jimmy, now joined by Charlie, giving one last united pull which succeeded in bring Flavia's torso over the edge of the wall. As Harlan' full weight came down, his hopes of taking Flavia with him were frustrated by the firm hold that her rescuers had managed to secure. Her hair ran through Harlan's wet, bloody hands like oily seaweed. Instead of taking her with him, Harlan succeeded only in ripping out a large junk of the poor woman's hair and scalp before falling into the blackness.

Harlan fell to his death in eerie silence. He had some

time ago prepared himself in not getting Samantha on the first try. His understanding that he might not be initially successful didn't disqualify him from another try sometime in the future. Any failure was really a matter of Sam not being up to receive and appreciate him properly. On the way down to the sidewalk below, Harlan took consolation in repeating an affirmation from one of the numerous self-help books he had purchased from a used bookstore in Fargo. "Set backs and missed opportunities are only minor detours on the road to self-actualization. Learn from your mistakes and above all, never allow them to get you down." As he reached the fifteenth floor he opened his server's jacket to help slow his descent; he would then land gently on the sidewalk and then proceed to…

The scene on the terrace was not much more uplifting. Flavia was alive, but with a large, ugly gash running halfway around her neck. She had also lost large sections of hair and scalp, and her front teeth whittled down to the gum line. When Demo came out and saw his disassembled, ragdoll of a wife he fainted dead away. Demo's place was immediately taken by a plastic surgeon, who recognizing a potential boon to his practice's cash flow, was at Flavia's side mumbling words of encouragement and promises of dramatic reconstruction.

Another doctor was administrating CPR to Bunny Leuven. Finding the efforts to save Flavia too taxing, Bunny without any fuss had quietly clutched his chest and then slumped down to the cold and damp stones, his head resting on one of the balustrade's supporting uprights. Rushing from Flavia's side, Charlie could hear the old man muttering something, but it wasn't clear what he was saying. After a few repetitions, Charlie could make them out to mean "it's the little things," softly repeated over and over again.

Chapter 22

HEROES AT HOME

Staring out from under the blankets, the first thing that Samantha recognized once her eyes became focused were the stacks of wall paper and fabric sample books, along with back copies of Architectural Digest and Better Homes, laying on an Empire settee off in the bedroom's sitting area, these reminders of her waning decorating mania now languished in mortified neglect, knowingly relegated to a lower level of importance given last night's harrowing disasters.

Charlie's call from the hospital about ten minutes before, saying that there was nothing more he could do and promising to return home shortly, had woken her from a fitful sleep. Throwing on a sweater and a pair of jeans, she made her way downstairs to the kitchen. She tried her best to avoid looking out at the terrace as she passed by the three sets of French doors, but her eyes refused to be averted altogether. The fog had returned and was now so thick she could barely make out the tables and chairs near the doors, let alone the more distant wall. On her way to the kitchen, Sam noticed that the main rooms had been clean and straightened by a combined squad of staff, guests and family members while she and Charlie were at the hospital. Relieved that housekeeping concerns could be excluded from her immediate lists of to-dos, Sam sleepily started to brew a pot of coffee. By the time she returned to the bedroom the red LED light on the bed table announced that it was 9:30.

Charlie arrived home five minutes later. Sam was struck by how haggard he looked when he walked over to her at the small table in the sitting room. In his tieless tuxedo he looked like a handsome cabaret singer after a long night of trying to whip up an indifferent audience. His drawn face sported the beginnings of a bristly beard; his eyes black and drooping. Charlie, however, was able to display a sense of authority that belied his spent appearance, which went some way in reassuring her that things would soon be set right. He kissed her gently on the lips as she tried to stand. Motioning her not to get up, Charlie fell into the chair next to hers, and let out a deep sigh.

"You didn't tell me much on the phone. Has there been any change? Are they going to be all right? Is your father out of danger? Should I run down and get you some coffee?" Sam asked hurriedly in a nervous voice.

"Please no coffee, I'm awash in it, any more and I'll never get to sleep," said Charlie, responding to the easiest of the three questions. His voice sounded scratchy, almost hoarse as if he was coming down with a cold. "Well, not a lot has changed since you left; that was about 4:00, right?" Accepting her nod, Charlie continued. "Things have just stabilized a little more, that's all. Everyone is going to be more or less all right but no one is going to come out of it unscathed. Father had a moderately severe heart attack. He'll stay at Lenox Hill for a few days as they do some more tests; after which, if everything checks out, he'll be sent home with a nurse. Jimmy has agreed to move in to help out for a while until Dad gets righted again. The doctor said that, at his age, not to expect a full recover anytime soon. We'll just have to see, I guess."

"And, Flavia, what's her outlook, Charlie?"

"Surprisingly good, once they take off her shroud of bandages. The doctors said they are confident that they can patch her up so you'll never know she was in a tug of war on the side of a thirty-story building. The cut to the neck, while pretty nasty looking, missed anything of importance. The scalp can be patched up with skin grafts and then reseeded with hair plugs and what have you. Plastic surgery will take care of the rest of it. When it comes time to getting her front teeth fixed, I hope to God she decides on doing something about her overbite. That improvement alone would it make it all worthwhile."

"Charlie, how horrible to say so," chided Samantha in a mocking tone. "I'll suggest it to her, darling, be sure of that."

"And now for the interesting part – the identity of our mystery assailant. You won't believe this but the cops ID'ed him as Harlan Zinter, Carl Troutmann's cousin!" said Charlie in a voice that still held a note of amazement in it. "I had forgotten, Zinter was never found after the storm. Everyone assumed that he was killed somehow, but his body never turned up. From what this detective was telling me, this guy was even crazier than Troutmann."

"How could they find out who he was so quickly?"

"His wallet, his ID was all in Harlan Zinter's name, amazing, isn't?" Charlie snorted in amused contempt. "Let's all hope this puts an end to the Leuven-Gartner feud. It struck me while in the waiting room that Harlan could be looked at as, amongst other things, a kind of dark paladin or nemesis sent by the Gartners to wreak vengeance on us. If so, I hope they're satisfied with his go-for-leather try, and we'll call it a day." Charlie looked at Sam to see how she reacted to his hypothesis of macabre retribution.

But she was more interested in learning about Zinter than Charlie's karmic musings. Sitting up straight and edging forward towards him, Samantha excitedly blurted out "I'd almost forgotten! When I was in that diner in Warroad, Troutmann was with this woman, well I thought it was a woman. She was slight and quiet, someone who could easily go unnoticed. I wonder if that wasn't Zinter in drag or something. Perhaps she/he stayed in Warroad that afternoon when I went to the Angle."

"Or perhaps he went along for the ride and watched the whole thing. But that begs the question of how he got out of there. He would have been stuck for at least a week to ten days before he would've been able to drive out of there. Who knows, maybe he walked out? Still, crazier things have happened," sighed Charlie again. "Well we won't have to worry about him. In a way he's the last victim of Storm Windigo."

"Speaking of victims, what really happened to Roger Gartner? I know you know. I could see it in your eyes when the reporter in Milwaukee asked you about him. So please just give me the unvarnished truth, I know you're not a saint, Charlie. If you were I would never have married you." Sam's question left her breathless, her fear of the answer only slightly out matched by her determination to finally clear the air on a question which had been nagging her since their return to Milwaukee from Duluth. All she wanted was a simple answer so as to get on with her life without the big question mark hanging over everything.

Instead of waiting to collect his thoughts, Charlie erupted in a short, barreling confession that satisfied no one. "Well, Sam let me explain. Roger attacked us with a gun and Jimmy had to run him over with the Cat, or he would've all been killed. It's really that simple."

"Please, Charlie, slow down and tell me the whole story."

Somewhat reanimated now, Charlie stood up and recounted the entire dreary saga of Roger's last twenty-four hours on earth, as best he could, being sure not to omit any of the sordid details, in the vain hope that a complete postmortem would satisfy his wife sufficiently so as not to bring up the topic ever again. Sam sat across from him, silent and immobile.

"...and when I flew up to Minnesota to rescue you, we put the body in the plane, and I dumped it out over Lake Superior. That's about it really."

"I see. I'm not surprised. So you threw him into the lake like an old tire. I take it back, I am surprised. You were brought up better than that. Jimmy I understand, but you?" she said, her voice rising as her mind produced a picture of Charlie struggling to get the bag of bones that was once Roger Gartner out the door of the Otter. She looked at Charlie hard, trying to figure out what went on inside the head of this man-child of a husband of hers. Then, in a calm voice, she spoke. "Charlie, you must promise me one thing."

"Sure, anything."

"Never do anything like that again, please, it's simply too American. Do you understand, never again?"

Charlie made the supreme effort not to bristle at Sam's condescending demand. At last, feeling he had his emotions under control, and wanting to end this uncomfortable conversation as fast as possible, he limply submitted to her demand. "Yes, very well, I'll try not to, I promise I'll jettison my bad old American ways."

Not waiting for Sam's acceptance of his

graceful capitulation, Charlie quickly moved the conversation on to related but less trying topics. "How are your parents? All your dad's prejudices about American barbarity must have been pretty much confirmed by the doings last night. I'm sure they'll want to head back home after this."

"Quite the contrary, I think. They were dears, staying up helping set the place right after we left for the hospital. When I came home I'm pretty sure I heard Father rattling on about staying on a bit longer so as to check out gangland activity in the South Bronx and 'Bed Sty', as he put it, with Jimmy. He'll never admit it but I am sure he experienced more excitement last night than at any other time since the Falklands."

"And Lionel and Anne, where are they?"

"Around someplace, when I got home around five, they were asleep on one of the sofas. They looked so sweet together. I'm making a bet that they will be married in six months."

Charlie let out an appreciative snort and then fell silent.

"Charlie, my love, I have something to say. Before you got back I was sitting here thinking about all the crazy things that have happened to me, or us, that I've experienced since I've been over here, the bad stuff like Cecil's murder, the Storm, Troutmann, the Gartners, and then last night. And also the good things like meeting you, and getting married and moving here. I must say Charlie I'm about spent. I need a break. Nothing appeals to me more than a dreary, boring winter in England. I'm sorry but that's the way I feel, darling. I know we can't run over just right now but after your Father is on the mend, could we get out of the good old USA for a while?" Sam said in her best imploring way. "Oh and by the way I'm preggers," she concluded with a self-satisfied expression in her voice as she leaned back into her chair.

Charlie sat stunned. Fatherhood... and so soon! It was wonderful and nuts at the same time. It was exactly the right antidote to banish the descendent gloom that had whirled around them over the last few days. A small tear formed in his right eye as he leaned across the table kissed and hugged Sam. They stayed in that embrace for a long time before they separated. "This is the best news I've ever had, when did you know?"

"Only this morning, when we were waiting in the hospital I corralled one of the nurses who looked bored, and as girls do we got to talking, and she ended up giving me a test and Voilà!"

"OK, England will be fine for a few months. It'll allow us to settle down and everything. Besides, I really can't find anything over here at the moment that's interesting. Maybe the break will give me a chance to think things through a little more clearly. Who knows? I'm thinking perhaps something in the way of an African-South American nexus. No, too dull. I know! Black Hole exploration via quantum super-positioning. What to do you think?"

Taking Sam's non-answer as a challenge to come up with something more realistic, and not exactly satisfied with his spur of the moment brainstorm, Charlie paused and tried to think of something really stupendous. He was interrupted in his fitful attempts when he turned and saw Sam with her head on one her arms snoring gently away.

About the Author

Photograph by Holon Videographer Nicholas Riccio

Peter Mason grew up in Grosse Pointe, Michigan and currently lives in Richmond, Virginia. His travels as an international business consultant and marketing executive have taken him to many far flung and obscure destinations. After concluding his business career, Mr. Mason has found writing to be an excellent vehicle for channeling his bountiful enjoyment of life pleasures.